rough fantasy

A HARMLESS WORLD NOVEL

ROUGH 'N READY
BOOK THREE

MELISSA SCHROEDER

HARMLESS PUBLISHING

contents

- Possession
- Surrender

Task Force Hawaii

- Seductive Reasoning
- Hostile Desires
- Constant Craving
- Tangled Passions
- Wicked Temptations
- Twisted Emotions-coming 2025

The Camos and Cupcakes World

Camos and Cupcakes

- Delicious
- Luscious
- Scrumptious

The Fillmore Siblings

- Hate to Love You
- Love to Hate You

Juniper Springs

- Wild Love
- Crazy Love
- Last Love
- Imperfect Love

The Santini World

The Santinis

- Leonardo
- Marco
- Gianni
- Vicente
- A Santini Christmas
- A Santini in Love
- Falling for a Santini
- One Night with a Santini
- A Santini Takes the Fall
- A Santini's Heart
- Loving a Santini

Semper Fi Marines

- Tease Me
- Tempt Me
- Touch Me

The Fitzpatricks

- Chances Are

THE MELISSA SCHROEDER INSTALOVE COLLECTION

Dominion Rockstar Romance

- Undeniable
- Unpredictable
- Unexpected
- Tempted

Mafia Sisters

- Stealing Destiny
- Guarding Fable

Faking It

- Faking it with my Billionaire Boss
- Faking it with my Brother's Best Friend
- Faking it with my Frenemy

The Fighting Sullivans

- Falling for the General's Daughter
- Falling for the Girl Next Door
- Falling for my Best Friend
- Falling for my Baby Mama

Also Included

- Kiss my Tinsel
- Dad Bod Rockstar

Texas Temptations

- Conquering India
- Delilah's Downfall

Hawaiian Holidays

- Mele Kalikimaka, Baby
- Sex on the Beach
- Getting Lei'd

Once Upon an Accident

- The Accidental Countess
- Lessons in Seduction
- The Spy Who Loved Her

The Cursed Clan

- Callum
- Angus
- Logan
- Fletcher
- Anice

The Sweet Shoppe

- Tempting Prudence
- Cowboy Up
- Her Wicked Warrior

By Blood

- Desire by Blood
- Seduction by Blood

Hands On

- The Hired Hand
- Hands on Training

Telepathic Cravings

- Voices Carry
- Lost in Emotion
- Hard Habit to Break

Bounty Hunters, Inc

- For Love or Honor
- Sinner's Delight

Saints and Sinners

- Seducing the Saint
- Hunting Mila

Lonestar Wolf Pack

- Primal Instincts

Texas Heat

- Scorched

Spies, Lies, and Alibis

- The Boss

SINGLE TITLES

- A Calculated Seduction
- Chasing Luck
- Going for Eight
- Grace Under Pressure
- Operation Love
- Saving Thea
- Snowbound Seduction
- Sweet Patience
- The Last Detail
- The Seduction of Widow McEwan

hawaiian terms

Aloha - Hello, goodbye, love
Bra-Bro
Bruddah- brother, term of endearment
Haole-Newcomer to the islands
Howzit - How is it going?
Kamaʻāina-Local to the islands
Mahalo-Thank you
Malasadas- A Portuguese donut without a hole which started out as a tradition for Shrove (Fat) Tuesday. They are deep fried, dipped in sugar or cinnamon and sugar. In other words, it is a decadent treat every person must try when they go to Hawaii. If you do not try it, you fail. Do yourself a favor. Go to Leonard's and buy one. You are welcome.
Pupule - crazy
Slippahs - slippers, AKA sandals

Edited by Noel Varner

Cover by Scott Carpenter

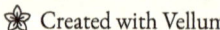 Created with Vellum

acknowledgments

Here we are again and I once again have a ton of people to thank. This book took longer than any other Harmless book, and I hope that you love it as much as I do. It would not have happened without the people behind the scenes who helped me in so many ways. Big thanks to Kendra Egert for redoing the cover to make it even more beautiful than before. Also, thanks to Noel Varner for jumping in and editing. A big hug to Gina Bauman DeWitt for reading over the first few chapters and another one to Heather Long for the formatting. Thanks to the three people I live with, Les and my girls, for reminding me that it is sometimes good to step away from the computer and be just Mel. Also, gratitude and love to the ADDICTS for supporting me always. And last but DEFINITELY not least, to Brandy Walker who keeps me on schedule and keeps me sane. Your love of the ridiculous is only out shined by mine.

dedication

In memory of Liz McChesney
You lived your last few years in the land of Harmless and I hope
you enjoyed every minute.
Aloha, my friend.

one

For the fourth time in less than ten minutes, Maura Dillon found her mind wandering. She looked out over the late afternoon Miami traffic and tried to concentrate on her brother's voice in her ear, and just spaced out. A second later, she realized that her brother had stopped talking.

"What did you just say?" She asked, leaning back in her desk chair closing her eyes. She felt herself drifting again, as if she were floating in the Pacific, enjoying the warm sun on her skin. She could almost smell the salt of the ocean and feel the breeze shift over her. It did nothing to help the pounding in her head. She felt as if she hadn't had a good night's sleep in three weeks. Probably because she hadn't.

"You sound distracted," Conner said.

Inwardly, she sighed. Her brother could always sniff out her mood, even five thousand miles away. It was one of his most irritating traits—and he had a lot of them.

"I'm not distracted. I'm just a little tired."

There was a beat of silence. With most men, it didn't mean anything. With Conner, it was a lethal situation. She turned her

1

chair back so she faced her desk waiting for the other shoe to drop.

"No, this is distracted, not tired. When you're tired, you're bitchy."

She ignored that comment, mostly because it was true. "I got the preliminary report on that group you want us to work with."

"You're going to ignore my question then?" her brother asked.

"Yes. When did you get all loving and want to talk feelings?"

"I didn't say it was about feelings. You just did. So you *are* distracted."

She was, but how did she tell her brother she was testy because she needed sex. She didn't. She shared a lot with her brother, much to his irritation, but this, she could not. It was hard enough dealing with the dream team of Zeke O'Brian and Rory McAllister.

"I'm distracted by this job. It doesn't help that I'm now a blonde." She shoved her hand through her now chin length hair. It had been a whim a few days ago and she had loved it. But, now she wasn't so sure.

Another beat of silence. "You only mess with your hair color when you're depressed."

She held the phone out from her ear and looked at it, then put it back. "This is Conner Dillon, right? Or has Jillian been giving you inside information?"

"Jillian hasn't and I know you better than you think I do."

That was probably true. Conner was devious that way. He seemed like the ultimate Alpha in any group, but one thing that had made him an excellent FBI agent was his observation skills. It was the bane of her existence when she was growing up—especially when he was left to raise her on his own. Nothing like having a criminal profiler watching your every move. Not that her teenage years had been that exciting.

"How do you know about the hair color thing, then?" she asked.

Maura recognized the aggravated sigh. She had first heard it when she was fifteen and asked her brother about lubricant. "The first boyfriend breakup you dyed it that disturbing bright red shade."

Of course he would bring up her breakup with Tommy Foster—otherwise known as the Scumbag from Boca Raton. "There was nothing disturbing about it."

"It glowed in the dark."

She remembered the look on Conner's face when she stepped out of the bathroom and chuckled. "Okay, I will give you that. It was pretty bad."

"If you aren't going to tell me, talk to Jillian when you get over here."

"I can talk to Jillian some other time, but there's nothing to talk about." Then she realized what he had just said. "Get over there? What are you talking about?"

"I want you to come over to Hawaii for a week."

Stranger and stranger. It was never a good idea to underestimate Conner, especially when he was scheming. And she definitely defined this as scheming. He was devious and most people wouldn't pick up on it. They would see him as being efficient. She knew better. Conner was born creating plots.

She cleared her throat and readied herself for battle. "I wasn't planning on coming over anytime soon. I was just there six weeks ago for your wedding."

No matter how much she wanted to run away from the office and her personal infatuation with Rory and Zeke, she would not use a trip to Hawaii to get away. Which, even as she thought it, made her crazy. Insane. Bonkers. Any sane woman would do it without much thought. She had gone over the edge.

And that is what those two had done to her. They had pushed her to the point that she was turning down vacations from her brother.

"I need someone who is good at being a nerd and it comes to you naturally."

Most people would be upset with that comment, but not Maura. She was a nerd and proud of it. It was one of the many things Conner had taught her. On top of it, she knew he was lying.

"First, you're lying. Big lying, but I love you for it so okay, I'll come see you and Jillian."

"And I want Rory and Zeke with you."

That made her to pause. Going to Hawaii would be a great escape. She could forget her problems; spend some time recharging her brain. Bringing the source of her problem with her wouldn't give her a break. Her concentration was already shot and now she had to deal with them dressed in trunks and all oiled up? She shivered.

"But who will run the office?" she asked.

"Jennifer is well trained and former FBI. I'm sending a few of the new hires from here to be trained in the office with her."

Which made sense, but it didn't explain why she needed to be in Hawaii. Maura knew she could definitely help with that and keeping the office running while Jennifer was training. Maura could also help with part of the training.

"The Petersen case is going to trial next week. Don't you think one of us should be here?"

"No. The federal prosecutor said he didn't need you. Which is for the best."

She frowned. She didn't think so. They did all the legwork and found out that Petersen had been funneling millions of dollars through the company he was CFO for. The owner had thought there was something hinky, so he brought Dillon Securities in to look it over.

They just didn't know Petersen had been working for the Columbians.

"Are you trying to get me out of the country?"

"Hawaii is part of the country. And when you get here, you would be smart to remember that."

She rolled her eyes. Conner had become more Kama'aina than Jillian who had lived there for a several years. Heck, he even took off early every Friday to celebrate Aloha Fridays. That was so not like Conner—and she was glad for it. Jillian had definitely loosened her brother up. Before falling for her best friend, Conner had been uptight—and he still was to a point. But now he had someone to tell him to take a break when he got too intense.

"Sure, sure. But, why do Rory and Zeke need to come with me?" she asked and then cringed at the whiny tone in her voice. It was worse that she didn't know what her brother's motives were. There were times she knew him better than she knew herself, but lately, he'd been acting very un-Conner like. If he wanted to talk about feelings, there was something very wrong. The idea that she had to spend a week with them in Hawaii didn't appeal. Okay, that was a lie. It did. But in the wrong way.

"Because they are associated with the case too. It would be best if you three are unreachable."

"So, Hawaii isn't connected to the rest of the world? I think the Hawaiians would be more pissed about your comments than some stupid haole tourist made." she asked.

He ignored her question. "And, there's that house I rented for us during the wedding crap—"

"Oh, how I love to hear my husband say our wedding was

crap," Jillian said in the background. The amusement in her voice had Maura smiling.

"Now you did it, Conner. And I'm not helping you with Jillian."

He grunted and Maura imagined that Jillian had plopped down on his lap. It was something that she did on a regular basis.

"I don't need help with Jillian. I can handle her all on my own."

The tone in his voice left little to figure out just what he was talking about.

"Ugh, ew. I am going to bleach my brain after that image suggestion."

He chuckled. "It's your fault. You sent me over here."

"Okay, moving onto other things, you said you had the house that you rented?"

"Yes. I found out someone backed out of the week's rent for it, and I jumped on it. Use the jet."

She wanted to argue with him, just for the fact that she didn't want to be with the two men while they were together. Zeke and she had mutually decided he could not give her what she needed, so they had split. It was hard enough working together, but seeing him with his old lover Rory, knowing the two of them were living together now, was a little too much to take. Worse, she was attracted to both of the men. Having them in the same house, day in and day out, might just be the death of any sanity she had left.

Before she could talk to Conner about not inviting the guys, Zeke walked through her office door, and of course, Rory followed behind him.

"Has Conner talked to you about this trip?" she asked.

"No I haven't," Conner said on the phone.

"Trip?" Zeke asked, his brow furrowing.

"Let me talk to him," Conner said.

"No. I'll tell him."

She didn't need her brother sniffing out her mood with Zeke. Both men were relentless and they would badger her. At least in Hawaii, she could ignore them and enjoy the sunshine. Not to mention, a trip to Rough 'n Ready would help.

"Maura—"

"Love you," she said and hung up.

She took a second to gather her composure. Maura had found it best when confronted by the dual assault of having both Rory and Zeke in the room to be prepared. If she didn't, her tongue stuck to the top of her mouth. When she felt she was ready to address them and not drool on herself, she looked at them.

"He wants us to be in Hawaii when the trial starts."

The men shared a glance. It irritated her on some level she didn't completely understand. What was she thinking? Of course she understood. It made her feel small and petty but she seemed unable to move past it. She hated they knew each other so well a glance was all they needed to communicate. Worse, she hated being jealous of it. She was envious of their intimacy and their secrets. It would be bad enough if she was just hot for one of them, but both of them had her hot.

Both of them—and that was the problem.

She was definitely mental. What sane woman would be envious of two men who obviously have the hots for each other?

What made it even crappier were the dreams she had started having about both of them. It was disturbing her sleep and now disrupting her work. That was not good. Going to Hawaii was going to make it worse—unless she could find herself a Dom to play with while she was there. It might help her work out the demons that seemed to be chasing her for the last few months.

She glanced at Zeke and tried to keep her mind on the conversation. It was hard to do because the man was beyond gorgeous. What made him even more tempting was the fact that he didn't see himself as attractive. His mother was Haitian and his father had been Irish, and both of them were easy to see in his character and his looks—not to mention his voice. His skin was dark brown, his eyes the color of milk chocolate and he had the body of a tough Irish fighter. All sculpted muscles and that stiff upper lip. Now that he had shaved his head and grown a goatee, he was even sexier. He was often times too serious, but maybe that is what appealed to her. He was hot and smart, two things that weren't always easy to find.

"Maura?" he asked, those dangerous lips turning down.

She pushed those thoughts aside. Thinking about his lips wasn't something she should do. Especially since Rory was now in the picture.

"As I said, he wants us there. It is kind of odd, but then, I can work on computer stuff there with no problem."

"And you agree with it?" Zeke asked.

She didn't really pay attention to the question. He had a baritone voice with that Irish lilt to it that just made her melt. She could remember hearing it first thing in the morning after their first night together.

"Uh, no. I would rather stay here because I have a load of work to do, but he wants us there. I will adjust. He's using the lame excuse that he needs us there and he's sending new hires for the upcoming Honolulu office here to be trained."

"That's actually a good idea," Rory said.

She forced herself to look away from Zeke to Rory. An Irishman himself, Rory was what most people would call black Irish. Dark hair, blue eyes, and a lanky muscular build made him a treat for the eyes, and she had been dying for a bite. He was unconventional in every way. He had dyed some of his hair blond, probably just because he wanted to. The tats made him stand out even today when everyone seemed to be getting one. She had only seen glimpses of them because apparently, Rory liked to have his tats in naughty places.

He had a quick temper and she had often wondered if that is why he got into BDSM. Zeke had said when they were younger that Rory had learned to control it.

They were opposites in a lot of ways. Zeke thought through everything. And, that is one of the reasons she had been sure he was a Dom. When she had found out he wasn't, even after he tried to play a bit, she had been disappointed. But, apparently, that was Rory in some capacity—from the rumors she heard.

Zeke was good at looking at the positive things and making the best. Rory had a jaundiced view of life that she truly appreciated. The few times he had been around her without Zeke, his sarcastic comments had gotten a chuckle from her.

And sadly, she wanted them both. But they were apparently interested only in each other.

"So, he thinks we can't protect you?" Rory asked with a sarcastic tone.

"I can protect myself, thank you very much," she said watching him settle in the chair in front of her desk and then lift his feet to the edge. "Feet off, McAllister."

Rory gave her a sweet smile, although there was nothing sweet behind it, and did as she ordered. She had a feeling he wasn't accustomed to women telling him what to do.

Zeke ignored the byplay. He crossed his arms and looked down at her. "Did he hear something about the Alvarez family?" he asked. Of course, Zeke would think of the case first.

"No. But he just thinks it would be best if we were gone. And you know Conner. If he has decided we need to be gone, that's the end of the discussion. He rented that house he had for the wedding."

"That sounds like a brilliant plan," Rory said. "Are we taking the jet?"

"Yes."

Zeke opened his mouth to ask another question but she had too much to worry about. And she needed them out of her office right now. The combination of sexy men was starting to give her the vapors.

"Call Conner and ask him anything. I am assuming we are leaving tomorrow morning. Can you boys be ready by then?"

"I've been ready for months, love," Rory said with one of those cute lopsided smiles that made her insides quiver. But she ignored it. Or pretended to. He had been saying things like that the last few weeks and completely confusing her. It was as if he was flirting with her and she didn't get it. She didn't have the time to even think about it.

Zeke did not like it from the look on his face. He gave Rory a warning glance, and said, "What else do you have on your agenda today? It's almost five."

"I'm going to meet with Jennifer. She needs to take over my meetings if I am going to be gone next week."

Rory nodded. "Right-o. I have a few calls to make too. Your brother doesn't like to plan ahead."

She laughed. "If you knew Conner before Jillian, you would never say that. But this was planned. He checked out the house, probably offered an obscene amount for it, and then worked it out with Margerie. He plans, but he likes to pretend he doesn't."

"And you let him do this?" Rory asked.

"I don't let Conner do anything. But, when all you have is each other, you learn to allow for your eccentricities."

She started to pull up some files on her computer. After a few moments, they were still there, both staring at her. She sighed.

"Go away."

Zeke opened his mouth but Rory chuckled. "Let's go, Zee. The lady has work to do. Let us know if you need anything."

Rory stood and headed to the door. With a worried glance in her direction, Zeke followed Rory out the door. When it clicked shut, she leaned back in her seat and growled. She couldn't stop herself. It was impossible. Every single day she had to deal with them and every single day she felt as itchy from the inside out. Worse, she had an idea that neither of them had any idea what they did to her. Zeke knew she loved him. They were going to drive her crazy. She needed to find herself a man in Hawaii and ignore the two men who had been driving her crazy.

She closed her eyes. If only she could listen to her common sense, she would be able to do it. Unfortunately, her common sense seemed to be on a holiday. The only thing that she could think was how much fun it would be to play with both Rory and Zeke.

She was doomed.

"You want to tell me what that was about in there, Rory?" Zeke asked as they walked down the hall to where their offices were located.

"What do you mean?" Rory asked. His attempt to sound innocent failed, at least with Zeke. Most people would never guess just how devious the man truly was.

"You questioning Maura about her brother like that." He didn't like it. He knew that Rory was planning something and it wasn't going to be good. Whenever Rory got crazy plans in his head, Zeke was always left cleaning up the mess and dealing with heartache.

"Nothing. Just wondered why she would do it for him. She's a workaholic."

That much was true, but it didn't sound like a reason Rory would be curious about something like that. He hated to admit it but Rory could be superficial with people in his life. Not the ones that mattered, but when it came to acquaintances, he kept everything on the surface. "But she loves Hawaii and a chance to see him, she will do anything."

They reached Zeke's office first and he stepped in his mind on the plans for the flight. He would have to make sure to get ahold of Michaels and tell him of the switch of staff on the job, although Conner probably already did, cheeky bastard.

"I get that. It's unnatural."

Zeke shook his head. Of course Rory would think that. With his fucked up family, Zeke understood why he never wanted to see them...or talk to them.

"To you and me, maybe. To them, no. They have always had each other's back. It's kind of heartwarming to see the way they look out for each other."

Rory said nothing as he leaned against the doorjamb.

"What?" Zeke asked.

"You have that tone in your voice when you talk about her. It's the same one I heard last year when you were involved with her."

Zeke bit back a sigh. He settled in the chair and looked at his oldest friend and lover. They had known each other for so long, it was hard to remember a time when they hadn't been together...or on each other's mind. Zeke had known that Rory hadn't been really happy about his relationship with Maura. It was hard to make someone understand his position.

"She wanted things I couldn't give her."

He hated to admit it, but that was the truth of the matter. He had never felt like such a loser as when he realized that he could not be the man she wanted in the bedroom. They might not be together anymore, but just being near her made him feel better. It was pathetic to even admit that to himself, but it was the truth. He might have allowed her freedom from their relationship, but he couldn't get her out of his head...or his heart.

Zeke could tell his honesty did not sit well with Rory. But they had promised each other that this time they would be honest. He loved Maura, maybe as much as he loved Rory. And, his heart still hurt when he thought about the night Maura and he realized it would never work.

"What kind of things?"

Zeke glanced over Rory's shoulder and saw Denise the office manager standing there. Six feet tall and plastic surgery perfect, she smiled at Rory. He smiled back, but Zeke felt no jealousy. She wasn't his type.

Maura was.

"Hey, Denise, did you need something?"

"No, I just wanted to leave these with you. They need to be signed by the end of the month." She slinked in and handed him the forms. She gave him a smile that he knew was an invitation. It was no secret he and Rory were involved. Worse, people had heard the rumors that they sometimes brought a woman into their bed. When that had made its way around the office, he had to deal with women who wanted to experiment.

One hard and fast rule that he and Conner both believed in was not fucking the help.

"Thanks. I have to make a few calls before six tonight."

"Oh," She said. "Have fun in Hawaii."

With that she left them alone. Rory stepped into the room and closed the door.

"What was it Maura wanted?"

He should have known Rory wouldn't let it go. "She's a sub. You know I don't do that."

He was busy looking over the papers Denise just gave to him, but when the silence extended, he looked up. The interest on Rory's face was enough to make him want to curse. *Dammit*.

"No."

"Why not?"

"Because you don't like her. Admit it, you never spend time with her alone."

He shrugged. "I got the vibe that she didn't want to have much to do with me once I moved here. I figured she was jealous of me."

He had known she was hurt when Rory had come back into his life, but it had been almost a year that they had called off their relationship. Still every now and then he would catch her looking at him with something akin to longing in her gaze. It made working with her very hard because he couldn't help wanting her.

Zeke walked to his desk. Rory hadn't liked her because Zeke had told him about their relationship. But, now, he might be changing his mind.

"A week in Hawaii just the three of us could be a lot of fun."

He stepped behind Zeke's chair and started to rub his shoulders. Zeke tried to resist the temptation. It was futile, he knew that, but he put up the fight for a few seconds.

"Think about it, Zee. You, me, a woman who likes to be tied down…"

Rory's voice trailed off then he turned Zeke's chair around. He leaned closer, bracing his hands on the armrests. The soap they had shared that morning in the shower permeated the air and brought back the memories. Zeke closed his eyes and shuddered.

Rory nuzzled Zeke's neck then he felt his teeth nip at the sensitive skin. He was a weak man. When it came to temptation there were only two people in the world who could get him to forget about the consequences. One of them had just dyed her hair blonde. The other was Rory.

"You know you like the idea, doncha, love? You're picturing it right now."

Of course he was. His cock twitched as he tried to keep his cool but he had never had control when it came to Rory. It was one of the things that both he and Maura had over Zeke. He couldn't resist either of them and right now, he wanted Rory. Needed him so much his hands were already shaking.

Rory kissed a path up to his mouth and then attacked his mouth. His tongue thrust into Zeke's mouth, over and over. How could it be that this man could make him come undone so fast?

When he pulled back, Rory smiled. "Come on, Zee. It'll be fun. Just think of everything that we could do. She's hot for it too, you know she is."

Zeke knew Rory was right. Knowing that he could watch her submit, one of his ultimate fantasies...Damn.

"Need a little relief, love?" Rory asked, his voice teasing Zeke as his fingers slipped down his chest.

His cock hardened further and his body yearned. He wanted that, wanted to feel Rory's talented mouth on his flesh. But...they were at the office and at the moment, the door was unlocked. They didn't hide their relationship, but having sex at the office was something else. As co owner he couldn't do something like that—no matter how much he wanted to.

"No. Not at that office."

Rory rolled his eyes but backed off. He liked to push Zeke's buttons and he had a lot of experience doing just that.

"There was a time when that wouldn't have stopped you," Rory said.

"I wasn't a boss then. Plus, we are about to leave for an

entire week, or more. I don't want anyone walking in on us starting our vacation early."

Rory gave him a smirk then walked away to the windows that overlooked Miami. There was something else bugging him, something that Zeke knew he was trying to work out in his head.

"You have to let it go with Maura. While she might be up for a little play, Conner would not be happy."

Rory rolled his shoulders. It was a sure sign that he wasn't happy with what Zeke had said. One of the best things and one of the worst things about Rory was that once he got an idea, he would never let it go. It was something that made him good at his job, but it also made him a pain in the ass lover.

"You think she would go for it?"

Zeke sighed. Rory wasn't going to let it go. "I think she might. It wouldn't be good."

Rory glanced over his shoulder and smiled. Those damned blue eyes twinkling at him. "I thought you said she was good. I thought what you said was she particularly liked..."

"I know what I said. It would cause problems here though."

"Problems? How?"

"Not everyone is like you. Especially women. The complications at work would be tough. It was hard enough last time when Maura and I decided to split ways. Besides, you know what happened last time we brought a woman into the bedroom."

"It was one hot fucking night, that's what I remember."

Zeke shook his head. Rory was right and with Maura, well, it would go beyond most of his fantasies. But their last experience had been very bad.

"So, you forget when she started to stalk you? How she threatened me? You always did have a selective memory."

"And you remember too. You remember watching me tie

Sherry down, don't you? The way she happily would do anything I told her. You liked to watch when she sucked me off."

Rory's voice deepened over every word and Zeke had to take a bracing breath to control his need. His body was throbbing and his cock was so hard he probably wouldn't be able to walk straight. Rory was one of the best at talking sex.

Rory walked toward him. Anticipation skated along his nerves. Zeke licked his lips. Instead of approaching him, though, Rory veered off toward the door.

"You think of that when you tell me you don't want to share her."

And with that he left Zeke, the door silently clicking behind him.

Even with the A/C on full blast, Zeke felt a small dribble of sweat slink down his back. He closed his eyes trying to calm the heat dancing over his nerve endings. Damn. The man could always control him.

It had always been like that from the beginning and Zeke had allowed it. Rory had his control issues because of his childhood and Zeke could handle it. They weren't Dom and sub. Zeke was truthful about that when he told Maura. And weirdly for Rory, he only liked to Dominate women. Of course, it fed into Zeke's need to watch. There was something about watching Rory work over a sub. With the right sub, Rory could send Zeke over the edge. And Maura would be perfect.

She was the right combination of sexy, smarts and submissive. He remembered the first day he met her. Never in his life did he have a reaction like that to a woman. She had smiled at him, her eyes sparkling from behind her glasses and his tongue had stuck to the top of his mouth. He actually stuttered. The only other person who had made him lose the ability to speak had been Rory.

It was inevitable that they get involved. Their arguing had only been foreplay to the bedroom. The sex had been wonderful, stellar. Still, he knew Maura had wanted—needed more. Something he couldn't give her.

But Rory could.

The naughty thought whispered through Zeke and he shivered. He wanted it more than he wanted his next breath. He wished life was easier, and he could have both of them. The need he had for both of them scared the shit out of Zeke. It almost overwhelmed him at times. He could give into the suggestion, but he wasn't too sure he would come out unscathed. He also had to think of Maura. He and Rory would still be together, and she would be left alone.

He just didn't think he could do that, no matter how much he wanted her. Needed her. He loved her too much to take advantage of her. And wasn't that just a bitch.

With a sigh, he turned his attention back to work. Zeke had learned a long time ago that life didn't always work out the way you wanted it to.

two

As Rory watched the traffic on Dolphin Toll Road buzz by, he wondered if he should have just gone home. He should be packing his bags for the trip, planning what kinds of things he would like to do while on Oahu. Their trip had been fast and furious for the wedding and he hadn't gotten to see much of the island. He'd only been to the beach to surf once. The only other time had been for the wedding. So, he had a lot he wanted to do in the short time they were there this time.

Instead, he was standing outside waiting on a woman.

He rolled his shoulders. This was definitely something new for him. As Rory thought about it, he realized he hadn't really done that for anyone other than Zee. In all his years, Rory had always been the one people waited on, even Zee to a point. It was six months ago when Rory realized that he was sick of waking up alone—even when he was in bed with someone else.

Rory was pulled out of his thoughts when someone honked their car horn. He shook away the regrets of the last ten years. Rory knew he'd been lucky enough that Zee took him back this one last time. In a way, this was for Zee. Rory knew he wouldn't be as interested in Maura if Zee hadn't been hung up on her.

He rolled his shoulders again as he thought about Maura. He had always thought Maura might make a good sub. From the moment he met her, Rory had felt a vibe from her that he was rarely wrong about. Zee had been mum on her bedroom personality, and Rory had avoided it—which was a first. Zee wasn't the kiss and tell type, but it was as if the two of them had never slept together. It was odd but seeing the two of them together the last few months told him all he wanted to know. Zee was still in love with her. Rory could tell. Every now and then he would catch Zee sneaking a glance at her. He hid it from everyone else, but Rory had witnessed the look of longing on his lover's face. Rory knew Zee well enough to understand he would never admit it. But it was there, and while he could probably get an answer from Zee about his feelings, it hurt a little too much to scratch at that scab. Now that he knew she was into BDSM, and that Zee thought she might be into it, all he had to do was propose the idea.

So he had waited thinking about her—which was dangerous. She was the kind of woman that many men overlooked because they couldn't get past her intelligence. Throw in her bulldog brother and the fact that she was a neurotic workaholic and well, she was a challenge. He smiled. Rory liked challenges.

He was leaning against his motorcycle when she came out of the building. Her mind was on something else, something that had nothing to do with him or Zee. Her head was down and she was rummaging through her purse for something. For someone so smart, she really did have a problem with paying attention to her surroundings. But, he couldn't complain when it allowed him to watch her without her knowing. She had a sidewalk-eating stride as if she always had something important to attend—even when he knew she didn't have anywhere to be.

Today, she was wearing one of those short little skirts that showed off the mile of leg she possessed. It was black and when paired with the stoplight red shirt, it made her stand out. She might have been a geek in college, but damn the woman had turned into a stunner. Add in the newly done blonde hair, she sometimes took his breath away. Okay, not just sometimes. All the time.

"Maura," he said, stepping in front of her.

She stopped, looked up and blinked. She had the most amazing green eyes. There were hints of blue in the iris. They were huge behind her glasses and there was always something very sexy about that. She looked like a prim librarian—although he knew better. It was going to be fun to reveal it.

"What are you doing out here?" she asked warily.

He understood her reaction even if he didn't like it. He hadn't been that happy when he'd found out Zee had fallen for the woman. It had come as a blow to Rory. He wasn't such as asshole that he thought Zee had no other lovers. They both had a history and he was sure Zee also had some people in his past he'd like to forget. When he realized just how in love Zee thought he was with Maura, he'd worried about what he should do. Over the last few months, Maura had grown on him a bit. She was sexy and now he knew she was a sub, she was even more intriguing. Without a doubt, Zee was going to end up back in her bed. Rory realized he didn't mind that—especially if he were around to control the situation.

"I was just wondering what you think I should bring with me."

She frowned and he felt her suspicions rising. It was a pretty lame reason to hang around, but he couldn't come up with anything else. It was just another sign that she had addled his brain—which wasn't normal. Women just didn't get to him this way.

"You were just there for the wedding. You know what to bring." Then she stepped around him and headed for her car.

She dismissed him, and Rory found he did not like that. It wasn't something he was accustomed to as a Dom, especially from a woman. It rankled him that she kept the hand's off attitude toward him. He wasn't that irritated that she didn't seem to return the simple attraction he had for her. Was it because of Zee or because she was a sub? Not all women did, he thought as he jogged after her. Maybe that was the reason he had been avoiding her. Now that he had decided though, he decided it didn't matter. All he knew was that he wanted her as a sub. Someone with her self-confidence would be fun to bend to his will.

She was already unlocking her Mini by the time he caught up to her.

"But, there are a few things I was thinking of that I didn't bring last time."

She threw her purse into the passenger seat. It landed there then fell over but she paid no attention to it. He'd never seen a woman with such little regard for her purse as Maura, but that was just part of her personality. And he kind of liked it. She might dress like a goddess but he knew beneath it all was a nerd.

"I'm sure whatever you want to bring will be fine," she said, her back to him. He used it to his advantage. He approached her as he enjoyed the view of her ass. His libido did a little tap dance as she bent over with a huff and picked up her belongs and stuffed them back in her purse. She had one amazing ass. The skirt pulled tight over it leaving little to his imagination. Rory could tell that she was either wearing a thong or nothing at all under the thin fabric. It took all his control not to reach out and press his palm against it.

He waited until she straightened out of the car.

"I have a few extra things I would like to bring."

She jumped and turned around, then backed up when she realized how close he was. Her eyes widened and her mouth was opened in a silent gasp. No wonder Zee had been so entranced with the woman. She was all sex and innocence in a luscious package any sane man would want to unwrap. As he stepped closer, he caught a hint of her scent. God, the woman always smelled like heaven. There was something so enticing knowing that in that nerdy package hid a freak in the bedroom. And he really liked freaks—being one himself.

She swallowed. "Uh, what kind of things? You don't need much there. I do want to do some diving."

She was talking fast and her breathing was erratic. A sure sign that he had rattled her, which he knew was hard to do. He wasn't proud how much of a rush it gave him, but it did. He could feel it singing through his blood.

He settled one hand on the hood of her car and leaned in. "I have a few toys I want to bring."

She swallowed. "Toys? Like...a boogie board?"

He shrugged. "And some other things. I do have a favorite pair of handcuffs I would like to bring."

Her face flushed and she looked down. "Bring whatever you want, Rory. I'm sure you and Zeke will have a bunch of time to play."

He heard something in her voice he hadn't heard before. Interesting that she was jealous, but there was a part of him that wondered if she was jealous of just Zee...or both of them.

"They aren't for him. You know he doesn't play." He paused and leaned closer. "But I hear you like to play." Even he heard the way his voice deepened over the words. His gut was twisted from the jolt of lust that had hit him. He drew in a breath and sighed when he recognized honeysuckle. He had gone from slightly aroused to almost overwhelmed with need for her. He pulled back.

Her face washed of all color. This wasn't arousal. She wanted to look anywhere but at his face. She was embarrassed. No—not embarrassed. She was mortified.

"I would appreciate if you wouldn't play sick games with me, Rory. I might not be as sophisticated as some other people, but I know you two are together."

She tried to turn and get into her car but he stopped her.

"We are together, but we have brought women into it before."

She stopped trying to get past him. "What?"

He couldn't believe that Zee had kept that from her. Of course, he had a feeling that both Zee and Maura had been hiding things from each other. That shit was going to stop in Hawaii.

"Zee told me why you broke it off."

She sighed. "Do we have to talk about this in a parking lot?"

He glanced around. "Tell you what. You live close by, right?"

She nodded.

"Why don't I follow you? That way you can pack while we talk."

Her eyes narrowed and she worried her lip. She really didn't trust him. He didn't know if he should think she was smart or be offended. Rory decided he was both.

"Maura?"

"I'm not sure that's such a good idea."

"If you tell me to leave, I'll leave," he said holding his hands up.

She blew out a breath that caused her bangs to blow up. It was an innocent gesture but for some reason, it turned him on. Right now, apparently everything turned him on.

She nodded. "Okay, but I *will* kick you out if you irritate me."

He smiled. "I've always liked a woman with a little spunk."

She rolled her eyes and slipped into her car.

Rory almost danced with glee on the way back to his motor-cycle. He didn't understand why but he knew he wanted her, and he wanted to share her with Zee. It would be delicious.

Now all he had to do was get her agreement and convince Zee.

And then the fun could begin.

three

M aura's stomach tightened as she walked up to her front door. Pulling in a deep breath, she tried to order her nerves to calm down. From the moment she ran into Rory in the parking lot, her hormones had been bouncing all over the place. She punched in the security code and cursed when the light flashed red. Dammit, he had her all crazy. It wasn't her fault. Since she'd seen him in the parking lot he'd been looking at her strangely. It was like she was his next meal.

She fought the shiver that worked through her body. Focusing, she punched in the code again and was relieved that she got it right this time. She opened the door and stepped in. Rory easily followed her. It was probably a bad move. Conner had always taught her to keep her suspect in front of her, but she was afraid of showing him too much from her expression right now. Another Connerism. Do your best not to let the enemy see if you're flustered.

And she did see him that way. The enemy. She didn't know what he was up to, but she didn't like it. Maura especially didn't like the way he made her react. Hell, her hands were shaking and that was just not like her. Why?

Because he'd been looking at her like he wanted to eat her up. It made her nervous. And hot. Very, very hot.

"Wow," he said as he walked in and looked at the entryway.

At one time she had the same reaction to the house that Conner had bought several years earlier. They had grown up middle class, their father the first to graduate from college. Conner had taken his job at the FBI and turned it into a very lucrative security company. She shut the door behind him then took off her shoes. He followed suit.

Not everyone did that but she figured that Rory understood the practice. Zeke and he had spent a lot of time in the Far East. "Thank you."

"No problem. I'm always happy to accommodate a woman."

She rolled her eyes trying to hide the way it made her feel to have him flirt with her. He had a little bit here and there, but nothing like this. It was a full frontal assault that she wasn't prepared for. If she thought about it too much she would definitely freak out.

"This is a pretty nice place," he said looking around.

"Thanks. I lived here with Conner, and he and Jillian always stay here when they come back." They stood in the entranceway staring at each other. The silence stretched and she felt the need to fidget—which would definitely let him know how nervous that made her. "Oh, would you like something to drink?"

He nodded.

"Come on. There's always beer here."

"How about some water?" he asked.

She shrugged as she led him into the kitchen. She had noticed that he didn't drink, at all. Oh, a nice wine from time to time, but only one glass. "Whatever you want is fine by me."

She retrieved a glass and filled it with ice and water. When she turned around, he was standing right behind her like he had at her car.

"Stop doing that."

He was looking at her mouth. "What?"

"Sneaking up on me. Zeke does it too and it drives me crazy. I hate that whole ninja thing he does."

His lips curved and she felt heat spiral through her blood. *Damn, he had a good smile*. Forget that, it was a freaking delicious smile.

"Ninja?"

Maura knew she shouldn't be so charmed, but it was hard to remember why. He was attractive even with the broken nose and the scar above his right eyebrow. The sexy Irish accent pulled her in every time. She needed perspective. She needed space.

Shoving the glass at him, she said, "You make no sounds at all. It freaks me out."

"You don't like me."

She should have expected him to make a bold statement. He was blunt and a lot of people didn't like dealing with him because of it. Funny, it was one of the things she liked about him. He wasn't really that rude, but she got the feeling he didn't like to tap dance around anything. Maura could respect that. She had the same problem and it was one of the reasons she had very few female friends. From the time she hit her teens, Maura had never been good at playing the social game.

She wanted to take a step back but the counter was there. She rubbed her temples. God, she was getting another headache. They were starting to be her constant companion the last few months. The stress of running the office without her brother was starting to get to her. The trip to Hawaii might be good for her in more ways than one. Sure, Zeke was Conner's business partner, but she couldn't let Conner down. He had done so much for her and now she could do this for him.

"Could you at least step back?" she asked.

He hesitated then did as she requested. "You're avoiding my comment."

She released the breath she had been holding. "No I'm not." Of course she was. She wanted this conversation like she wanted to wear pantyhose in August. "I like you, Rory. I'm just not comfortable around you."

"Honesty." He nodded. "I knew that Zee wouldn't be involved with a woman without integrity."

She'd had a feeling Zeke had told him they'd been involved. If not, someone in the office would have. They had been discreet, but people weren't stupid. And for all of Zeke's faults, he had been candid with her before they hired Rory.

"Listen, I know you two are together, that's fine."

He cocked his head to one side and studied her. It was different than most of the other times he had looked at her. Before, he had barely taken notice of her. No, that was wrong. He did pay attention, but not any more than he did anyone else. Now, though, he seemed to be looking at her with an interest she had never seen before.

Finally he spoke. "But it isn't. Not for you...and not for Zee."

"You give Zeke something I cannot." And that hurt more than she would ever let anyone know. It always felt like someone had taken a knife to her chest. She blinked when her eyes started to burn. "I want him to be happy."

He straightened and set his glass on the counter beside him before approaching her. With every step he took toward her, her pulse increased. Having Rory concentrate on her and only her was almost too much for her to take. Her nerves were sparking with an energy that she hadn't felt before in his presence.

"Zee didn't call it off because you couldn't give him what he needs."

She snorted to hide the pain. "I don't think you know what you're talking about."

He settled one hand against the counter then the other, effectively caging her in. She felt trapped, but for some reason, she didn't want to escape. Her nipples were hard against the lace of her bra and her mouth was suddenly dry. It was just like when they had been at her car.

"Zeke never explained it to you, did he?" Rory asked, his voice drawing the words out, his Irish accent thickening.

She shook her head because she could not speak. All the air in her lungs seemed to back up and her throat clogged. He was looking directly into her eyes and she felt herself melting.

"Zeke doesn't like to play at BDSM."

She sighed and inwardly cringed at the wistful sound. She hated that she sounded like a little lost girl.

"I know."

"I do though."

She shook her head even though she knew it was true. She had heard the rumors, but she had never believed it because Zeke hated BDSM. He didn't like playing either role with men or women.

Rory nodded, one side of his mouth curving up. God he was driving her crazy with small gestures. No wonder Zeke was so in love with the man. He could probably seduce the most conservative man into bed.

"And here's a little secret," he said, his voice rougher than before. He leaned closer until his mouth was against her ear. His warm breath feathered against her skin and she shivered.

She needed to get some control over the situation and, not to mention, her body. "What's your secret?"

He chuckled and she realized he had been waiting for her to ask. "Well, love, Zee likes to watch."

He teased her earlobe with his teeth as her brain shut down. God that felt good. She hadn't had a man since Zee and it had been so long.

"He what?" She asked closing her eyes enjoying the way his teeth grazed her ear.

He took his sweet time answering her. Of course, she didn't really care because what he was doing to her ear lobe had her entire soul humming.

"He likes to watch me tie a woman up and dominate her."

The image he was creating was a little too much for her to deal with, but it was there now and there was a good chance she would dream about it tonight.

"R-really?" she asked.

"Yeah, and then, we fuck her until she can't walk."

She shivered again and tried to swallow. "Umm."

"Or...we drive her crazy by making her watch us. Zee really does like a cock up his ass."

Her brain was melting. And her body. That was melting too. Her panties were beyond damp and every sane thought she had evaporated. He tickled her lobe with his tongue. He smelled like sin and that is all she wanted to do. Sin. With him. And Zeke.

"Do you think you would like that, love?" He asked, his Irish lilt deepening over the words even more. Oh, lord, he was going to make her come just by talking to her and playing with her ear. What kind of man could do that? Apparently an Irishman because Maura was just about to lose it. He was dangerous with that mouth. She could just imagine what he would do with it on different parts of her body.

"Maura?" he asked and there was a hint of something else there. It was more of a demand and of course she responded.

"I-I'm not sure."

He chuckled as he nuzzled her neck. Tendrils of need unfurled through her blood. He slipped his fingers along her jawline, then down to her breast. He hummed when he came in contact with her nipple. "I think you are, love."

That was the truth. She could picture what he was describing and her body yearned. Her hormones were telling her to just hop on him and enjoy the ride. Hell, the man had her glasses fogged up. She wanted it so badly it scared her.

Maura grabbed onto what little sense she had left and said, "I--I need you to move."

He paused. "Are you sure?"

She nodded. And, true to his word, he stepped back.

"You're not playing games?" she asked.

"I wouldn't have gotten both of us worked up if it was just a game, Maura. I don't play that way...unless it's for the job."

He glanced down. She followed his line of vision and she saw his hardened cock easily through his jeans. She blushed.

"God, you are a joy," he said. He leaned forward and brushed his mouth over hers. The simple kiss sent another jolt of lust racing through her blood. He pulled back and smiled. "You think about it. It's a week. We can try it out, play...no worries. I have a feeling that you'll have a really good time."

"I don't know."

"Just think about it." He took her hand and kissed her fingers. "I'll see myself out."

She didn't move, couldn't. She was so turned on she didn't know if she could walk. She finally gathered herself enough to take a couple of steps. The glass he had drunk out of sat on the counter still. She grabbed it up and drank the remaining water down in one gulp.

She set it on the counter. The ideas that Rory had conjured up in her brain were never going to go away. Closing her eyes, they flashed there, tempting her. It was everything she could hope for. Zeke, and a hot Dom to make it all happen just as he had said.

She *would* have a really good time, but would her heart survive?

four

Zeke rolled up his swim trunks and stuffed them into his
suitcase with more force than he needed. Irritation
inched down his spine. Zeke knew he should have
known this was going to happen, but he thought this time
would be different. Rory had promised, had told him that he
was there to stay. It was one of the reasons he had hired him.
They needed dependable people, and when he was there, really
there, Rory was the most dependable person in the world.

Zeke heard the door open, knew it was Rory and said
nothing.

"Zee," he yelled.

Zeke hesitated. He wasn't sure he was in the mood to deal
with his lover at the moment. Rory had a habit of disappearing
for long periods of time right before he vanished for several
months. Zeke promised himself it would be the last time for
that shit. This time, if Rory walked out of his life, he was
cut off.

Rory stepped into the room. "You seem to be doing some
damage to the clothes, there. What have they ever done to you?"

His tone told Zeke he was trying to keep that tone light.

Zeke wasn't in the mood. He didn't even look at him. If he did, Zeke was pretty sure he would punch him in his fucking throat.

"What's up?"

Zeke rolled up a shirt and stuffed it in with his other clothes before answering. "Nothing. Just wondering where you were for two hours."

"I had some things to pick up."

Rory had never cheated on Zeke. *Never.* It just wasn't in his character. When he was there, he was there just for Zeke. He might be a bastard when it came to sticking around, but that went with the package. Rory had commitment issues to the extreme. Zeke understood them, he was just sick of dealing with them. Sometimes, it was too fucking much to ask.

"When are you leaving?" Zeke asked. As soon as he said the words, he regretted them. He wasn't really in the mood for the truth. He wasn't sure he ever was but he was pretty sure he wasn't now.

When he said nothing, Zeke looked up at him. Rory was frowning. "What the bloody hell are you talking about?"

Of course, Rory had no idea what he was talking about. They never addressed the issues they had. Not the ones like this. He would start to discuss it and Rory would disappear. It was the way he had dealt with things in the past.

"Look," Zeke said as he went into the bathroom and started to shove things into his shaving kit, "I know what's going on. This time though, I'll have to replace you at the office if you are going to disappear, so at least give me a head's up."

Rory said nothing. Zeke wasn't sure if he was confused or stunned that he had confronted him on it. He brushed past him back into the bedroom.

"Stop," Rory said.

Zeke shoved his bag into the suitcase. "I'm not in the mood to have a fight, but if you're leaving, I need to know."

Rory walked to him then and took his hands. "Stop."

Zeke shook his hands away. "This is my life here—my reputation. I can't let you drop off the side of the earth because things got too intense." He couldn't look at him. Zeke knew if he did, Rory would talk him back into bed easily. He was sick of that. Hard truths had to be said.

"What the fuck are you talking about? I'm not planning on going anywhere."

With a sigh, he turned to face him and felt a sharp punch to the gut. The pain in Rory's gaze was enough to undo Zeke. It was his downfall to love stubborn people. Maura was just as bad. And when he shoved them, Zeke tended to hurt their feelings.

"I'm not leaving you. Not now, not unless you want me to."

Zeke wanted to believe him. The sincerity in his voice was genuine. And he understood that many times when Rory left, it wasn't because of their relationship but of the ghosts he fought from his past.

Rory skimmed his hands up his arms and then cupped his face.

"I am not leaving. *Ever.*"

Then he leaned closer, brushing his mouth over Zeke's. The taste of him, the feel of his lips against his pulled a sigh from Zeke. He rested his forehead against his. Rory sighed.

"I can't leave you, Zee. Not anymore."

The words tightened Zeke's heart. Desire and love threaded Rory's voice. So many times he had watched the one man he had always loved walk out of his life. This time...it might kill him. But never before had Rory promised him not to leave.

Rory kissed him again, invading his mouth. Zeke's heart raced as his cock hardened, his blood heated. Rory's tongue brushed against Zeke's as he slid his arms around him and down to his ass, pulling Rory tight against him. The feel of his cock against his own, even through the layers of clothing, was enough for Zeke to start losing control. Rory was already hard and Zeke groaned. It was difficult not to. For over ten years, it hadn't changed for them one bit.

Just like the first time, Zeke felt himself falling. Rory always did this to him, could always make it impossible to resist him. He needed him like an addict needed their favorite drug. Every cell in his body urged Zeke to surrender to him. All the concerns he'd had just minutes before dissolved under Rory's sensual assault.

Rory kissed a path down Zeke's neck as he grabbed the bottom of Zeke's shirt and practically tore it off. Then, Rory started to work his way down his body, kissing and nipping at his skin. Zeke's cock hardened further and he shivered when he felt the hard bite of Rory's teeth against his flesh.

There was an urgency to Rory's movements and it fed Zeke's need. He needed the connection, needed to feel flesh against flesh. Rory grabbed the waistband of Zeke's jeans, yanked it free of the button then jerked down the zipper. Zeke wasn't wearing any underwear and his cock sprang free. Rory wrapped his hand around it and gave it a few long pumps.

"Like, that, do ya, love?" Rory asked. He didn't wait for an answer. He took Zeke's mouth in a hard, punishing kiss as he continued to pump his shaft. Fuck. With each stroke, Rory pulled him closer to the edge. At that moment, he was completely and absolutely under his spell. Rory bit down on Zeke's bottom lip before pulling back and releasing his cock.

Rory dropped to his knees and wrapped his hand around his cock. He gave it another hard pump before he lifted it up and slipped his tongue over Zeke's sac. Zeke curled his toes into the carpet and tried to control himself. He was so fucking close to coming.

"Beautiful," Rory said as he leaned forward to lick up one

side of Zeke's penis. His breath feathered over Zeke's flesh and he shivered. Then, Rory looked up at Zeke and slowly, took the tip into his mouth. Rory swirled his tongue around the tip, as he pumped his cock. He pulled back, licked down one side, teasing the tip of his penis, then down to his sac again. Little nips against his sensitive skin pulled another drop of precome to the surface and Zeke could feel his orgasm approaching. As Rory continued to pump him with his hand, he took Zeke's penis into his mouth fully. His other hand was on his ass, his fingers digging into his skin as if he was afraid he would go somewhere. There was no chance in that.

Closer and closer, Rory pushed him toward that edge, but just as Zeke was about to come, Rory pulled back.

"Fuck," Zeke muttered as he watched Rory pull off his shirt. Rory stood and attacked his pants. He was naked within seconds. Not able to resist, Zeke skimmed his hand over Rory's chest then slipped it down to Rory's impressive erection. Rory leaned his head back and groaned as Zeke stroked him a few times. He wanted to make Rory lose control. Before he could though, Rory tumbled them back onto the bed. Zeke heard a thunk and realized the suitcase had fallen on the floor. He ignored it.

Rory wasted no time. He straddled Zeke's face and took his head in his hands. Zeke eagerly opened his mouth and took him in. Deeper and deeper Rory thrust into Zeke's mouth. His fingers dug into Zeke's scalp as Zeke slid his hands to Rory's ass. A drop of precome danced over his taste buds.

Each time he took him in his mouth deeper and deeper. He wanted that, wanted to taste him as he came, but Rory had other ideas. He pulled back and then moved off him.

"Fuck."

The exasperation was easy to hear and Zeke smiled. It wasn't often he could push him that far. Rory scooted down

Zeke's body so they were lying groin to groin, their cocks pressed together. Zeke closed his eyes and sighed. Rory cupped his face and kissed him. Frustration and desire filled the gesture.

When he pulled back, he looked at Zeke for a long while.

"I love you, Zee."

The words were whispered but without hesitation. It had taken him so long to finally tell Zeke of his love it was always a joy to hear. Zeke smiled.

"I love you too."

Rory smiled at him. It was almost embarrassing how his heart flip-flopped. He really did love this man, almost more than he loved himself. He had never really been serious about another man in all his life. There had been others, but there was only one Rory. There was a part of his heart—part of his soul—that had known that all along.

Rory slipped out of bed, and offered his hand. Zeke took it and stood, his heart hammering against his chest. Rory knelt down in front of him, kissing and nipping at the skin as he went. Zeke slipped his hands down to Rory's head and fucked his mouth. God, it felt good, the damp, warm recesses of his mouth, the way he moved his tongue over the tip of Zeke's cock always got to him. He continued pumping in and out of his Rory's mouth, but his rhythm quickened as he felt his orgasm take over. One hard thrust and he came, holding Rory's head still as he thrust one last time in his mouth and giving over to the pleasure.

Rory gave Zeke's cock one last lick before he kissed his way back up his body. Then, he turned Zeke toward the bed. He skimmed his hands down Zeke's back. God, the man had the hands of a god. Just one little touch and Zeke was turned to jelly. Rory trailed his fingers down to Zeke's ass. Zeke settled his hands on the mattress as he felt Rory pull his cheeks apart before he entered him in one hard thrust.

Fuck, that felt good. The connection was stronger than ever. Rory thrust in and out of his ass, his groans were music to Zeke's ears. It didn't take long before Rory was groaning Zeke's name. He leaned over him, his chest against Zeke's back. He could feel his lover's heart hammering as Rory kissed the back of his neck.

He pulled out of Zeke's ass and they fell onto the bed but unlike all the years before, Rory held onto him, tightly. Zeke could be pissed, he could be worried, but he couldn't say that things hadn't changed between them.

Zeke just hoped that this time Rory was there for good.

five

R ory didn't always enjoy lying around in bed with lovers. He rarely seemed to be able to settle even after a good bout of sex. With Zee, it was different. No matter where they were, Rory could find himself at peace if Zee was beside him.

The sun had set and the only light in the room came from the hall light. His mind seemed to relax, his body felt...right. Something just seemed right here in bed with Zee. After years of fighting what he finally accepted, Zee was his home and there was no way he could fuck it up. And that was the reason he wanted to give him Maura, even if it was for a week.

"So, do you want to know where I was?" Rory asked him. He knew Zee was worried about their relationship. The man was a worrier and that was probably why Rory found him so attractive. He knew he didn't have to deal with the worrying; Zee worried enough for the two of them. It was also nice to have someone, anyone, worry about him. He'd only had one or two people in his life like that.

Zee's sigh was long and there was a bit of loneliness to it.

Ever since his return a few months ago, Rory felt that there was something more going on with him.

"I figured you were starting your regular pattern."

That brought him up short. Rory shifted in bed to get a better view of Zee. His eyes were closed and the little bit of light that was in the room shimmered over his skin. Damn, the man was still fucking hot.

Rory shook his head. "What do you mean?"

Zee sighed again. "Every time before you bug off, you start disappearing for long stretches."

Rory pulled himself up so he could look down at Zee. Rory knew Zee was close to falling asleep, but Rory had a point to make. He had been a shit a huge part of his life and Rory knew that the biggest mistakes he had ever made were pushing Zee away when they got too serious. He was done with that. Almost dying did things to a man and it made him look at life differently.

"Zee." He waited for his lover to open his eyes. They were deep chocolate with a dark gold encircling the iris. How could anyone resist a man who was so fucking sexy and loving? He couldn't and thankfully, Zee hadn't given up on him. "I'm not leaving. I know you don't believe me and I have a lot to prove, but I'm not leaving this time."

He said nothing. Rory needed something else, some kind of connection. He leaned down and gave him a kiss. It was sweet and hot and he never took his gaze from Zee's.

"You know I love you," he said. It was still hard to say the words. Zee was the only person he had ever said them to. Each time he did, Rory expected him to throw them back in his face.

Zee lifted his hand and cupped his face. "I love you, too."

Rory let loose a sigh of relief and laid back on the bed. At one time, the words would have sent him in a panic. Now, it was a comfort.

"So where were you?" Zeke asked.

"I went shopping."

There was a beat of silence. "For what?"

Right now, Zee wasn't ready to go for the threesome. Strike that. Zee was ready, he just needed a little push. Zee wanted it and Rory wanted to be the one to give it to him. Rory knew watching Maura submit was going to be the ultimate turn on for Zee. Even thinking about it right now had his blood heating.

"For our trip to Hawaii. Easier to buy what I wanted here, than trying to find a place there. Since we don't have to mess with the TSA, makes it even easier."

Zee sighed again, this time it was filled regret. "She won't go for it."

"She will."

"How do you know that?"

Rory closed his eyes and remembered her reaction to him, to the picture he had painted for her. "I talked to her about it."

"You what?" Zee almost shouted and sat up. "I told you to leave her alone."

His reaction was over the top. It was one of the reasons that Rory thought Zee needed to work the woman out of his system. "Hold on, lover, I just talked to her. That's it."

Zee laid back down with a huff. "Do you ever listen to me? Do you ever listen to anyone?"

"Not when I'm right. And buddy, believe me, I was right about Maura."

Zee said nothing for a moment. When Zee was quiet like that, Rory knew his mind was working the issue. "What did she say?"

"I told her to just think about it. It's a week where there can be no rules."

"She doesn't need you tempting her into something that would end up hurting her."

That caught his attention. "What?"

Zee sighed. "I guess she heard a rumor about us and suggested a threesome. She immediately took it back."

"When were you going to tell me this?" Rory asked. Silence. "Were you ever going to tell me?"

"I'm not sure."

And that chaffed at Rory. He knew they both had secrets, but, still...it rankled him.

"I don't know," Zee admitted. "You don't understand her very well."

"How do you know that?"

"If you did, you wouldn't be so flippant about this. Bloody hell, anyone who knows Maura well knows she wouldn't handle this."

"Explain."

Zee shot him a look, but said, "She doesn't like change. You've seen how she is at the office. She doesn't live in the moment. She likes everything to go as planned. She probably planned on hooking her brother and Jillian up."

He filed that bit of information away. "Maybe she's at a point that she wants to make a change."

"And what about when we get back, working with each other every day."

Rory shrugged. "I don't think that will matter."

"Of course you don't," Zee said, his voice sounding weary. "You never think about the consequences of your actions."

Annoyance had his gut tightening, along with a healthy dose of worry. And that aggravated him even more. He had never really worried about the consequences of his personal life and now Zee had him worrying. Dammit.

"Don't make me sound like a shit. I might make a few mistakes here and there—"

"You mean the mistake like in Tokyo where I almost got my bloody head blown off."

"That was five fucking years ago. I can't believe you're bringing that up." Rory drew in a deep breath trying to gain hold of his temper. He didn't want to fight about something that happened when they were both so green they didn't know what they were doing in the field. "I have thought this through. I left it up to her. You know you want it, Zee. I do too. We haven't done this in a long time."

"Because every time we do, you disappear. It's the sign you are freaking out."

"No it's not." Rory frowned. "Are you serious?"

He huffed again. Zee was always kind of a huffy guy and most of the time, Rory loved it. Not now though, not now that he was ripping his character to shreds. "No. I'm making shit up. Of course I'm serious."

"I think you've been smoking weed again."

"I haven't had that in years. And you are avoiding the subject I brought up."

"And that is?"

When he spoke, Zee's voice was weary. "Quit being a dick, Rory. I've seen this pattern over and over. You're freaking out."

He was, Rory knew that. But it wasn't just a sign that he was leaving. Wanting Maura with them was a preemptive strike. Zee was infatuated with her and that infatuation was a bad thing in Rory's opinion. There was nothing but heartache on that path. It was better that both Maura and Zee work out their need for each other and get over it. He'd been waiting for an opportunity and this seemed perfect.

He leveled a look at the man he'd loved most of his life. Sure he had just figured it out, but better late than never. He would do anything to keep them together now.

"Other than that, what are your other objections?"

Zee didn't say anything for a long time.

"Zee?"

"I worry about Maura."

Zee could have stabbed him in the forehead with a fork and it would have hurt less that those four words. Rory knew Zee was half in love with the woman. The fact that he was more worried about her than either of them was enough to piss him off. He would never let Zee know just how much it hurt because the way Zee was, it would make him hurt too. He had never met someone who had so much empathy for the people he loved. That's the reason he had fallen in love with the man.

"She's important to you."

Zee looked at him, searching his face. He hated that. Hated Zee could pick his brain, but it was one of the things he loved most about him. "She should be important to you too. She hasn't had an easy time of it."

Rory snorted. "Yeah, I saw the house, looked tough."

"You've always been cynical but you're worse now than ever before. When did that happen?"

It had nothing to do with being cynical. There was a deep-set panic in his gut that told him that Zee cared more about Maura than any other woman he had been involved with. That alone had him being nasty, but Rory was having issues himself. The woman had drawn him in before, but now...he was hooked. Other than Zeke, he couldn't get the woman out of his head.

He ignored his worries and smiled at Zeke. "I'm not any more cynical than you are, my love."

"Yes you are. Besides, money won't bring her parents back."

Shit, he hated that admiring tone Zee got when he talked about Maura. He knew he was jealous and hated that too, but there didn't seem to be a damned thing he could about it.

"She had Conner." Fuck, now he sounded defensive. He

didn't like when they had discussions like this. Zee always got hurt and Rory ended up ticked off.

"Yeah, but she was in the car with them when they died."

"She survived."

"Just to watch her parents die."

"Is that what she told you?" he asked, not able to keep the snarl out of his voice.

"No. Conner told me she used to have nightmares. I do know she was stuck in the car with them for three hours after. The bastard drunk who hit them just sped off and left them there. When..." Zeke glanced at him apparently not wanting to reveal too much. He sighed. "When we were together, every now and then, she would have the nightmares. She tried to hide it, but they disturbed her. If she's under a lot of stress, she tends to have them. It's another reason Conner probably wants her over there."

Rory said nothing to that, mainly because now *he* was starting to admire her. She never mentioned anything about it. And, she did work like she was just like everyone else at work. Tonight had to be one of the few nights she left before anyone else, and she worked as if her brother didn't own the company. That made him like her even more. Not once did she act as if she expected something to be done for her. *Dammit.*

"Then, add in that she is a geek, a woman with a mind so sharp it's scary. She was always an outcast. In college at sixteen...it wasn't easy."

"That doesn't sound so bad."

"Stop being an ass," Zee said without much heat. "This isn't a one night stand or even just a week. If we pull her into a threesome, then we just go on together without her, she'll be an outcast again. She doesn't need that. No one deserves that."

Rory knew he spoke of his mother and father. Zeke's father's family had never accepted the wife and child he had brought back from Haiti. They were pretty much left on their own when his father had died.

"Okay. We'll be careful, but I already put it out there. Besides, we don't have to end it when we come back."

It was dark but he sensed Zee's glance. "What are you saying?"

"Maybe we leave it up to her at the end?"

Even as he said it, it sounded so wrong...but so fucking delicious. Having a sub that enticed Zee the way Maura did in the relationship would be beyond anything they had done before. She wouldn't go for it probably, but there was always the slight chance she might.

"I have a feeling she'll say no anyway."

Rory said nothing. In their line of work, he had learned a long time ago how to read people and what he saw today told him that there was at least a good chance she would say yes. Of course, arguing with Zee was like arguing with a brick wall. Once he set his mind on something he just would not let it go. The only way to prove Zee wrong was doing it in front of his face. He wanted it as bad as Rory did, he was just afraid. Worrying about it tonight. They had an early start to their day and there was no reason to keep debating what Maura might or might not do. Rory turned toward Zee and slipped an arm over his waist. With Zee's even breathing filling the air, Rory followed him into sleep.

six

I rritation slipped down Maura's spine as she hurried along the tarmac. She was late. She was never late, ever. It always made her feel as if she had lost control. Her stomach clenched. Her head was pounding, her eyes scratchy and her basic attitude was crap. Seriously, if someone challenged her on something, there was a good chance she would punch the person in the throat. This was not how she wanted to start her day off. Normally she liked to be up with the sun. Today, not so much. Maybe she would sleep for the entire seven days she was in Hawaii.

Her phone buzzed with Zeke's ringtone. She flipped it open. "What?"

"Well, top of the morning to you, darlin'."

She sighed. "Sorry, I'm on my way to the plane right now."

"Are you alright?"

No, she wanted to scream. She had spent most of last night thinking about Rory's invitation. When she had grabbed a few hours of sleep, she had been haunted by the idea of having two sets of hands on her, two mouths and two voices thick with an Irish accent as they drove her crazy.

"Yes, just had some things that caught me off guard. I can see the jet."

He said nothing for a moment. She sensed he wanted to ask her questions. About what? Did Rory tell him what he had asked her? Of course he probably did. Those two shared just about everything.

And they wanted to share her.

Heat slipped through her blood and danced over her nerve endings. She stopped in mid step and ordered herself to calm down. She had decided not to allow it, right? She had thrown the idea out to Zeke when Rory had moved in but it had been desperation. She had been scared of losing Zeke once and for all —even as a friend. Knowing that now, she would be beyond pathetic. Her emotional well-being would be damned to hell if she agreed to it. She had thought about how it would hurt when they returned and that had been the deciding factor. She would never be able to work with both of them after that. Seeing them together now was tough enough. After seven days in their bed, it would be too painful.

She started walking again and watched as he stepped out onto the steps.

"I can see you and this conversation is ridiculous."

She didn't wait for an answer; she just turned her phone off.

He was watching her, his gaze on her as she approached. At least, she thought he might be, because he was wearing those aviator sunglasses. God, she loved them. He looked so fuckable when he was wearing them. If she had time to think about it, Maura would probably worry more about her attraction to him as an authority figure. When he stood there like that, those badass glasses on, it reminded her of a cop or a military dude. What the hell was wrong with her?

He jogged down the stairs and Rory appeared behind him.

Her heart did a little jerk, then her stomach muscles clenched again. Dammit, how was she going to be able to ignore the temptation that they represented?

Zeke walked out to meet her and took her bag. "I'll take your bag around."

She nodded.

"Are you sure you're okay?"

"Yeah, I'm just a little off. I have been the last few days." She didn't want to talk about the insomnia that seemed to be her constant companion these days. If she told him, he would tell Conner. Then, there would be a talk. Lord help her if Conner wanted to talk. "I think I just need a week in Hawaii to rest. And see Conner."

He nodded, then turned, taking her arm to walk her to the jet. Rory was still standing there, waiting and watching. Heat slid down her spine and it had nothing to do with the fact that she was on a Miami tarmac. She could smell Zeke's musky aftershave.

"There isn't an attendant," Zeke said when they reached the stairs.

"I didn't think we needed one, do we? There's food on board, right?"

It was odd that he would bring that up because it had never really been an issue before. They rarely had an attendant on board when they used the jet for leisure. It just wasn't in her nature to be waited on.

"Sure." He handed her up the stairs and there was Rory, waiting still. She got a very odd feeling that Zeke was handing her off to Rory. Just the thought caused her to shiver.

Rory held out his hand and she hesitated. It wasn't as if there was a final decision. She had decided not to do anything, right? This wasn't a good idea because...

Okay, she couldn't remember why it was a bad idea, but she was sure it was.

"Maura?" Rory asked, his voice threaded with concern. She shook herself and took his hand.

"Sorry. Not enough sleep last night."

He led her into the plane. "You can just doze in the bedroom until we get there."

"I have to call Conner first." As soon as she said it, her phone rang.

Rory shook his head. "It's the middle of the night there."

"He's waiting to go to bed until I tell him we are on our way." She clicked the phone on. "Hello, Conner."

"Hello, Maura. Everything fine?"

"Yep. Zeke is just putting my case in the storage compartment and there he is," she said when he stepped into the jet. Maura collapsed onto a couch. "We should be leaving pretty soon."

"Good. Get some rest. I want to talk to Zeke."

"I love you too, Conner."

He sighed. "I love you, Maura."

She smiled and handed the phone to Zeke. "Grumpy bossman wants to talk to you."

"Hey, Conner."

He walked off to the back of the jet as they pulled up the stairs to close off the jet. The copilot smiled at her. "Morning, Ms. Dillon. We should be in the air within ten minutes."

"Thanks, Henry."

"Let us know if there is anything you need," he offered with a smile before he returned to the cockpit. Zeke was still in the back talking to Conner so that left just Rory and her. She glanced at him and he was staring at her.

"Did you get any breakfast?" he asked.

His voice sounded normal. How could someone act

normally after what he suggested the night before? She had to think extra hard just to make conversation. All she could think about was having both of them touching her. Being in a plane for the next ten hours was going to be tough enough.

"Uh, no." She rolled her eyes. "And you can tell from my very intelligent conversation that I haven't had any kind of coffee either."

He grinned at her and for a moment, her brain just completely shut down. Part of it was the lack of sleep and caffeine but the bigger part of it was him. Rory was a stunning man, but when he smiled...he stole a woman's breath. He was wearing a black t-shirt another pair of jeans. He looked badass and fuckable.

Lord, she saw them both as authority figures. And she wanted them. What the hell was wrong with her?

"We can remedy that. You take it black, right?"

She nodded and he went off to get her a coffee. Why was she so stupidly happy that the man remembered such a small detail? Maybe because it was one of the things she liked about Zeke. So many guys took her for granted. She wasn't a women who enjoyed flowers or extravagant gifts. Simple pleasures were all she needed. Zeke had understood that, and now Rory did too, apparently.

They would make good partners in bed...especially both of them at the same time.

You are not here for that. For him, or Zeke. Do not make yourself crazy wishing for something that is not going to happen. Probably.

If she could remember that when either of them smiled at her she would be better off. She could save herself from playing the fool. But was she a fool for letting an opportunity like this go?

He poured her a cup and brought it to her. After setting it

down, he settled on the couch next to her. This time, she was enticed by the citrusy aftershave that Rory preferred. It teased her senses and turned her on as much as Zeke's had just a few moments ago.

"Your brother needs to learn to relax," Zeke said as he walked back to them.

"You have to admit he's better since he and Jillian became involved."

"He's worried about the Petersen case. More worried than he has to be," Zeke said. "I told him this was silly."

The plane started up and Zeke sat down on the chair across from the couch. All of them buckled their seatbelts.

"Why are you two complaining? We get to do a little consulting and spend a lot of time in a million dollar house for the week. Sun, sand, tropical drinks."

"We live in Miami. You can go the beach any time," Maura said with a smile.

"When was the last time you went? Or any of us? We all work so many hours we don't have time. And when we do, we're so damned tired, we just want to sit on the couch or sleep."

That was true. Living so near the beach they all took it for granted. And all of them had been a little overwhelmed by running the office without Conner.

"Okay, I agree with that. I'm really looking forward to seeing the new office though."

"Nope, you are not talking about work. Not now. We are going to enjoy the trip over as if we are just going to be on vacation," Rory said. "What do you say, Zee?"

God, it always turned her on when he called Zeke by his nickname. She had resented it at first but after awhile it started to get to her. There was something very sexy about knowing these two men had an intimate relationship. Every time Rory said it, Maura could imagine what it sounded like when he said it when they made love. His voice dipped every time he said it too. It was easy to hear the love and desire between the two of them.

Zeke was watching her as if waiting for her to object. But she didn't.

"Sounds like a good plan to me," Zeke said slowly.

The next few minutes were taken over by getting ready for take off. It came off without a hitch. Once she knew it was safe to move around, she undid her seat belt and stood.

"I think Rory's right," she said. "I'm going to catch a few more hours of sleep. Knowing Conner and Jillian, they'll want to keep us up for hours."

Rory took her cup of coffee. "Call if you need anything."

Maybe she had gone insane but she was pretty sure it was a loaded offer.

"Sure," she said, before escaping to the back. She shut the door to the bedroom and collapsed on the bed with a sigh. She closed her eyes trying to forget Rory's offer yesterday.

She had known for a long time she was a sub. When she had become curious about it, she had researched it. It was the way she could deal with things. It was always the way she dealt with life. After the trip to Rough 'n Ready while on an assignment, she knew without a doubt she was. The problem was, the man she was in love with wasn't a Dom.

Zeke had tried, but it hadn't been in him. He just did not get into the life like she had. It had hurt—more than she would ever let him know. But their relationship at the office was more important, especially now that they were running things without Conner there. Oh, her brother still had his hand in everything, but he had been the buffer for them. Now, it was mainly them, with a little help from Rory. Jennifer was good at her job, but Maura and Zeke were now the face of the company. She couldn't let her brother down.

She opened her eyes and stared at the ceiling. A shower would clear her head. With a huff, she pulled herself out of bed and headed for the small shower stall. And if this didn't help, she didn't know what she would do.

Seven

R ory's blood was humming. Just being on the plane alone with Zee and Maura had him ready to jump both of them. It wasn't like him at all. He might not practice BDSM with Zee, but he could always control himself for the most part. Sure, he didn't have a problem with getting down and dirty in places they shouldn't—like the office. But he could control those urges if he needed to. Now he seemed unable to keep his mind on anything else. It was hard not to think about Maura, about what kind of sub she would make.

He wasn't a Dom who liked a pushover. He didn't know many Doms or Dominatrixes who liked a sub who didn't present a challenge.

"I can hear those little wheels turning in your head," Zee said without looking up from his computer.

"What?"

"She didn't say anything. So, it's a no go."

"No, saying nothing does not mean no. It means she hasn't decided. Or maybe she wants to wait until we get there."

With an aggravated sigh, Zee leaned back. "Will you stop talking about it? Bloody hell."

The outburst surprised and delighted Rory. Zee held onto his emotions too tightly. If this is what Maura did for him, it was a welcome change for the two of them.

Rory smiled. "Sorry, love, but I can't stop thinking about it."

"Well, neither can I. You aren't making it any better."

Rory jumped up from his seat. "Maybe we should check on her. She's been asleep for awhile."

Zee rolled his eyes. "Stop."

He knew that tone. Zee's temper was getting the best of him. It had nothing to do with anger though. No, that had to do with his frustration...and with Maura. He knew Zee wanted it as bad as Rory did. That was a very good sign.

"It won't hurt to ask."

Zee shook his head. "Leave her alone. Didn't you see how tired she was? She was barely making it across the tarmac. She's been under a lot of stress."

"And what is better stress relief than sex?" he asked.

He meant it as a joke but even Rory heard the dark need in his voice. Zee gave him a dismissive glance, then looked back to his work.

"You need to give her space. She's not like you. Maura is more like me."

He frowned. "What the fuck does that mean?"

Zee tapped a few more keys, then looked up at him. It was easy for Rory to see the irritation in his lover's eyes. It was a rare day when one of them hid their emotions any more. "She doesn't rush into anything. Maura has always thought things through. If she hasn't decided to spend the week as ours, then you have to give her the space to decide. If you crowd her into a corner, there is a good chance she'll shut the whole fucking thing down. It's the way she responds to things like that."

He grunted while Zee went back to work. For a few moments, he watched him work. Zee had always intrigued him, even before he had known either of them were bisexuals. Even after all these years, the need to have Zee in his life overwhelmed everything else he wanted. It only took him ten years to really get his shit together, but once he realized it, Rory didn't want to wait any longer. He had been lucky that Zee had welcomed him back. There would be consequences if he fucked it up this time. Rory was pretty sure Zee would never speak to him again if he did.

He glanced toward the door to the back of the airplane again. He couldn't remember ever wanting a woman this much. He had been attracted to others. There was something so...soft about women. He liked the way they felt, the way they smelled, and God, he loved to watch a sub when she finally gave into him. But...there was an edge this time. The lust was on level with what he felt for Zee when they first got together. It was odd, but Rory figured it was because Zee wanted her and he wanted to be the one who gave her to him.

"I tell you what. I'll peek in on her, make sure she doesn't need anything."

Before Zee could stop him, Rory opened the door. He knew better than wait for Zee. He moved like an old man. Coming from a man who was a Dom, that meant a lot. Rory knew how to control his emotions and his needs, but Zee had his own issues. He overthought everything, and it was one of their main problems.

He heard Zee following him, but Rory ignored him. The door opened silently and Rory found her snuggled beneath the covers. She looked so...contented. There was a quality to her that he couldn't seem to figure out. The woman was sexy, but there was something that seemed so...untouched. Zee didn't kiss and tell, but if she kept Zee occupied—and still had him interested—she liked to let loose in bed. God, she was so fucking irresistible.

She sighed in her sleep and he felt a little tap in his chest. It was like something had pulled on his heart. Zee was right. Looking at her face it was easy to see the dark smudges beneath her eyes. He was going to back away and let her sleep, but she shifted in her sleep and then her eyelashes fluttered, then her eyes opened. God, she was gorgeous. Her hair was a mess, her face flush

Her lips curved. Something tightened in his test.

"Hey," she said.

"Hey, yourself."

She blinked. He didn't blame her. Desire threaded over one of his syllables.

She cleared her throat. "How long have I been asleep?"

He stepped further into the room, shutting the door behind him. "About two and a half hours."

Her eyes widened. "Really? I haven't taken a nap that long in forever."

Rory smiled. She looked so sweet and innocent sitting there in her oversized shirt. He wanted to do nothing more than to crawl up into the bed and hold her.

What the bloody hell was he thinking? Of course there was something he wanted. Still there was part of him who wanted nothing more than to feel her body next to his...and Zee's.

"Why are you staring at me like that?" her voice had dipped lower.

He shrugged. The hum in his blood was now a full-bodied opera. He slipped his hands in the back pockets because his fingers itched to touch all that soft, soft skin. And taste. Tasting would be fanfuckingtastic.

"Can't seem to help it. Although, I'm not sure just how I am staring at you."

"Hmm."

"Listen, we don't have that much time before Zee comes beating on the door. He told me to leave you alone, but I think it is best just to get it out of the way."

She licked her lips and he groaned.

Her eyes widened. "What?"

"You're just driving me crazy, here."

Then, silence.

"Well, are you going to answer me?"

"I had decided to say no."

The door opened before she could finish her thought. Zee smacked Rory in the back with it.

"Bloody hell, Zee," he said, his back stinging from the blow.

"Grow a set, Rory."

Rory looked from Zee to Maura. The heat in the air went from simmering to boiling hot. Damn, he had never felt that kind of reaction from Zee for a woman before. No wonder he was so hung up on her. There was something between them. He knew part of him should be worried, and it was, but fuck it was so sexy to see Zee fall for a woman.

"So, we both want an answer. Zee doesn't want to admit it, but he's more than a little interested."

Zee shot him a dirty look.

"I-I was going to say no," she repeated.

For some reason, that had his heart sinking when she said it again. He had thought that maybe she had changed her mind by the tone in her voice. But now she sounded more resolute. He glanced at Zee who wasn't looking at him. He was looking at Maura.

"But?" Zee asked.

She licked her lips again.

"I'm not sure why I was going to say no."

Rory wanted to scream but he didn't. He held it all in as she looked from one to the other.

"I think we're pressuring her too much," Zee said.

"No, you aren't. I'm going through all the reasons I had for not accepting the invitation. I had a really long list."

"Of course you did," Zee said, his voice low and soothing that made Rory want to ring his neck. Now was not the time to go soft.

She sighed. "Now they really don't seem that important."

"Yeah?" Rory asked, his lips curving and his heartbeat sped up.

"I'm just a little nervous."

"About?" Zee asked.

She snorted and rolled her eyes. "I have two Alpha males, one of them who wants to make me submit, standing in a very small space, and you are wondering why I'm nervous?"

"How about this? How about we just do a little play? No heavy stuff. Then, we can decide," Rory said.

"I've played before. Not with Zee, but with others." She glanced at Zeke. "Sorry."

"I knew."

She sighed and picked at the blanket. "I worked with a Dom. I had to know if I was right about what I wanted in the bedroom."

"So, you know how it goes, but it's different with us," Rory said.

She looked at him. "Yes, and I don't want it to be weird when we get back."

"Again, let's just play, then you can decide from there. If not, we will have a fabulous time in Hawaii, then go home."

He started to pull the blanket off her and her eyes widened. "What are you doing?"

Zee chuckled. "Rory isn't going to wait another seven hours before we land now that you said you would play."

"But...the pilots."

Zeke smiled as he rose from the bed. He flipped the lock.

"That takes care of that."

She sighed again and the sound of it sent a wave of heat through his blood. Rory caught a whiff of her scent and his cock twitched. Dammit to hell, she smelled like cinnamon. She always smelled like that, almost every day. It made him think of dessert, and that had him thinking of whipped cream, which led to all kinds of naughty thoughts.

"I just..."

"What, love?" Rory asked as he nuzzled her neck, drinking in more of that cinnamon scent. He nibbled at the tender flesh just behind her ear. She moaned.

"Maura," Zee said as he joined them on the bed. He kissed her as Rory continued on to her ear.

"Guys," she said holding up her free hand in protest.

They pulled back and waited. Rory's gut tightened as they waited. Maura studied them and he could tell nothing from her expression. Her cheeks were flushed but her mouth was unsmiling.

Rory could feel Zee's anticipation shimmering in the air and it urged Rory's need to new heights.

She looked from one of them to the other then a small, slow smile curved her lips. His breath tangled in his throat as she held out her hands.

"Okay."

eight

*Z*eke's heart almost stopped at the sound of that one little word. No one said anything for a moment, but he was sure they were all shocked. That might be the wrong word but he had hoped for this moment for so long his mind took a second to assimilate. His body had no problem responding. Lust and love rushed through his blood as his heart smacked hard against his chest. Lord, he was amazed that everyone didn't hear it. Zeke just couldn't help it. The fact that she agreed was the one dream he thought would never happen and now, just like that, he had the two people he loved most in the world in his bed.

"So..." Maura said. It was easy to hear the nerves in her voice. He wasn't accustomed to seeing her unsure of herself. He knew she always had doubts, but she hid them so well, he never really saw them. That alone told him how worried she was about this.

He glanced at Rory who smiled at him then looked at Maura. As lovers, he and Rory had done this before, but this was different. He sensed it more than probably both of them, but he knew Rory understood. His lover might not be ready to

64

admit it, but Zeke knew it was going to change everything. It was something he had been worried about, but now...none of that seemed to matter. Her agreement seemed to dissolve the worries he had. All that did matter was Maura and Rory.

"There's no reason to be nervous, love," Rory said, his voice a low hum.

Zeke studied him, surprised by his soothing tone. Rory had always been good with women, but normally, they didn't initiate anyone. He had added another level of reassurance to his voice that told Zeke he knew this was something special.

Granted, Maura wasn't a true initiate. He knew for her, she would have studied BDSM to the extreme. The rumors of whom she had worked with had reached him. It hadn't been easy to ignore what had been going on, but he had for both their sakes. They had already called it quits by that time, so it hadn't been any of his business.

Still, working with a Dom was different than putting it into practice. Even if she had, she was still a novice and every experience was different based on the people involved. No matter how many relationships she had been in, this one would be different. Rory and Zeke were different. Their needs were unique and many women didn't go for it. And apparently, Maura had some reservations. His bold, take anything on Maura clutched the sheet as if it was a magic shield. Apprehension etched her features.

He shifted his weight from one foot to another and she looked up at him. She was rumpled, her face flushed and she looked so damned unsure of herself. His heart melted right there. The fact that she could show him her worry meant they had moved another big step. Damn, he loved the woman. He could have died right there and been the happiest man on earth. He cupped her face and leaned forward to brush his mouth over hers.

"We'll go slow. You tell us if we push you too far."

She drew in a deep breath and nodded. Then, she leaned into him and deepened the kiss. Just like always, she took him by surprise. She was anxious but she was a woman who never second-guessed herself. Once she made a decision, Maura jumped in headfirst.

He slipped his tongue into her mouth and she took it willingly. He was soon losing himself inside her. From the first time he had kissed her it had been like this. It was how he had known they had something special. No one other than Rory had really affected him this way.

Zeke pulled back and smiled at the picture she made. Her lips were swollen and wet; her eyes were still closed. God, she was a delight. Zeke forgot just how much she loved kissing.

Rory leaned forward on the bed and kissed her neck, then slipped his fingers beneath her shirt and pulled it over her head, tossing on the floor behind him. She wasn't wearing a bra. Of course she wasn't.

"How did you concentrate at work knowing she looked like this," Rory said, admiration vibrating in his voice.

Zeke smiled at Maura's blush. "It was pretty hard at times."

Rory grinned at him and Zeke caught the double entendre. He chuckled as he watched Rory settle on the bed behind her. He brushed her hair aside and kissed her neck again. The sight of the two of them sent another jolt of need racing through him.

It had been months since he had touched her. When he sat next to her, he could feel his entire body shake inside. He needed to touch, to taste. He leaned forward and kissed her throat as Rory shifted moving down her back. Zeke took his time, savoring the taste of her skin. With small nips and pecks, he worked his way down to her breasts. Right there, he could smell the scent she always sprayed between her breasts; tart and summery, much like the woman herself. Whenever he smelled citrus, he got hard thinking about her.

Slowly they leaned her back onto the bed. As Zeke continued to pay attention to her breasts, Rory worked his way down her torso. He moved to settle himself between her legs. Kissing up one thigh then the other, Rory pressed his mouth against her pussy.

He gave her one leisurely lick as Zeke watched. Damn there was something so fucking sexy about seeing Rory between her legs. Rory pulled back and then slapped her mound. Her gasp was loud and arousing and Zeke had to fight the urge to take her right then.

"I like a woman who shaves. Of course," he said pausing and looking up at both of them, "Zeke and I do like to shave pussies ourselves."

Rory set his mouth against her again and started to eat her out.

Zeke slipped his arm behind Maura's neck and cuddled her against him. "Look at that, babe."

It took her a second, but she finally opened her eyes.

"I think he likes the taste of you," Zeke said unable to keep himself in check. Kissing her, he immediately plunged his tongue into her mouth.

She was trembling by the time Rory moved away from her mound and started a lazy journey back up her body. Zeke watched as one lover touched the other and felt something shift in his world. Rory and he had done this before, many times, but this...was different. He had thought it would be. They hadn't even started their BDSM play and he was already more entranced than he had ever been with his lovers before. He knew without a doubt, he would do everything he could to keep them together.

Zeke watched as Rory bent his head and licked one of her nipples.

"Damn, she's responsive." He smiled at Zeke. "And she tastes like heaven." He leaned forward and kissed Zeke. The familiar taste of Rory rushed through him, but it was more seductive this time. Maura's own arousal was now intertwined with Rory's familiar taste. Zeke felt lightheaded by the time Rory pulled back.

"You should have a better taste," Rory said as he leaned down to kiss Maura. She was watching them with such avid interest before. As he watched Rory kiss her, he knew just how arousing it had been for her to watch. Just watching their mouths moving together had most of the moisture drying up in Zeke's mouth. Maura closed her eyes and moaned as Rory deepened the kiss. For a second, he watched, mesmerized by the scene. Rory cupped her face, the gentle gesture spoke of the dual personality of Rory. He was caring, loving with women, but he also liked being in control. Witnessing his behavior with Maura was beyond anything he ever imagined.

She moved her legs restlessly. Zeke sat up and leaned down to taste her pussy.

The taste of her hit him full force. He knew that she loved oral, getting it and giving it. It was one of the things that would make her an excellent sub for Rory. Just thinking about that had his dick hardening. It was getting very uncomfortable in his pants. He added a finger and pressed his thumb against her clit and teased it with his tongue. She bowed up off the bed. He did not let her come though. Zeke wanted to savor her release. He had given her up months earlier and he wanted to draw this time out—to watch as she gave herself over to pleasure.

He sat up and Rory did too. They shared a look then both smiled. Zeke knew that Rory was going to let him take the lead this time. In the future, Rory would be in charge most of the time. But in this, Zeke knew Rory was giving him a gift. He smiled down at Maura, then leaned closer to kiss her.

Zeke slipped off the bed, pulled off his shirt and pants in record time. He was hard and he wrapped his hand around his cock as he watched Rory undress. Rory looked at him for permission and Zeke nodded. He definitely wanted to watch a little. Rory got up on the bed on his knees. He stroked his cock then smiled down at Maura.

"Want a taste, love?" Rory asked.

Maura licked her lips and Rory groaned and looked over at Zeke.

"Does she do that on purpose?"

Zeke smiled. "No. She is completely oblivious. And, she loves oral."

She was frowning at him. "Don't talk about me like I'm not here. I don't like it."

Rory returned his attention to her. "I'll allow that tone for right now, but after we get to Hawaii, you aren't going to be able to give your opinion."

She turned her frown to Rory, but Zeke knew she was aroused by Rory's tone. She said nothing, though and in turn probably turned on Rory by her submission. It wasn't much, but Zeke knew Rory was feeling her out. She wasn't inexperienced as a sub, but Rory was a very experienced and hardened Dom. He didn't believe in jumping in with someone like that.

Rory held his cock in front her mouth. "Come on, love. I want to feel that delicious mouth around my cock."

She shivered slightly and leaned forward to take his cock in. He watched. Entranced, Rory slipped his hands around the back of her head and fucked her mouth.

"Shit," Rory muttered.

Zeke knew what that meant. Maura was especially good at giving head. In fact, he had often joked that she was as good as any male lover he had before. Soon, though, he saw the signs. Rory's strokes were deeper and faster into her mouth.

Zeke grabbed a condom and rolled it on. He joined them on the bed and wrapped his fingers around her thighs. He could barely contain himself as he slipped his hands to her hips. She wrapped her legs around his waist. Slowly he eased himself into her warm core. He rested himself on his hands on the bed and began to thrust. Each time he pushed inside of her, she moaned against Rory's cock. He knew from experience just how that felt. Rory pulled out and offered his cock to Zeke.

With eagerness he took Rory's cock into his mouth. The taste of Rory's musky precome hit him full force. Combined with Maura's arousal it was intoxicating and overwhelming.

"You like that, Maura?" Rory asked. Zeke pulled back and noticed that she was watching him. Capturing her gaze, he took a long stroke into his mouth. He gagged a bit against the tip of Rory's penis, but he didn't care. In fact, it turned him on more, it always did. Still he was more aroused by the fact that she was watching them. He could feel her avid attention and it spurred his own arousal to new heights.

Rory pulled his dick out of Zeke's mouth then leaned down to kiss him. It wasn't a frantic kiss. Instead, it was slow and wet. It grabbed Zeke by the heart and tugged—as Rory could always do to him. Rory moved behind him, settling on the mattress. He used a bit of lube to ease his finger in. Zeke paused and groaned as Rory thrust his way into his ass.

"Fuck, that feels so good, babe," Rory said, his voice low and rough.

Rory started to move and Zeke let him take over. Using Rory's set rhythm, Zeke reveled in the connection to both his lovers. These two people were such a big part of his life, and now, together they were linked. Arousal and overwhelming joy was the feeling of being connected to both of his lovers; each time Rory pressed into his ass, he thrust into Maura. Over and over they repeated the motions. Her moans grew louder. He leaned down and took her mouth in a bruising kiss. With every bit of power he had in him, he wanted her to know that he loved her. Without words. She returned the kiss, slipping her hands up his chest then to his shoulders. At the same time, Rory bent down to kiss Zeke's neck. Right then, it was as perfect as Zeke thought life would ever be. Intoxicating, addicting...he didn't think he would ever get enough of these two people.

In the next instant, Maura came on a scream, surprising them all how fast she came. Her muscles clamped down hard on his cock, pulling him deeper into her core. Still, he held back. He wanted this to last as long as they could make it.

They continued, pushing her, holding back themselves as she came two more times. When she was still shivering from her third orgasm, Zeke allowed the pleasure to wash over him, through him. He thrust one last time into her and surrendered to his needs. A second later, Rory thrust into his ass and followed both he and Maura into bliss.

nine

Maura woke a short time later when she moved her foot and came in contact with a hard, muscled leg. "Watch it there, girlie," Zeke said, his voice thick with heavy satisfaction and sleep. "I need that shin."

He was curled up behind her, his arms wrapped tight around her. She snuggled back against him enjoying the feel of his bare flesh against hers. As she drew in a deep breath, she smelled both men's natural scents and felt her heart jerk. She was in way over her head, not sure just where this was heading. But, dammit, she was loving it at the moment.

She opened her eyes. There was a wide expanse of bed open before her. She knew that Zeke was on the edge of the bed on his side. Rory wasn't in bed with them. She heard the shower running.

"Sorry," she said.

He kissed the back of her neck. "How are you feeling?"

She loved his voice always, but she particularly loved it when there was a bit of husky sleep in it. The intimacy of it always made her toes curl. "Like I have just been to heaven and back."

He chuckled. Maura could feel the vibration of it against her back. "And we've just started."

She shivered then turned around to face him. His eyes were barely open, but his mouth was curved. She had wanted to be back in his bed for months, but knew that it wouldn't have worked—not forever. Everything in her soul wanted to be near him, but their issues in bed would have overwhelmed the relationship. Before she had worked through whether it had been the best decision or not, Rory had arrived to work at the company. She had known then she could never compete with the love of Zeke's life.

Mentally, she shoved that thought away. Regret was something she was trying to avoid. During this week, she was going to live in the moment. Still she had to be sure.

"You sure you want this? I mean, you and Rory have a pretty great relationship. I don't want to cause any problems."

He brushed the hair back away from her face then slid his fingers down her cheek and along her jawline. The endearing touch had her heart turning over.

"You aren't causing any problems. And while you might think this was amazing...I promise you, you haven't seen anything yet. Your submission will be..." he closed his eyes and drew in a deep breath, "sweet. I can't wait."

He opened his eyes and looked at her. There was an emotion in his gaze that she couldn't figure out. The man had always been open with her, but she knew there were parts of his life he hid, even from her. She understood that. Very few people knew about her bouts with insomnia. So she understood that Zeke might keep certain things to himself. This, though, might have solved their problems in the bedroom.

"Why didn't you tell me before that you had this...kink?"

He took a second or two to answer her. As always, Zeke chose his words carefully. "I don't do this with any other man."

She thought about that. She knew that Zeke was bisexual when they went to bed, before actually. And, she knew about Rory. He had always been very open about his love for his fellow Irishman. It had been intriguing, not just because of his open sexuality. There was an element of acceptance and love in that. Zeke was a man who loved to the most extreme.

"So, you never share a woman with anyone else?"

He shook his head. "Truly, other than the women we've slept with, Rory is the only other person who knows about this."

She sighed. "There's already rumors at work."

He frowned. "How did they find out?"

Rolling her eyes, she snorted. "Oh, good Lord, there are a bunch of former government workers there. They gossip better than the little old ladies at church."

He chuckled. "You're right there. What I meant is that... well, people don't realize that this is something that Rory and I share together and with no one else."

"Oh."

"And now we're sharing it with you. No one else knows but the three of us that it's something just for us."

She nodded.

"If you are still in the mood to move forward."

She was surprised by the uncertainty in his voice and her heart melted just a little bit more. She loved this man. From the moment he had touched her in Hawaii she knew that he was the one for her. Or she had thought he was. The crush she'd had on him had exploded into all encompassing love. The one thing she never did was hide that. He had known from the beginning and she knew he understood how she felt about him. The fact that he needed reassurances was a glimpse into the soul of the man.

"I would have to be crazy not to want to at least try more. I love you."

His gaze softened. Her throat closed up at the look on his face. She wasn't accustomed to sharing so many of her private thoughts. Zeke had told her once he would read her like an open book, but still, she was uncomfortable telling a man she loved him.

She swallowed. "I mean...Rory is an amazing Dom, I can tell already."

"Is that so, love?" Rory asked.

She looked past Zeke and found Rory watching them. She wondered how long he had been standing there, but in the next instant her brain went blank. All he had on was the towel he held anchored at his waist. A small bead of water slipped down his chest. Lord, the man was a god.

Rory was a man who had lived a hard life, just like Zeke. But for some reason, it seemed more pronounced on Rory. Zeke was lean lines, like a swimmer. Sculpted, yes, but not so damn big. There were a few scars here and there but the one that held her attention was a long thin line from his chest to abs. She had also seen a little pock mark on his ass earlier that she knew was from a bullet but she had been disappointed to find out that the rumors of tattoos on his naughty bits had been exaggerated.

"Doesn't he look good?" Zeke asked, his voice already deeper, the arousal easy to hear.

She nodded because she couldn't say anything, again. Seeing the way Rory was looking at them and hearing the lust in Zeke's voice had her body heating. Hell, her nipples were already so hard they hurt. She had never had a problem with talking until she had gotten involved with these two men. They undid her at every turn. They seemed to get under her skin so easily.

Zeke moved closer and pressed his wet mouth against her

throat as Rory dropped the towel. His cock was longer than Zeke's. It curved up against his belly, rock hard and ready for another round. Of course, Zeke made up for that in girth.

She felt her face start to burn and Rory laughed.

"You are so easy to read, Maura. Don't think of ever lying to us because we'll know." He leaned down and cupped her face with one of his large hands. "What naughty thoughts are going on in there, love?"

Her face turned even hotter.

"Not tellin', huh?" he asked his voice deepening over the words. He slipped his finger beneath her chin and forced her to look up at him. "I will allow this right now, but soon there will be no secrets of this nature, do you understand?"

She nodded, still not able to speak. She was only catching a glimpse of the Dom he was holding under control and what little she saw intrigued her. For a man who seemed to be able to walk into danger without a thought, he seemed controlled in the bedroom. If that was the only place he practiced control, that was fine by her. Sharing him with Zeke, well, that was icing on the cake.

Zeke kissed his way down her back, his open mouth wet against her skin.

Rory stroked his cock drawing her attention away from his face. She licked her lips thinking of the taste of him.

"Naughty Maura, not me this time," he said. His voice had roughened and she felt a little sense of satisfaction that he was affected as well.

Zeke moved away and laid her back on the bed. He offered up his cock to her and she gladly took him in her mouth. He leaned his head back and moaned. The glide of his shaft into her mouth sent little bursts of lust popping through her blood. Damn, the man always got to her.

She hadn't realized Rory had left until he returned with a

vibrator. It was large and pink. Maura looked at him as he smiled down at her, then looked up at Zeke. He picked up the lube and put it on.

Then, he spread her legs out.

She had paused but Rory didn't like that.

"You keep sucking on that big cock of Zeke's. I know how good it tastes, and I know he deserves a good mouth fuck. You show him how much you like having it right there."

"Ahh, thanks, Rory," Zeke said. His voice was dark now and he sped up as he continued to thrust in and out of her mouth.

Rory turned on the vibe, but Zeke didn't let her look. He held her head then straddled her and started to fuck her mouth in earnest. He kept pushing himself deeper and deeper into her mouth, bumping up against the back of her throat making her gag.

Rory pressed the vibe against her pussy lips and she almost came then and there. She moaned against his cock as Rory then slipped the vibe into her cunt. The vibrations filtered out over her. She could almost come then, but he would not turn the vibration higher. Because of that and the angle he had put the vibe, she was kept right on the edge of her release.

"Why don't you move, love. I want to turn her over and get a piece of that ass."

Zeke did as Rory asked, and before she could respond, they were turning her over. Zeke reached for the vibe to apparently make sure it was still inside her. He moved against her clit and she felt a rush of her orgasm but he moved it back away again leaving her frustrated.

Rory smacked her ass playfully. "Not yet. You've had anal sex, yes?"

She nodded and could barely contain her excitement. She actually loved anal sex and one of her fantasies was to be taken at the same time. Rory got a condom out and then grabbed the lube. He stopped to kiss Zeke. It was long, wet and she was mesmerized. Bisexual men had always been a turn on for her, but watching it in person, damn. Rory cupped Zeke's face much the same way he had done to her and deepened the kiss. She let her gaze slip down their bodies to take in the whole package. They were almost equal in height and their groins matched up well. Zeke slipped his hands down to Rory's ass and pressed him closer. She watched as their cocks touched and licked her lips.

Oh, mama, she was one lucky woman.

Her concentration was interrupted by Rory's chuckle. She glanced up and found both men looking at her. Again, she blushed. God, she was too old to blush as much as she did with these two but there was something so deliciously decadent sharing them.

"I think she wants another taste of your cock, lover," Rory said. He kissed Zeke and moved to the foot of the bed.

Zeke gave her a smile. "Rory knows what I like, and I think he already knows what you like."

Rory moved her so she was across the bed diagonally. Zeke joined her on the bed again, his cock in his hand and sexy smile on his face.

She opened her mouth and took him in.

Rory moved behind her and she jolted just a bit when he slipped a lubed finger into her ass. He worked her over and soon she was moving with him, enjoying the way he teased her anus. She sucked in a breath when he added another finger. A lot of guys didn't know exactly how to do that. She figured being bisexual gave the guys an advantage over her former lovers.

"Oh, she does like to be ass fucked, doesn't she?"

"Hmm," was all Zeke said. He had her head in his hands again and he was thrusting in and out of her mouth. She wasn't truly submitting but it felt so good to have two men take her this way. Giving herself up to the moment was so freeing.

Rory slipped the vibe out of her pussy and then spread her cheeks, slowly entering her ass. Zeke had stopped his movements, but still had his cock in her mouth.

Tears burned the back of her eyes. She had anal sex, but not with anyone as big as either of them. This wasn't going to be easy.

He slipped past the tight ring of muscles and he groaned as she moaned against Zeke's cock. He started to move, slowly at first, then into a steady rhythm. Over and over he thrust into her as Zeke started to move in her mouth again. The men moved in tandem again, and it was wonderful. Over and over they thrust into her. She was frustrated because she had nothing in her pussy, but they kept moving and she felt her arousal shift into another area she had never been in before.

Zeke thrust into her mouth one last time holding his cock inside her mouth as he poured himself into her. Just a few moments later, Rory's movements sped up.

"Fuck yeah. God, her ass is amazing," he said. "Maura, fuck, so fucking unbelievable, love."

He thrust one last time, his fingers digging into her flesh as he groaned her name.

Zeke pulled out of her mouth and then Rory did the same.

She collapsed, her body still shaking, her need for release leaving her almost in pain. Zeke turned her over as Rory removed his condom, then returned back to the bed.

"Maura," Zeke said.

She opened her eyes and found them smiling at her.

"You want to come, baby?" Rory asked. Zeke gave him a look she couldn't discern but he didn't say anything. She nodded.

"Your wish is our command," Rory said. He slipped onto

the bed beside her, taking her nipple in his mouth as he teased the other. Zeke moved between her legs and licked her.

"Damn, she tastes so good. You need to come bad, doncha, love? She's so fucking wet, Rory."

Rory smiled up at her and this one had not one ounce of cynicism or calculation in it. He looked about ten years younger and even as frustrated as she was, she felt her breath catch in her throat.

"Really need to come?"

She nodded and he kissed down her stomach. Then, they drove her out of her mind. Her pussy was sore, her clit swollen, her body screaming for relief. Zeke gave Rory room to tease her clit. He took it into his mouth and sucked lightly as Zeke slipped a finger into her pussy and continued to slide his tongue over her labia.

It didn't take long and she was coming. She moaned both their names over and over as they continued to tease her. She couldn't even finish her first orgasm when the second one was on the way, slamming into her.

Minutes later, they collapsed on the bed on either side of her. She felt the warmth of their bodies, their hands moving over her flesh and felt that strange contentment she felt after their first bout of lovemaking. She didn't know what to make of it and right now, she was too damn tired.

"Rest," Zeke said, turning her toward him. She snugged under his chin as Rory moved closer behind her. She thought she felt the brush of his mouth against her neck as she drifted off to sleep.

ten

"**D**o you think the bossman is up yet?" Rory asked as he leaned against the back of the Jeep and enjoyed the sweet Hawaiian air.

Zeke had offered to drive and he was happy for that. Zee and Maura knew the island better than he did. Just getting to Jillian and Conner's little slice of heaven was difficult for a local to remember how to get there. It was off the beaten path—way off—which had struck him as odd. Both Jillian and Conner earned a lot of money and Jillian was the heir to a huge corporation. Still, in over thirty years, he had seen much stranger things and he just chalked it up to different strokes.

"Of course he's up by now," Maura said. "He probably had one or both of the pilots call him when we drove off. You know what a control freak he is."

He could tell she was nervous about seeing her brother and he couldn't understand why. Of course, a person with his fucked up family life wouldn't. He was an odd Irishman, avoiding his family or any mention of them. He was sure he had siblings out in the wild knowing his bastard father the way he did, but he had never met them and didn't want to. There was a

81

good chance they were as fucked up as he was—or worse. If he hadn't been discovered by Zee's ma, there was a good chance he would have ended up just like his da.

He brushed those thoughts aside and realized Maura was still talking about her brother. There was something between the siblings that was endearing and perplexing at the same time. She saw him as a brother, which Rory understood, but she also acted as if she needed his approval like she would a father. It was odd that she tied so much in her life to his approval.

"I just want the key to the house, then I want to go to sleep," Zeke said when Maura stopped long enough for him to comment.

Rory nodded as he leaned back and let the environment take control of him for just a little bit. He needed this time off, all three of them did. And this...connection they all seemed to have was definitely one that he was going to enjoy. They did need rest and he could understand why Zeke just wanted to go to sleep. Rory was exhausted in one way, but there was a part of him that was completely exhilarated. Who couldn't be with two lovers like Zee and Maura?

He watched Maura from the back seat. He liked women. They had been his first love until he hit twenty and had his first encounter with a man. Still there was something about Maura. Something in her tugged at him. He had sensed it before they had been in bed. Zee had a thing for her and now...Rory wasn't so sure he didn't have a thing for her.

Whoa. What the hell was he thinking? Sure, the sex had been stellar. She hadn't really submitted yet and he was already a little tangled up in her. But, that was all it was. One week for Zee to work her out of his system, and then they could move on. That was it.

She turned and smiled at him. "How many times have you been to Oahu?"

They'd removed the top of the Jeep because Maura had insisted it was the only way to enjoy Hawaii. It had surprised him. She seemed closed down at the office, all business. But here, in this setting with them, she was open as if she feared nothing. It seemed so...intimate. Something about her he didn't know. And now, her hair was flying around her head. She pulled it out of her face and smiled at him. Something hit him hard and clutched at his heart. He rubbed his chest hoping to rid himself of the feeling.

"Only when your brother and Jillian got married."

Her eyes widened. "Really? I thought maybe you and Zeke had been here before. Like for work."

His lips twitched. "Not a lot of security work here on Oahu for us."

Her smile turned into a grin. "I hope there is since my brother insists on opening that office."

He didn't want to tell her that the type of work Zee and he did for years wouldn't be the type of high-level security they now handled. It was down and dirty, some of it more than a little questionable. He didn't think much about the earlier jobs these days. Truth was, if Zee and he didn't have the protection of the British government, they would probably be in prison somewhere. But, they had done it for—what was it the Americans liked to say—God and country. That was it. Those days were long gone, but he didn't regret them. They had done what needed to be done.

Shaking himself from his thoughts again, he found Maura staring at him still.

"No, it's actually smart. You have a lot of work here thanks to the movies plus, it gives Dillon Securities the ability to work their way into the Pacific Rim. There is a lot of need for security. More and more US companies are moving into these new market areas and we can provide them security for their executives and their offices."

"I'm just the nerd who works on the technical aspect," she said shrugging. "I don't think there's a need for me to be here."

He didn't like the fact that she downplayed her abilities. It was something that her brother and Zee allowed all the time. Zee always dismissed it as a joke, but Rory still did not care for it. He knew the truth of it. Their company wouldn't be able to function without someone like Maura. She was the reason they were gaining more and more clients in every area.

"Computers are a huge part of the problem today. So much terrorism happens online, or the ability to hack into systems, easy way to steal millions."

She nodded and then gasped when Zee took a hard right turn.

"Dude," she said punching him. "Slow down."

"You know that Conner is going to want to keep us there forever. I am ready for bed."

He heard the way Zee's voice dipped over the word and understood that Zee wasn't just planning on sleeping. He was as ready for a submission from her as Rory was. She had been so fucking responsive to him on the jet; he could just imagine what she would do when he pushed it to the next level. The fact that she liked watching Zee and him together was even more arousing. Not every woman they took to bed did like that part of it. In fact, he was pretty sure she was the only one who looked forward to that part of it. He couldn't wait to tie her down and make her watch.

He shifted on his seat trying to ease the tightness of his jeans. Fuck, he was getting a hard on. Not a good idea. Part of it was Maura's fault in a way. The woman intrigued him more than anyone before, except for Zee.

"And, here we are," she said, her voice bubbled, excitement

filling every syllable. Zee had barely put the jeep in park when she jumped out of it and ran to the house. The door was already slamming open.

Jillian Dillon came running out squeeing, her braids flying behind her. As the two women embraced, Rory realized just how opposite they were. Sure, he had seen Jillian a couple of times at the office and then at the wedding, but seeing them together told him just how odd a pair they made.

Jillian was a tall black woman, tattooed and pierced, with long dark braids. She lived life on her own terms as an erotic romance writer. Dressed in a pair of cutoffs that had seen better days and a red tank top, you would never know the woman controlled billions with her family's company. If you looked up free spirit in the dictionary, you would probably find her picture. He often wondered just how they made it work as friends, but there was some kind of connection between the two women.

Conner came out behind her, a frown on his face. Rory wasn't sure that he had ever seen the man smile other than the day of the wedding. From the moment he met his new boss, there had been a patent distrustful air about him. At first, Rory had assumed it was his relationship with Zee, but he soon found out that Conner could care less about that. He looked at everyone that way, which is one of the reasons he was good at his job. But the moment Conner saw Maura, his entire expression softened. That was family—something he would never understand.

She untangled herself from Jillian and launched herself into Conner's arms. "I missed you so much!"

Conner, in a display Rory would never expect, pulled her up off the ground into a bear hug.

Zee must have read his expression. He walked up beside him. "They are very close."

"You don't have to tell me that, Zee."

"No, I guess not."

Jillian shaded her eyes. "Come on boys. I just put on some Kona and I think we can scrounge you up something to eat."

"I'll cook," Conner said, his arm now draped over Maura's shoulders.

Rory knew he was just her brother and was not a competitor for her sexual affections but it bothered him. He had never been possessive except when it came to Zee. Not like this. He had to control the need to tell her brother to get his damned hands off her. He shook his head and smiled at Jillian.

"I would love a good breakfast," Rory said.

"Then I better cook because while Jillian is good with writing books and making coffee, her idea of breakfast is usually leftover pizza."

She shot her husband a nasty look. "I can cook. But when I have a man trained to do it so nicely, why should I bother."

He growled and for the first time in a few minutes, finally let go of his sister. Rory barely kept himself from walking up the steps to the porch and slipping his arm around her waist. For some reason, he wanted everyone to know she belonged to him and Zee. It was an odd feeling, but maybe it had more to do with the lack of sleep than anything else.

Conner swatted his wife on the ass. "While I would like to argue with her, Jillian is right. I do a lot of the cooking because someone gets too caught up in work to notice that we have nothing to eat."

She shook her head and gave Zee a hug. "Hey, Mr. Man, how are you doing? I like the baldhead. It gives you a real 'The King and I' look, especially regal with that goatee."

Zeke laughed. "As long as you don't expect me to sing, we'll be fine."

She gave him a smile and Rory felt the power of it. She

didn't downplay her attributes, but she was so laid back he forgot just how powerful they were. When she turned all that attention on him it was hard to miss.

"Hey, there, Rory."

"Hey, yourself."

Jillian patted her heart. "Ohhh, two men with Irish accents. How ever do you concentrate at work, girl?"

Maura laughed. "I use my super intellect and lots of coffee. And where is that coffee I was offered?"

"Make sure to give her some soon, or we could be dealing with a monster," Conner said. She elbowed her brother.

"You have no room to talk, Conner. But, I would love to have some coffee, and I am definitely famished."

He sighed following them in. Zee gave him a warning look. Rory nodded. He knew they had to be patient to get her alone again. If he spent any time thinking about it, Rory was sure he would be worried. He'd never been this into a sub before, but he was going to keep going in the spirit of their week.

There would be plenty of time to worry when they got back to Miami.

"So, how's work really going?" Jillian asked when she and Maura were finally alone walking on the beach.

Maura shrugged as she tried to sort through her feelings. She was still feeling slightly overwhelmed by the two men and her body was buzzing. Once they got to the house, they were definitely going to want to play. Just knowing that made it really hard to concentrate on talking. "It's going."

"Girl, don't even try that with me. I picked up on the vibe with the three of you."

Maura looked out over the water trying to come up with a way to describe what was going on. She knew that Jillian would know right away. Now was the time to decide just what she would tell her best friend.

"And don't even think of telling me nothing's going on, because Jillian sees all."

Maura chuckled. "I can't believe I bought that in college."

She smiled at her and Maura was thrust back into the memory of meeting the worldly Jillian the first time. She had been so young and scared to death. Jillian had made life so much easier—even if she had lied telling her she had spies all over campus.

Jillian tugged on a lock of her hair. "Yeah, quit stalling."

She looked out over the water again. Maura didn't know if she was ready to explain what happened. Hell, she didn't know what was really going on. Sure, there was sex. Amazing sex. Hell, just thinking about it right now had her blood heating and her hormones hopping. Something else was there though, something that she worried about.

"Stop pondering and share before Conner gets done with the guys."

"You know Rory and Zeke share women sometimes."

"You said that before, or you suspected it."

"There were rumors, but I wasn't entirely sure. You know, people in the office talk."

"They haven't been doing it with people at the company, have they?" Jillian asked. "Conner would kill them."

"No. No, not until recently."

Jillian didn't say anything for a second. Maura glanced out back over the water again, but she could feel her friend's attention. Then, Jillian chuckled. "Good for you Maura Dillon."

Maura looked over at her. From the moment they met, they had been friends. So odd because Jillian had been so, well, cool. Maura had been years younger in age and even more naïve than the average teenager. She hadn't known just how to take her roommate, but after awhile she realized she had been handed a gift. Jillian was the older sister she had always wanted.

"No recriminations?" she asked worried that for the first time in her life she let her best friend down.

"Of course not. You're an adult. You know what you're doing."

"Do I?" she asked, still unsettled by the lovemaking earlier. They had just started and she found herself enthralled with both men. She had a really bad feeling that things were going to get out of hand pretty fast and at the end of the week, it would be over. She already loved Zee. She didn't even want to think about what would happen if she fell for Rory also.

Jillian sighed. "How did it happen? When?"

"How—Rory approached me. Seems that while Zeke is not into BDSM, he does have a kink."

"And that would be?"

"Voyeurism."

Jillian hummed. "Ohhhh, mama. That is hot. I mean, really hot."

"Apparently, he also really likes showing off for the sub. Like if the sub likes to watch the guys together, it turns him on more." And that was one thing she liked. She loved the way they touched each other. Their openness to express their affection for each other was so sexy. Even right now the heat was building in her blood thinking about it.

"Wow. Well, right up your alley then. How long has this been going on?"

"Are you going to go tell my brother?" she asked.

"Of course not. I might be married to him, but I know better than that. He needs to let go and let things happen. His control freak nature is the reason you're here. I'm going to warn you though; your brother might sniff it out. He might try and pretend it isn't happening, but I have a feeling it will hit him if you spend any time with him while you're here. It will be hard on him to accept. I think in his head he still thinks you're a virgin."

Maura shook her head. "He does not."

"He pretends at least."

She rolled her eyes. "Men. You should have seen the way he reacted when I told him I had lost my virginity."

There was a beat of silence. "Wait, when was that?"

"You know when that happened. I told you about it."

Jillian waved that away. "No, not losing it. When you told him?"

"Oh, when I went up to DC to see him a few weeks later. He didn't take it the way I thought he would. I mean at the time. Now, I understand."

"I would have paid a thousand dollars—and I mean it—to have seen that."

"Yeah, he didn't look at me for over a whole day."

"I can imagine. Guys don't like hearing stuff like that about their sisters, especially with him being the authority figure in your life."

"Well, I told him I didn't know what all the fuss was about. I mean, it was over so quickly with Jed."

Jillian snorted. "Oh, please tell me you said that to him."

She blinked. "Of course I did. I thought he could tell me what was wrong. He got a weird look on his face and just walked away."

Jillian laughed. "Why didn't you ask me?"

"Well, if you want to know the truth, I was embarrassed. I mean, he was so fast I thought it had something to do with me, or that I was frigid because nothing happened for me. I did research but it was all so vague so I asked him later about a woman being frigid."

"Thank you. I am going to use that against him in the future." She crossed her arms beneath her breasts. "So, spill, when did this start?"

"On the ride over."

Another beat of silence. "Oh. My. God. Woman, when you let loose, you really let loose. Little Maura Dillon a member of the Mile High Club. And not just one guy in a small stall. Two guys, a bed, and a private plane. You do me proud. How was it?"

She sighed. "It was actually very wonderful. And we haven't even started playing with submission. Rory is a Dom, but only with women, and well, the one thing Zeke likes to do is watch him make a woman submit."

"But?"

She looked at Jillian then out over the water again. "I'm not sure what I'm getting myself into. They're together, this is just for the week that we are here."

"Are you hoping for more?"

That scared her. Even now she didn't want to think about going back to Miami and being left behind. It would hurt, probably more than losing Zeke the first time. Resisting would have been futile though. They would have just overwhelmed her at every turn. And now, she wouldn't just be losing one of them. She would be losing Rory too. She wanted both of them so much now. She closed her eyes as if that would help.

Jillian said nothing, so Maura opened her eyes.

"Are you?" she asked again.

"God, I don't know. You know how I feel about Zeke."

"You love him. You have for a long time," Jillian said quietly. She had been the one who had picked up on Maura's feelings before Maura knew what was going on.

"Yeah, and I find Rory over the top attractive. To make it worse, he's a talker."

"Oh, wow. A Dom who is a talker, and they like to do each other. Talk about Maura's dream come true."

She didn't regret telling Jillian her fantasies, but her friend was always so bold in stating them. While Maura believed in being cautious, Jillian thought it best to face your desires head on. Telling her that she had a thing for bisexual men probably hadn't been the smartest thing Maura had done, but they had been drinking at the time.

Jillian frowned at her. "Don't look like that. There is nothing wrong with your needs. Who are you hurting?"

Maura shook her head and smiled. "No one. I just hope that at the end of the week I'll be able to walk away."

"I would just play it by ear." Maura's spine stiffened and Jillian rolled her eyes. "I know that's hard for you Dillons, but in this one week, let it go. Have fun, enjoy. You might learn a lot about yourself."

She nodded feeling a little better. Jillian always put everything into perspective. "Why don't we head back? The boys have been playing shop long enough and all of you look like you need a nap."

She snorted. "I doubt Zeke and Rory are going to let me sleep."

As soon as she said it, she blushed. Jillian laughed and slipped her arm over Maura's shoulders.

"You go, Maura."

twelve

Z eke leaned back in the chair irritated he didn't have eyes on Maura. He knew she could handle herself, but something in him made him want to have his attention on her and not her brother. He kept going on about work and for the first time in a long time, he could care less. He wanted Maura. Now.

"I heard from a source that Petersen is finally ready to deal," Conner said.

Zeke brought his attention back to his friend. "About fucking time. The guy was an idiot. The cartel was letting him go down for the laundering and they were threatening him and his family."

"I think the bastard was waiting for a better deal," Conner said.

"No. He was expecting to be saved by his Columbian connection," Rory said. "Zee and I saw it a lot in Ireland, but then the mob there is much more family oriented. Sure, they have families here, but they have lost that in the last few decades. I doubt they would have hired out like that. And if they did, it would have been someone they considered family.

Now, they don't have give a damn who they hire as long as they do their job. That way, the people who work for them are expendable."

Rory knew better than most. Zeke didn't know much about it, but he knew Rory had worked undercover for the British government in Ireland. His knowledge of the Irish mob was considered one of the best in the world. It was one reason he had money to spare. Many intelligence agencies paid him well to consult on cases. Hell, he didn't even have to leave the confines of their apartment. They sent him a secure file, Rory told them what he knew, they paid him.

Conner rolled his shoulders. "Anyway, I heard from a friend that his lawyer finally got him to sit down with the federal prosecutor. I hope he takes it."

"You want scum like that to walk the streets?" Rory asked.

"No," Zeke said surprised that Rory didn't pick up on it. "He knows that if Petersen turns evidence over, the three of us will be off the cartel's hit list. They'll go after him."

"Or that's what I hope. I know bringing the three of you here isn't much, but it allows for some space. And here, especially in the places locals love, people take notice of a new face. Miami is such a melting pot."

"Honolulu is too," Zeke pointed out.

Conner shrugged. "But the house is in an area not a lot of tourists go. And the streets aren't that easy to set up a stake out. It is safer."

He understood his concern, but Zeke didn't like the idea of his friend doubting his ability to protect Maura.

"And before you argue with me, I know both of you can protect her. She's had enough lessons from you and me both for self-defense so she will argue that she can take care of herself. But this way, she is close during this time. Just removing you from the area is good. It also puts pressure on Peterson. Plus, we have the office to talk about here. I want to come up with some planning for expanding here in the Pacific Rim."

"We could do that online."

Conner looked at Rory. "Is he really bitching because I brought him to Hawaii for a week?"

"I do believe he is," Rory said chuckling. "You know our boy, Zee. He likes to work."

Conner shrugged. "That's why we understand each other and why we do well on the business front."

"So, you want to talk that over today?" he asked not really wanting to. His every thought was getting Maura to the house and watching what Rory would do to her. He hadn't seen what kind of toys Rory had bought, but Zeke was sure it would please Maura. Just concentrating on Conner's words was getting difficult. Of course, anything was difficult when you were walking around with little blood in your brain.

"No. In fact, I have an idea that Jillian would yell at me."

"Tsk, tsk, done in by a woman," Zeke said with a smile.

Rory shook his head. "Being done in by a woman like that, I can see why the man is busy."

"She's worried about Maura. She thinks something's going on with her."

Of course there was, but he couldn't tell Conner that. They had been friends for a really long time. He had no problem when Zeke and Maura hooked up. Okay, Conner had a few but he had gotten over them, especially when they ended it. Rory and him bringing Maura into their bedroom that might be the end of their friendship if he didn't handle it the right way.

And, there was part of him still trying to figure out what the hell he had been thinking. What he did know was he had been thinking with the wrong part of his anatomy. Still, he didn't regret it. Couldn't.

"She thinks she has a lot to live up to," Rory said. Zeke

glanced at him somewhat surprised that he had picked up on that tidbit. "What? I pay attention."

Conner sighed. "Maura has always been an over achiever. Even before Mom and Dad died, she seemed destined to blow through school. I always felt like I was trying to catch up with her."

"You're older," Zeke pointed out.

"True, but the fact still remains that she read full books at the age of three, could do multiplication at the age of five. It was a bit daunting to be struggling with school myself, and she was showing me how to do algebra."

Rory laughed. "You're kidding."

Conner's eyes narrowed and Zeke knew why. There was something in Rory's tone that wasn't just being amused by a teenage Conner asking his sister for help on homework. A hint of admiration threaded Rory's tone, and it wasn't just admiring her math skills. It was almost intimate. They didn't need Conner picking up on what was going on—not yet. If Zeke had his way, he would definitely like to continue the relationship, but he needed to be patient for that. And they definitely didn't need Conner butting in.

"So, I think that we need to just keep an eye on the Peterson trial. He will probably take a deal and if he does, he'll be the target," Zeke said, trying his best to deflect Conner's suspicious study of Rory. Of course it worked, because work always caught Conner's attention.

"Yeah. The word I hear is he is about to cave. They've threatened him and his family, so that will probably push him to turn."

The door opened. Jillian stepped in first, Maura followed behind her. She was smiling and already looked more relaxed. Her hair was already wavy from the humidity and her cheeks were rosy. Zeke always forgot how happy Maura was in Hawaii.

She would never move there, but it was hard to ignore the way she was already flushed from the sun. You would never know they lived in Miami by the way she worshiped Hawaiian beaches.

"What have you two been up to?" Conner asked as he crossed the room to pull Jillian into his arms for a kiss.

"Just talking. Plus she was talking to Adam about his bike. Maura had a lot of questions about where to get a rental on the island."

Conner leveled a look at Maura.

"No."

She crossed her arms and frowned at him. Zeke knew then that Conner knew exactly what she had been thinking. It was odd that he used to feel left out when they did that. Now, though, he knew exactly how her mind worked.

"I can do what I want. I *am* an adult."

"I do not want to get a call from Zeke about you being in a wreck."

She made a face. "I don't know why you think I would get hurt."

Panic tightened his gut. Maura was good at most things, but riding a bike would be a disaster. She wasn't all that great at driving her car because her mind was always on something else. Panic had him stepping in. Maura was exceptional at everything but balance. "No. I don't think you should do that."

Conner was now giving him that narrowed look he had just given Rory. He didn't blame him. Zeke knew he had sounded proprietary but at least they had a longer history together.

Zeke shrugged. "I don't want to deal with Conner. He'll blame me."

"And then, I'll have to kill him."

She rolled her eyes and huffed. "Fine."

But he knew she was still working it out in her head.

"I think we need to get to the house, get settled. If we get some sleep, then we can go out tonight," Maura said.

"Where do you think you're going for the night?" Conner asked suspiciously. Of course he would know that Maura was going to want to pop into Rough 'n Ready and while her brother might not have a problem with it, he wouldn't want to be there for anything.

"I wanted to drive around later today. Rory saw little to nothing of the island when y'all got married a few weeks ago. So, if we can get some sleep right now, we can get out in this evening."

Conner nodded. "Okay, but make sure you check in. I don't want to hunt you down."

"Don't worry about it boy-o I think we take care of her," Rory said.

"I can take care of myself," she said, as she walked to Conner. He took her in his arms and gave her a kiss on the cheek then pulled her close. He whispered something that had her smiling, and she pulled back. Conner handed Maura the keys.

"Don't goof off too much while you are on the island." He looked at Rory and then Zeke. "Keep an eye out. I doubt they'll come out this way looking for you, but be careful."

Rory rolled his eyes, but Zeke understood. Conner and Maura were closer than most siblings because of what they had been through, and with the age difference, Conner looked at her more like a daughter.

"Don't worry, Conner," Zeke said, after catching his eye.

Jillian laughed. "That's like trying to tell the world to stop spinning."

They headed out the door to the Jeep. He slipped into the driver's seat and stared at his friend. He had been happy that Conner finally found a woman tough enough for him, who wouldn't take any of his shit. But, now, seeing Conner with his arm around Jillian, he felt a tug of jealousy. He wanted nothing but happiness for his friend, but he wanted some of that himself. Zeke had never thought he would be the home and hearth kind of guy, but now, he wanted it. More than anything he would like to find some middle ground with Maura and Rory. Maybe, this week would allow them to find it.

He sighed and pushed those thoughts aside. He had to live one day at a time right now and worry later.

Once they were out on Kam Highway, Rory asked, "Do you think we need to stop for food?"

"No," Maura said. "Jillian told me she got the essentials. We can go out later and pick up particular things we want."

"I thought you would want to get out on the beach," Rory said.

She laughed. "If I wanted to spend more time on the beach, I could do that in Miami, although I do prefer the beaches here. No, I like the nighttime here. There is something about the way the air feels on your skin here at night. Plus, why would I want to hang out on a beach? I have two very sexy men who have decided to make me their play toy for a week. I would be an idiot to want to spend more time on the beach."

Zeke smiled as he glanced up in the mirror. He could tell that Maura had stunned Rory a bit, but that was a given with Maura. She was very open. She had secrets, but Zeke understood that she would never play coy with them. She had accepted their terms and she saw no need to pretend.

"Why indeed?" he asked and gunned the Jeep. The sooner they got to the house the better in his opinion.

It only took them twenty minutes to get to the estate where they were staying.

"Why doesn't your brother have something like this? He can definitely afford it." Rory asked.

Maura smiled. "Jillian is a creature of habit. She doesn't really like change and has that temperamental writer personality. It doesn't show up that often, but man, does it rear its ugly head when you change her home base. I think he might be planning to add on. She owns all that land down to the beach."

Zeke laughed. "Did he clear that with her?"

"No. He knows how to handle her. He'll reveal it in stages." She shrugged. "He understands her and she understands him. He's so happy with her."

Zeke unlocked the door and they stepped into the foyer. It was a fantastic house, one with a view and he knew to buy it, several million dollars would have to be plunked down on it just for the down payment. He didn't even want to know what Conner had paid for the week.

"I forgot just how freaking big this place was," Rory said. He glanced at Zeke. He knew they were both remembering the little flat where Zeke's mother had raised them. It would have fit in the living room of this house. Hell, there were times in their careers they had both slept in the street thanks to the work they were doing at the time. Never would he have thought they would make it to some place like this.

"God, it feels good to just be here. I can't wait to get my clothes changed," Rory said.

She collapsed on the couch and smiled up at them. "I'm assuming we'll be able to use the master bedroom. It has a California King in it."

"Let me guess, you called dibs on it," Zeke said with a chuckle.

"But of course. He was spending every night over at Jillian's anyway. Her cousin and his husband stayed here with us though. They were so damned sweet. Newlyweds. So, what was I saying?"

"That there is a California king in it, so we can fit in it," Rory said.

"Sounds good."

"We probably should have stopped off for some food. I think there might be milk, but now that I think about it, Jillian's idea of staples is coffee, creamer and cold pizza. A Whole Foods just opened up over here."

She smiled when she said it and Rory gave him a look. Zeke smiled. "Give it up, babe. Either we go for coffee now or we go later."

She bounced off the couch. "Great. I'm going to go freshen up."

She gave them both a kiss and then dashed up the stairs.

"Does she do this a lot?" Rory asked as he followed him out to the Jeep.

"No, and that's why I don't get pissed. Maura hardly ever asks anyone to do anything for her, so she needed some downtime."

"You think she's changed her mind." Rory said as he followed Zeke to the Jeep.

"No. She hasn't. Maura is kind of a loner. She has a few very close friends. Everyone else she could take or leave. When she's surrounded by a lot of people it overwhelms her brain sometimes. She'll regroup and then...watch out. I have a feeling for once, Rory McAllister, you're about to get your fingers burned."

Rory laughed as he climbed into the passenger seat. "Good. There are a few things I would like to get...especially whipped cream."

thirteen

Maura leaned back under the shower head and sighed. She always liked to have a shower right after she landed. Sure, she had one on the plane, but she needed to relax now. It was hard to really loosen up wondering what was in store for her. Rory had already shown hints of his inner Dom and she would be lying if she didn't admit to being intrigued. Just thinking about what he would be like once he fully unleashed it sent heat racing over her nerve endings.

With a sigh, Maura turned off the water. She had been in the shower so long, the glass had fogged up and she couldn't see out. She opened the door just enough to slip her hand out to grab the towel she had put there and found the hook empty. Frowning, she eased the door open not wanting to let too much of the cooler air into the stall. That's when she saw Rory standing a few feet away, her towel hanging from his fingertips. Zeke was sitting on the counter smiling at her.

"You took your shower without us," Rory said, obviously not happy with the situation.

She looked at Zeke. He said nothing, but there was a sparkle in his eyes.

"I'm talking to you now, Maura, don't look at Zee."

She turned her attention back to Rory. His tone was no longer one of the playful lover. This was the Dom out in full force.

"I didn't know you wanted to take one with me."

"When it comes to you being naked, I want to know about it." Rory said.

She glanced at Zeke and he was no longer smiling. He was watching them. His avid interest had her responding. A shiver of need slipped through her, heating her blood. So, the D/s was about to start. She had been with a Dom before, but...this was different. The other had been more about exploring her desires and it had been all professionally handled in a club. This was more familiar.

"Step out," Rory said, holding his hand out. She did as he ordered but she was surprised when he threw the towel at Zeke. He caught it easily and came forward to dry her off.

"Now that we are starting this," Rory said moving back to lean against the counter. "I need to know your safe word. Zeke said you'd played before, so I'm sure that you know what that means."

She nodded. "Bulldogs."

"Good."

Zeke started to dry her off but he was taking his time. With each soft stroke of towel, he was teasing her. She looked down at him.

"Look at me," Rory snapped. She gave him a disgruntled look. "You don't want to play by my rules, we can call this off."

Just as he said it, Zeke moved the towel up her leg just barely brushing her pussy. The small touch had her knees going weak. Maura was embarrassed to admit that she was already growing damp. The combination of the two men was already driving her crazy and they had barely started.

"Now," Rory said as he walked toward her. "I have a little fun planned this afternoon."

Zeke moved behind her and started to slip the towel up her legs. Sinful pleasure spread through her as he continued to dry her skin. He moved up to her ass, cupping both cheeks through the towel and squeezing.

"You liked watching Zee and me, didn't you?" Rory asked.

More than she could ever express in words. "Yes."

"I know you've played a bit on D/s, but I want to leave some of the...rougher stuff until we do a few sessions. Is that all right with you?"

She nodded. He smiled and kissed her. It wasn't that sensual, but his lips felt cool against hers. She understood it was a reward for following his instructions. He pulled back.

"Then, let's get started."

She turned to grab up her clothes, but he laughed.

Zeke smiled as he tossed the towel on the floor. "You aren't going to need them, love."

He bent at the waist and picked her up to carry her into the room. The windows were open but they were in a private area so she didn't have to worry about that. She wanted to play in public, but she didn't want to get arrested.

"Put her on the bed, Zee."

She swallowed as excitement rushed through her every cell. She wanted to know what he had planned but part of her didn't. Not knowing heightened the anticipation.

"Stop thinking," Rory ordered as Zeke put her on the bed. "Spread those legs and let us see our pussy."

Oh, God, Rory was such a talker. With that thick Irish accent, she was ready to come right then. She did as he ordered. Cold air hit her pussy and she shivered. Fuck.

"Hmm. All pink and wet. What you think, Zee?"

"Yeah, I like that almost as much as I like eating our pussy."

Shit. He had turned Zeke into a talker somehow. She heard the excitement in Zeke's voice. The combination of both men talking about her cunt like that was almost too much to bear. Even now her labia was damp, her pussy aching to be touched.

"Yeah, she likes that. Look how fucking wet she is. Damn," Rory ground out. He let his gaze travel up her body and it was if he had touched her. Her skin tingled. "From now on, no talking from you. You can say your safe word. You can answer my questions. And, you can moan our names as we fuck you. Never hide your pleasure. But, you are now under my control, you understand."

"Yes."

He stepped forward and slapped her pussy. She was unable to control the gasp. The sting shocked her at first and any other time she would have been pissed. No one had ever done that not even Sebastian, the Dom who had trained her. She shifted her bottom on the mattress and he slapped her again. The sting hurt just as much, but now pleasure rolled over her.

"Yes, what?"

She looked at him and he slapped her one more time.

"Maura," he said, a warning threading his voice.

Then, she realized what he was waiting for. "Yes, Sir."

"Good." He stepped back. "She said that fast enough give her a little reward, Zee."

Zeke smiled and bent down. Placing a hand on each of her thighs, spreading her legs even wider, he licked her sensitive pussy, three times. The slight brush of his goatee against her labia heightened her arousal. He slipped his tongue in before pulling back.

He stood up and licked his lips then looked at Rory. "Yeah, that's good. You should have a taste."

He smiled and stepped closer to Zeke. Rory kissed him, slipping his hand down to Zeke's crotch. He stroked him through his pants. Zeke leaned his head back and moaned. Rory attacked his throat, nipping at Zeke's skin. When he pulled back, all three of them were breathing heavy.

"Hmmm, our pussy does taste good." He gave Zeke another little kiss, they both looked at her. Rory's gaze dipped down to between her legs. She fought the urge to close her legs to relieve the pressure. "Oh, she is going to be a joy to play with."

"Maura's always fun in the bedroom."

Okay, she shouldn't be so turned on that they were talking about her this way, but for some reason, it was making her hotter. She always did like a man who liked to talk dirty. Zeke had never been big into it. Rory apparently brought it out in him.

"Really?" Rory asked as he approached her. "I know she likes to suck cock, doncha, love?"

She nodded unable to speak. Rory squatted in front of her and set his hands on her thighs.

"What other kinds of things does she like, Zee?"

She couldn't look away from Rory. She knew he wouldn't like it, and she knew enough about the D/s relationship to follow his orders. He had specifically told her to keep her attention on him. Of course, that made it harder to accomplish. Zeke chuckled and she glanced at him. Rory smacked her pussy. The slight sting filtered out over her skin. Maura looked down at him.

"Eyes on me, Maura, or you will regret it. Do you understand?"

"Y-yes."

"What was that?"

She swallowed. "Yes, Sir."

Zeke climbed on the bed behind her but she didn't dare look at him. Rory's mouth twitched.

"Apparently you do."

He pressed his hand against her pussy, slipping a finger inside her. She sighed but the relief was short. He removed his hand just a few seconds later.

"Now, I want to make sure you understand all the rules. You are in control of how far we go. You can say your safe word at any point if it gets intense."

She shook her head but he frowned.

"I'm not kidding here, Maura. If you cannot understand your boundaries, we can't go any further. You are new to the life and I don't want you to be hurt because of something I did. And don't just agree with me because I'm a Dom. In this, I have to have a promise you take it seriously."

For a moment she didn't say anything. She couldn't. The sincerity she read in his expression had her nodding.

"What are you agreeing to?"

"I will use my safe word. I promise."

He smiled then. Again she was struck on how much younger he looked when he did. For some reason, she felt she won an award.

Zeke had moved closer and started to nuzzle her neck. She shivered.

"Good," Rory said.

He rose but not before giving her a brief but passionate kiss. It was just a few seconds, but the effect it had on her was substantial. He moved away and walked to the dresser. He picked something up, but she didn't know what it was. Zeke slipped one hand through her hair and pulled her face around to face him. He kissed her then, a little more aggressively than he ever had before. She didn't know if it was because he thought he was competing with Rory or if being here with Rory made him more forceful. Maura really didn't care. By the time he pulled back, they were both breathing heavily.

"Such a pretty picture," Rory said as he approached them. She didn't hear any cynicism or jealousy in his voice. She looked at him and saw the intensity in Rory's gaze. It struck her then that he was as aroused by watching her byplay with Zeke as she was when she watched them.

"I have something special for you. As I said, we are going to start slowly, and one of the things I want to do is take away one of your senses. Easiest is sight."

Rory was holding a red slip of material in his hands.

He approached her and she was struck again by both men being fully clothed and she was bare assed naked. Apparently, that didn't bother either of them. For her, it added another level of naughtiness to the play. She knew Rory probably planned it this way. It was all about control, especially in the beginning of the D/s relationship. Testing boundaries...and this was one. Rory wanted to establish who was in charge.

Without saying a word, he slipped the silky fabric over her eyes. She thought she would be able to see a little bit, but instead, she was thrown completely into darkness. Immediately all her other senses went on alert.

"Now, I'm ready to play. How about you, Zee?"

"Yeah, babe. And I think Maura is too." She could hear the smile in his voice.

"I have a few more toys I brought with me, love."

Because she couldn't see who Rory was looking at, she didn't know whom he was talking to.

"What do you think of spanking, Maura?"

She shivered as Zeke started to kiss her neck. "I like it."

There was a beat of silence as she assumed the men were digesting that information.

"So you did this in your training?" Rory asked.

She hesitated, not because she didn't want to tell him. She didn't want Zeke to hear. She wasn't ashamed of her needs, but she didn't want to hurt him. Another swift swat to her sex had her gasping.

"Answer me."

"Yes."

"What was your favorite item?"

She sighed. "The paddle."

"And?"

"And the bare hand."

There was another pause of silence. She didn't know what Zeke was thinking but he continued to kiss her neck.

"I think it's time for a little spanking."

"Hmm," Zeke said. He gave her neck one last nip then slipped off the bed.

Rory approached her and took her hands. She could tell it was him because of his footsteps against the wooden floor and the scent of his aftershave. He eased her off the bed then turned her to face it. She really didn't like not being able to see what was going on around her. It was something that made her feel... out of control.

He placed her hands on the mattress and situated her so that her ass was sticking up. Lord, now she was happy she couldn't see herself. Totally naked, her ass up for both of them to look at. Of course, from the hum in his voice, Rory apparently liked the position he put her in.

"I think that is a position you will be in a lot," Rory said. He spread his hands over her ass, rubbing it then squeezing it. "I do like a woman with a nice full ass. I have never liked skinny women."

He stepped away and she felt another set of hands on her. Zeke, of course, but she would have known by the touch. It wasn't that he was softer than Rory but he was a bit more gentle.

"Now, move away love. Our girl likes to be spanked, and I want to see how she reacts."

Zeke gave her one last long caress and stepped away. She had no warning before Rory's hand came down hard on her flesh. The smack was loud in the room, the pain of it slipped over her skin. She drew in a deep breath in reaction.

"Oh, she likes that."

"Yeah, she does," Zeke said. "Smack her again."

The arousal had deepened his voice and there was an element in it that she had never heard before.

"First, though, Maura spread those legs further apart."

It took some effort, but she did as ordered. He wasted no time. His hand came down on the fullest part of her butt cheek. Again the sting hurt, but there was a bit of pleasure because of it.

"Zee, why don't you get up there on the bed...give her a little stroking while I paddle." There was a pause as she felt the mattress dip under Zeke's weight. "You like that idea, Maura?"

"Yes, Sir."

Zeke's fingers spread her labia as he caressed her. "You look so beautiful, babe. You should see yourself. And fuck, you're wet."

She shivered as she listened to Rory's feet retreat then return. In the next instant, the paddle smacked her hard.

"Fuck," she muttered. Zeke chuckled as he continued to tease her. Rory started to paddle her in earnest. In a series of hard and soft swats, he spanked her, not allowing any part of her ass to be left untouched. Her flesh stung, her pussy was so fucking wet she was embarrassed, and Zeke continued to torment her.

Rory's hand went to the small of her back before he hit her

one last time. It was such a hard smack that tears welled up in her eyes. Oh, damn. She wanted to come. Her whole body was electric with need; pulsing and she thought she would go insane.

"Hey, Zee," Rory said, his voice rougher than usual telling her he had been just as effected as she had been by the spanking. "Give her another little taste."

"Gladly," Zee said as he slid his head between her legs. The touch of his tongue against her labia almost had her coming. She was so fucking aroused she didn't know if she could hold back. Of course, Rory hadn't ordered her not to come.

Zeke moved away taking away any chance of that.

"Your ass gets so damned pink," Rory said, admiration threading the words. She didn't have time to bask in the glow. He slipped his hands around her waist and pulled her away from the bed. She gasped then laughed when the tossed her back on the bed. She bounced twice before he was on top of her. Rory didn't hesitate. He set a hand on each of her thighs and pushed them apart. He set his mouth on her pussy and slipped his tongue inside her. Over and over he thrust inside her. She was unbearably wet, already shaking with her need for release, but he never let her have one.

He gave her one long lick then pulled back and moved off the bed. In the next instant the blindfold was removed. She blinked at the sudden light that almost blinded her. Rory must have sensed it stunned her.

"Sorry, love," he said leaning down.

When her eyes finally adjusted to the light again, she noticed that Zeke was standing by the bed and he was totally naked.

Oh, lordy. His cock was long and hard, already bobbing up against his stomach as he crawled onto the bed. She licked her lips and Rory laughed.

"I will never doubt Zeke again." She glanced up at him

frowning. "He said there was never a woman who liked a cock in her mouth as much as you, and I have to say he was right."

He leaned down as he cupped the back of her head and kissed her. She could taste herself there, the muskiness of her arousal and the unique taste of Rory. He pulled back and nodded to Zeke. She watched as he came up to his knees and took his cock in his hand. He kept looking at her as he stroked himself.

She sighed.

"Wanna taste, love?" Rory asked her. She looked at him.

"Yes, Sir."

He smiled at her, then looked up at Zeke. "You heard the woman, Zee."

She started to get up but Rory stopped her.

"No, Maura, you stay right there, I didn't tell you to move. You can come up on your elbows though."

Zeke moved closer, his hand on his cock as he offered it up to her. Needing that connection, she took him in fully, sucking him so deep she gagged a bit. She didn't care. As she started to really get into giving him oral, she heard the buzz of a vibrator a second before Rory set it on her sex. She moaned around Zeke's cock.

"Yeah," he groaned. "Just like that, love." He slipped his hands into her hair taking over the depth and rhythm of his thrusts. As he fucked her mouth over and over, Rory tortured her with the vibe. He used varying speeds to tease.

"No coming, Maura. I'm going to be inside you when you do," he muttered as he moved the vibe away and replaced it with his hands and mouth. At that point, she let go. She let both men take over.

Zeke's strokes went from long and deep to fast and short. Soon, he thrust into her one last time and came. His cum filled her mouth as he held his cock in her mouth. When he was finished, he pulled out and leaned down giving her a toe tingling, soul changing kiss. When he pulled back, he rested his forehead against hers.

"Thanks, love."

Rory moved off the bed and grabbed a condom. She had been so into giving oral to Zeke she hadn't noticed Rory had disrobed. He was rolling a condom on. He didn't hesitate as he joined her back on the bed. His face was flush and she let her gaze travel down. Damn, how did she get so lucky. Both men were works of art. All hard muscle, and, she thought as she licked her lips, hard cocks.

He kneeled between her legs and pressed his hand against her pussy. She shivered. She needed a release, but for a moment all she had cared about was pleasing them.

"You're so fucking wet, sweet. Poor thing needs to come so bad."

He stroked her a few times and dammit, she almost came a few times. Just the touch of his fingers had her arching off the bed. He moved closer and slipped both hands under her ass. He entered her in one, hard, swift thrust. She moaned his name.

He stopped and she looked at him. "I like my name on your lips. I'm going to make you scream it in just a few minutes."

Rory rose to his knees and went about driving her completely mental. Over and over he thrust into her. Every nerve in her body seemed to be focused on him and what he was doing to her. Soon, the headboard slapped against the wall and her moans did turn into screams. Zeke added another level as he took a nipple in his mouth then pinched the other. The slight pain shot right down to her pussy.

"Oh, please, please, please, Rory," she moaned.

"Please what?" he asked, his voice labored as he continued moving. The smack of their bodies against each other and the springs in the mattress filled the room.

"Please, let me come. Please." She screamed the last request.

"Properly."

She was out of her head. Her body hurt from top to bottom with the need to come and he was expecting something she just couldn't figure out. She growled.

"You need to call him Sir, love," Zeke said as he skimmed his hand over her stomach.

"Please, Sir. Please may I come?" She barely had the words out of her mouth and Zeke had his hand on her clit. Rory continued his long deep strokes as Zeke pressed his fingers against her.

"Come, now, love. Maura, come," Rory said. She did then, her torso bowing up off the bed further as she screamed Rory's name. Tears filled her eyes and slipped down her cheeks. She didn't care.

"Fuck, yeah, that's it. All those little ripples, Maura," Rory groaned. "Look at me."

Maura forced her eyes open as Zeke moved away. Rory thrust into her one last time, his gaze on hers and came.

Moments later, he released her and settled on top of her. He threaded his fingers through her hair and smiled at her. It felt as if she had just won another award. Without taking his gaze from hers, he bent his head and brushed his mouth over hers.

"Thanks, Maura. That was truly special."

She felt the mattress move beside them and she looked at Zeke who was smiling at them. He leaned forward and gave her a kiss too.

"It was. How do you feel?"

She sighed. "Satisfied."

Rory laughed and kissed her neck.

"And tired," she added.

"We all need rest."

She looked at Rory. "Thank you." Then she looked at Zeke. "Thank you both for that."

"You're most welcome, love," Zeke said.

Rory slipped out of her and then off the bed. Zeke pulled her into his arms.

"You sure you're alright?"

She nodded as Rory joined them in bed behind her. He scooted up behind her and rested is arm across her and then over Zeke's back.

"Good. Now everyone shut the bloody hell up. I need rest."

Zeke and Maura laughed. The concerns she had were still there, but at the moment, she felt too damned good to care.

fourteen

Maura woke up a few hours later. She kept her eyes closed while she snuggled against Zeke.

"Well isn't that the cat ate the canary look?" Zeke said, his voice a low rumble against her ear.

She opened her eyes and found him smiling down at here. There was very little sun shinning through the windows, so she knew the sun was setting. Was there anyone who could resist this man? Why would anyone want to?

"Sorry, but after that, any woman in her right mind would feel that way."

He chuckled and she lifted herself up off his chest. The bed was empty except for them. "Where's Rory?"

"Went out for a run."

"Ugh, don't tell me he is some kind of fitness geek."

"No, but I have a feeling he couldn't stick around."

She blinked knowing she was missing something by his tone. Before today, she would have never asked, but now she would. "Why?"

Zeke slipped his hand up to cup her jaw. "He knew that you might have been a sub, but he is...a little more extreme than what you are accustomed to. He didn't push you that far today."

She shivered in delight. She had a few things she wanted to try and she hoped that Rory was up for it.

"Damn, it's a good thing he's not around to see that look. We would never make it out of the house tonight if he did."

"Yeah?"

"Yes. Plus, for him, it is all about control."

She snorted and dropped back on the pillow. "Nice of him to think of that now."

Zeke didn't laugh like he normally would. Or she would have thought he would.

When he looked at her, he was studying her with a very serious expression.

"What?"

He hesitated, then asked, "Are you sure that you are okay with this?"

"Why wouldn't I be?"

He hesitated. "I don't want you to think you have to do this to make me happy."

"Do you think I would do that?"

"You might."

"Are you happy?"

His lips twitched. "Yeah. Having the two people together I love the most, of course I'm happy."

Her heart did that little jig whenever she heard him say that. He didn't do it often, but before now, it had hurt so much. When everything had fallen apart and they realized they would be more friends than lovers, she hated hearing him say it. Knowing just how much he loved her, sharing this with him, seemed to make it so special.

"Then why are you worried?"

"I don't want you to do it just for me. I want you to do it for yourself."

She smiled. "Oh, I promise you, it was all for me in a way. Besides, you need to get over yourself. I might do a lot of things for you, but this isn't one of them."

He chuckled and leaned down to kiss her. Soft, innocent kisses, gliding over her mouth. He deepened the kiss. Her body came alive; her mind completely lost any train of thought. It had been two years since their first time together and he still could do this to her. He touched her and she was lost.

Within moments, the kiss turned hot and she couldn't control herself. She rose up to deepen the kiss, trying to pour all her emotions into it. She straddled him. She needed the connection, just the two of them.

"This is allowed, yes?" she asked as she kissed him. His cock was already hard against her sex.

"Yeah, I would say so," he said, a bit of humor and desire filling his voice.

She kept her eyes opened as she kissed him again. This time, it was slow, sweet and wet. Maura had said once that he made her toes curl every time he kissed her, and it hadn't changed. That link was still there, still strong.

He reached over to the table and grabbed a condom. She took it out of his hand and sat up.

"I think I can help you with that," she said smiling as she opened the package. Positioning the condom on the tip, she unrolled it. She took her time, caressing his flesh as she rolled it on his penis. He was groaning by the time she finished.

The power it gave her to do this, to give this to him, coursed through her veins. She raised herself up to her knees then took him inside her. He let her have her way for a few moments but he rose up, wrapped his arms around her and took a nipple into his mouth.

As she rode him, she felt that connection grow stronger. She did her best to let him feel the love she had for him. Soon, Maura moaned his name as she came, her body convulsing with her orgasm.

She continued to ride Zeke and leaned down to kiss him.

"Come for me, babe, do it," she said against his lips. She cupped his face. "I love you, Zeke."

He thrust one last time inside her and came whispering her name as he did. He fell back on the mattress taking her with him.

Maura settled her head against his chest and felt herself being lulled back to sleep by the beat of his heart and the warmth of his body.

fifteen

Maura loved the nighttime in Hawaii. She had access to decent beaches in Miami, although she preferred Kailua Beach to them, but the nighttime was truly beautiful. Zeke and she thought it best to take Rory down into the heart of Waikiki for the night. She liked to walk along the beach as the sun was setting and the tiki torches were being lit. And she loved the fragrant, balmy air. She smiled as Rory turned onto H-1.

"So, you haven't thought of moving here now that your brother's moved over here," Rory asked.

She shrugged. "I don't think so. It's fun, I love the island, but I'm afraid that I would go stir crazy. I need change every now and then. If I can't see fall foliage, at least I can fly to it relatively easily, I would be unhappy."

"Where are we going?" Zeke asked from the backseat.

"I thought we could hit Ala Moana tonight. I'm in the mood for a pork ball."

"I should have known. We haven't been on the ground for 24 hours but you feel the need to grab one of those clusters of cholesterol."

She smiled. "You know that it's my addiction."

"What's a pork ball?" Rory asked.

"They are heaven on earth," Maura said.

"They're filled with fat," Zeke said.

"He pretends to hate them but then he always eats them," Maura said.

Rory laughed. "Yeah. He likes to pretend he's all Mr. Health, but when you get him near something greasy...all bets are off."

"Well, these are not really greasy. It is sort of a savory sweet dough with a pork filling. One of them is enough to fill me up for dinner. I have no self-control when I get them. It's probably a good thing I don't know how to cook them."

"Face it, you don't know how to cook anything," Zeke said teasingly.

She frowned at him. "I can cook macaroni and cheese."

"You can't count using the blue box as cooking."

She stuck out her tongue and he laughed. He was often too serious so she treasured when she could make him laugh. "You can't either. I don't know why a woman is expected to be a great cook and men get awards when they boil water."

"Nope, you know my skill is in cleaning up the mess others leave behind. But, Rory here can."

She glanced at Rory who seemed to be concentrating on the traffic with renewed interest. "You can cook?"

He shrugged as if embarrassed that Zeke had told her about it. "I like to dabble in the kitchen."

"Dabble as in I know how to throw a steak on the grill or--"

"As in, Rory here can make a soufflé you would kill for," Zeke said, pride infusing his tone. It was hard not to smile at the way Zeke talked about Rory as if he were some kind of wonder. But even as she did, she felt a little twinge of jealousy. These men were going to go back to the way things were before they came to Hawaii. When she got home, it would be just her.

"What's wrong?" Zeke asked.

She glanced at him and gave him a smile even though it felt forced. "Nothing. I think the jet lag is getting to me. Plus, I'm hungry."

He looked like he didn't believe her, but he let it go. Zeke was always good at giving her space.

"There's Ala Moana," she said and gave Rory instructions on where to park. When he parked, she slipped out of the jeep and felt something stir the fine hairs on the back of her neck. Maura looked around but didn't see anyone looking at her. She walked a little further, listening to the guys talk about nothing of importance and she felt it again. This time, she stopped and looked around the parking garage. It was well lit and busy with tourists and locals on a Saturday night.

The guys walked a few steps before they stopped too. They were both frowning.

"What's wrong?" Rory asked.

She shook her head. "I think I'm just tired."

She fought the urge to look behind her as they walked into the shopping center's food court. The place was filled with a wealth of locals and tourists. It was large, housing at least 20 places to eat. She didn't pay attention to anything else. Maura made a beeline for her favorite Asian eatery. She heard Zeke chuckle behind her.

"What if we don't want to eat that, Maura?" he called out.

"You can feed yourself, Zeke," she said, but didn't turn around.

He didn't follow but Rory did.

He grabbed her by the arm. "Slow down, love. You sure do eat up the ground with those long legs."

"What's the use of walking slowly when you know what you want?"

He shook his head and his lips twitched. "To enjoy the journey?"

She rolled her eyes as she stepped into line to wait to give her order.

"So, you don't eat all the healthy stuff?"

"I watch what I eat but I have been blessed with good genes. Zee's father had all kinds of issues."

"But he didn't die because of that. He died in a bomb, right?"

Rory looked surprised that she knew. She tried not to take offense to it, and she really shouldn't. Rory and Zeke had known each other for so long. She was pretty sure that Zeke rarely got involved with women the way he had with her. Their relationship was different for him...for her. They always seemed to have that connection, the ability to call each other in the middle of the night just to talk.

"What is going on in your head?" he asked.

She shook herself out of the funk. "What do you mean?"

"Zeke said that you have a computer in there," he said smiling at her. She usually hated when people talked about her intelligence that way. But when Zeke did, it didn't bother her. And, apparently, it included Rory now.

"When I get tired, I can't keep my thoughts organized. I'm trying to do that right now."

"Ah," he said, but she knew he knew she was lying.

This was their first night in Hawaii and she didn't want to ruin it with sad thoughts or regrets. Living in the moment... that's what she told Jillian she would do. And dammit for once in her life, she would.

"Ready for the best thing on this island next to pineapple and malassadas?" she asked.

Rory studied her for a second then grinned. "Bring it on."

sixteen

R ory finished off his second pork ball and realized that Maura had just finished eating one.

The sweet, savory taste lingered in his mouth as he tried to figure out just what went into the delicacy. When he had left Ireland, he had discovered an entire world of different tasting food. Granted, he did have a soft place in his heart for bangers and mash, but a lot of their food was really bland. Thanks to the job, he and Zee had travelled the world over. They'd eaten in dives starving dogs would avoid and five star restaurants that had served presidents and kings. He was always intrigued in the way to cook things up, how they were made up. It was one of the reasons he had been good at making bombs once upon a time. It was all about what went into it and the execution...just different ingredients.

When he licked his last finger, he nodded. "You're right. Those are heaven. I need to figure out how to make them."

Zee looked at them from across the table as he ate his salad. "You two are disgusting."

"You're just jealous, Zee," Rory said, but his mind went

back to the treat they had just eaten. "I'll have to play with it a little, but I think I can figure it out."

Maura smiled. "Then, I will do anything for you if you can. I love those things but I have yet to find a place in Miami that makes them this way."

"Hmm," he said. "Just what would I get in return for making you these?"

She frowned and then again, he was reminded how literally she took everything. "I could clean your house."

"No." Zeke said. "You are not cleaning our house. You don't know how to clean."

She glanced at him and was going to open her mouth but something caught her eye. Rory followed her line of vision and saw a tall man striding down the row toward them. Waist length hair and strong Native American features of his face made him look fierce. Maura squealed and jumped up and ran toward him. He opened his arms and caught her in a big hug.

Rory couldn't hear the man's voice but he caught the smile and was on his feet before he knew what he was doing.

Zee caught him, wrapping his fingers around his forearm to stop him. "Slow down, love. It's just the owner of Rough 'n Ready."

He glanced at Zee.

"Who?" he asked looking back at the man holding his woman.

His woman? Shit. That was not smart to be thinking. He looked at Zee again and noticed the way he was studying him. "What?"

Zee shrugged. "I don't know if I ever saw you freak out over a woman before."

Rory knew what he was talking about, but he ignored it. If he argued with Zee it would make him more suspicious. It was bad enough it took every ounce of his control.

"So, he owns the club. Does he have to paw all over her?"

Zee's face went blank, then he laughed. "Oh, my, God. You're jealous."

"I'm not jealous." He knew he sounded desperate as he counted backwards from ten. The man was still touching her and Rory's fingers curled into the palms of his hands. Zee was still chuckling and with more than a little desperation, he said, "Conner wouldn't be happy if we didn't protect her."

"Sure, love, you keep telling yourself that. Some day you might just believe it."

Rory tossed Zee a furious glanced and headed off to Maura. He tried not to look so intent on reaching her, but something pushed him forward. He watched as Maura took a seat next to a rather largely pregnant woman. Zee caught up to him.

"That's Micah's wife, Dee. He is very happily married, so you don't have to worry about them."

"He wasn't one of the Dom's she was involved with?"

Why did that matter? It had never bothered him before but for some reason he couldn't get the idea out of his head that this man had touched her. From the look he was giving Rory, he knew that he was being sized up.

"No. We met him when we had to came over on one of Conner's old cases."

He nodded as they finally caught up to the trio. "Micah, how's everything?" Zee asked.

The man was tall—taller than either Zee or him and that was saying a lot. He continued to stand behind his wife's chair. He didn't appear to be doing anything but Rory sensed that the man continued to scan the area looking for threats. No matter.

"Everything's going well, except that someone had a need to come get some frozen yogurt."

The diminutive brunette smiled up at them then glanced at her husband.

"Stop looming like the Grim Reaper, Micah, and sit."

His lips twitched before doing what his wife ordered.

She turned her attention back to them. "I think I met you at the wedding."

Then he did remember meeting them. She hadn't been as pregnant then.

"Yes. We did. I'm Rory McAlister and this is Zeke O'Brian."

"Oh, I know Zeke well since he turned me into the feds."

Zee shook his head. "I didn't turn you into the feds. Just into Conner."

She laughed then turned back to Maura. "So, I like the blonde hair."

And they had been dismissed. He had an idea that the woman was a sub with a husband who ran a BDSM club and the fact that he screamed Dom just by his actions. But she really did run things in her own way.

"Yeah, and yours is completely brunette now. I don't know why you would have changed it before."

She laughed and he watched as Micah turned his head slightly, his expression softening a bit.

"So, you boys here for a vacation?" she asked.

He would usually take offense at being called a boy, but he had a feeling Dee Ross didn't mean anything by it.

"Yeah."

Then, her and Maura started talking.

"Are you here because of Peterson?" Micah asked.

Zee nodded. "In a way. I don't think we have anything to worry about, really. We turned everything over to the FBI, they took it from there. We aren't even mentioned in any of the papers. They conducted their own investigation. Conner just thought it best if we were removed from the situation at least during the beginning of the trial. Plus, he was worried about other things," he said looking over at Maura.

Micah followed his line of vision and nodded in understanding. "What flavor did you say you wanted, babe?"

"Chocolate. But I can get it."

"No, you sit. You remember what the doc said about staying off your feet as much as possible. Maura?"

"Vanilla, waffle cone."

He signaled with his head and they followed him.

"She's not looking very good."

It wasn't an accusation, but it still felt that way. He bit back the retort, but apparently Ross picked up on his feelings.

"And don't be getting upset with me. It's just an observation. Since everything that went down with Conner, I know that she has been on edge. Dee said she sensed it in her voice when they would talk. She's been a little worried about Maura. Running the office by herself is hard."

"I'm there and I hate to have to keep pointing this out, but I'm partners with Conner," Zee said. Rory sensed he was mildly irritated.

Ross sighed as he stepped in line. "I get that, but you know that girl. She's so focused on not letting Conner down. The fact that she's changing hair color is a sure sign."

Rory frowned at him. "What are you talking about?"

Ross eyed him. "Dee has said in the past that Maura changes her hair color when she is upset."

Zee nodded. "I picked up on it, but at least she didn't go dark. When Conner and Jillian were in that mess, she died it black. That wasn't pretty."

He glanced back at the table and smiled when he watched her throw her head back and laugh.

"Does Conner know?" Ross asked.

He had to pull his attention away from Maura to concentrate on Ross. He found the Dom watching him without an expression on his face.

"What?"

"No, he doesn't know," Zee said. "And we would rather not have to deal with that."

Ross crossed his arms and stared them down. Rory had dealt with more bastards than he wanted to remember, but at the moment, most of them paled in comparison to Micah Ross.

"There is one thing I want both of you to understand. I love my wife."

"Nice to know," Rory said, sarcasm dripping from his words.

"My wife has a soft spot in her heart for Maura. I do too."

"And, what does this mean to me?" Rory asked, not able to keep the sneer out of his voice.

"This means that if you hurt her in any way, Dee will give me permission to beat the shit out of you."

He glanced at the woman again. She was very petite and small boned. She had one of the sweetest faces. He turned back to face Ross.

"She's too sweet."

Micah snorted. "You got that off the what fifteen minutes total you've spent with her?" Rory opened his mouth but Micah stopped him. "Sweet Dee is the daughter of Tony Rizzoli. Yeah, that's right. And, she hid for years, all the while learning how to defend herself. The only thing she got from that bastard of a father was that you mess with one of her family —either one of your choosing or blood—she will happily order me to hurt them. Ask Zeke here."

He glanced at Zee and he nodded.

"Your problem is that you don't see women as a threat," Ross said. "You make too many misconceptions."

"And you figured that out after fifteen minutes in my presence?"

Instead of getting mad, Ross smiled. "Hey, just trying to

help out. And I'm good at reading people. Part of my former life as a bounty hunter. Just remember that women aren't as helpless as you think."

Rory was irritated but he did his best to hide it. "Yeah, and how did you come to that observation?"

"Who's standing in line waiting to get yogurt and who's sitting at a table talking?"

Rory laughed. "You have a point there."

SEVENTEEN

Maura held her hand on Dee's stomach and giggled when she felt another kick against her palm.

"Wow, you have a future soccer player in there, woman," she said.

"You don't have to tell me. All night long, every night. I'm blaming Micah because he's so damned tall."

She sat back and smiled at Dee. It was hard to remember her as the young woman her brother had hunted for years. When her father put a hit out on her, Dee didn't just give up. She survived and now, she was getting rewarded. A woman who was married to Micah Ross and had the man knee deep in love with her was one lucky woman.

"You look so happy."

Her smile widened. "I am happy. I never thought I would be, but I am. Before Hawaii, I'd move within a year."

"Yeah, I know," Maura said, wryly. "I am pretty familiar with your disappearing act."

Dee threw back her head and laughed.

"Sure, you think it's funny. I had to deal with Conner. You

know how many times we almost got to you? There was a time in Chicago...I thought Conner was going to come unglued."

"Well, I guess I can't complain too much. I found my brother thanks to that little excursion. And I think because you came in here with big, bad Zeke, you got to hook up with him. So, I think you kind of owe me."

Maura laughed. "You would say that."

"Well, I have to say, you have more energy than I do," Dee said as she glanced toward the men standing in line.

"What are you talking about?"

Dee looked at her, one eyebrow raised. "Oh, please, woman. They look like they were ready to eat you alive. Plus, that Rory, he wasn't too happy with Micah manhandling you that way."

Maura snorted trying to ignore the way her heart did flip-flop when she thought about it. Sure, they were playing, but there was nothing permanent. "That pregnancy of yours is starting to mess with your head."

Dee leaned forward, her smile fading. "You better know what you're doing, Maura."

She opened her mouth to argue but Dee stopped her. "I do not judge you. Seriously, I wouldn't mind living out a fantasy. But that's how things started with Micah. I thought, I'd just have fun for a while. Then I fell in love."

Air backed up in her lungs and she suddenly found it hard to breathe.

"Maura, are you okay?"

Maura shook her head. "I'm not in love."

Understanding moved over Dee's features. She said nothing as she took a sip from her water bottle.

"Okay, I love Zeke, I probably always will. But that isn't that important."

"Really? Maura Dillon, who are you kidding? You are head

over heels in love with Zeke, and I'm guessing you're falling for that other big Irishman."

She wanted to deny it, but she was really afraid it was true. Dee looked behind her, and Maura turned to find out what had caught her eye. All three men were walking toward them. Micah usually garnered the most attention, but all Maura could see were Zeke and Rory. They were both tall, strong, and undeniably sexy. And she was in love with one and desperately falling in love with the second.

Shit, she was in a lot of trouble.

eighteen

Maura sniffed at the air and smiled. "God I love the smell of plumeria. It's fantastic."

Zeke couldn't help but smile as they walked along the path next to the Hilton. "Yeah, there is something here you can't get anywhere else, especially on the mainland. It's like being in another country in a way, they're so unique."

She looked at him from the corner of her eye. "Don't let the locals hear you say that."

"Hey, I thought they liked to be known as one of the most original states."

"They do, but I don't blame them for having a little chip on their shoulder about being considered the US. You hear people say when I get back to the states...it is kind of annoying."

"That's the truth."

"So, Rory, what meals do you plan to make for me."

That was Maura. While her figure was trim, it wasn't due to her lack of eating. She'd been graced with a high metabolism. And now that she knew Rory liked to cook, she would badger him until he made her several meals.

"I don't know. I thought we would be eating out more often."

She lifted her head and grinned at Rory. "That was before I found out you could cook. Tell me, how are you at Italian?"

Zeke groaned. "Oh, god, she is going to have you making pasta every night. I can't handle the carbs."

"Suck it up, Zeke," Maura said. "So, what can you make me?"

"Are you more of a Northern or a Southern Italian lover?" Rory asked.

Maura let go of him to clap. "Anything, all, I want it all."

"I'll make a lasagna this week."

"With béchamel sauce?"

"Of course," Rory said.

"I will be your slave for life."

Rory gave him a look then leaned closer to her. "I'll make sure to remind you of that next time I have you naked."

Her face turned red, then she looked around them.

"What?" Rory asked. "You're not embarrassed, are you?"

She shook her head and shrugged. "I feel like someone is watching me. Weird."

Immediately, Zeke's alarms went off. Maura wasn't a woman who worried about being followed on a regular basis. He knew Conner didn't get calls in the middle of the night from Maura.

"What?"

"When we got into Ala Moana, I felt it, but it's gone just like that. Might be my imagination."

He looked back at Rory who was already looking around. The fact that neither he nor Rory felt it was enough to satisfy him, or it should be.

"You don't have an imagination."

She rolled her eyes. "Way to romance me, Zeke. The flattery is going to make me faint."

"Maura," he said, lowering his voice in a warning.

She patted him on the cheek. "It's probably because I'm tired. It's been such a long day. Even with a few cat naps, I need some rest."

"Yeah, that's probably it," Rory said, but Zeke wasn't too happy with it. He knew not to blow it out of proportion and coming to Hawaii had only been a precaution, but still, it was something he would have to think about.

"It *has* been a long day. Let's head back."

She sighed and set her head on Zeke's shoulder as they walked. "That sounds great."

nineteen

B y the time they got home, Zeke had mostly dismissed her worries. She went to the bathroom leaving them alone.

"What's bothering you?"

He looked at Rory. "Maura doesn't have things like that happen to her."

Rory shrugged. "So, she felt someone staring at her. She's probably tired."

Zeke thought about it and realized he might be blowing it out of proportion. How much of it had to do with their relationship?

"I see those wheels turning, so what the hell is going on in there?" Rory asked.

"Nothing."

But he was lying. He was in love with two people who made it very hard to choose. Not that they had asked him to, but he could feel them dancing around each other trying to figure out the relationship. There was a small part of him...okay a big part of him that wanted to make it permanent. He wanted both of them forever.

That thought hit him hard. He blinked.

"Zee, are you okay?"

Rory's concerned voice reached him. He nodded.

But he wasn't. Shit, he had promised himself that he wouldn't get bogged down on what would happen when they returned home, but somewhere in the back of his mind, he had been. He had been hoping that they could be together forever.

"What's up with him?" Maura asked as she walked into the kitchen.

"Not sure."

"We just need to get to sleep."

Maura smiled, but it wasn't her usual brilliant grin. Zeke realized just how exhausted she was. He patted her shoulder.

"Come on, love, let's get to bed."

She nodded and he practically carried her up the stairs to the bedroom. By the time she was in PJs, she was almost asleep. He tucked her into bed then looked up at Rory.

"She's wiped out," he said.

Zeke nodded and waited. It was going to be a real test if he wanted to sleep with her. Zeke wanted to, but Rory tended to avoid sleeping with other lovers. The intimacy was something he could not handle. Zeke was pretty sure he was the only lover Rory had ever really slept beside.

Rory pulled his shirt up over his head, and dropped his pants. He climbed into bed with Maura as if it was the most natural thing in the world to do. Zeke was so happy, he didn't even mention that Rory had left his clothes on the floor.

Zeke undressed and then brushed his teeth. When he walked out of the bathroom, he stopped and just looked at the scene on the bed. Maura had rolled all the way over to Rory. Both of them were fast asleep and she was snuggled up against him. Rory had his arm wrapped around her as if to protect her.

Zeke's heart melted. The two of them probably didn't even

realize what it meant to him to see them like that. In their sleep, they accepted each other. He slipped into bed behind Maura, snuggled up close to her and sighed as he closed his eyes.

It wasn't a huge step, but it was at least a step in the right direction.

twenty

Z ee was already dressed by the time Rory and Maura crawled out of bed. Rory was glad to finally have a partner with them who enjoyed snuggling in bed rather than getting up and going to work. Zee always berated him for it. Rory was just sitting down at the kitchen bar when Maura came stumbling in.

"There has to be some coffee, and it better be hot."

Zee sighed as he poured her a cup, handed her sweetener and retrieved the creamer from the refrigerator.

"She takes it black, Zee."

Zeke looked at him and there was a flash of irritation in his eyes before he hid it. He put the creamer back in the fridge.

"You two are pathetic."

Rory opened his mouth and laughed. Maura flipped Zee off.

"Well said, love. Anyone who wants to work with the ocean view like that one out the window is an idiot anyway."

Zee frowned at him. "I'm just going to spend this morning going over some figures with Conner. I don't know when we'll be able to sit down in person again."

Maura snorted. "You can do a teleconference any day."

"And for some reason, I don't want to hang around with you two this morning. Not that your shiny personalities don't do it for me, but I am not in the mood to deal with two grumpy lovers."

He picked up the keys and walked around the counter. First, he kissed Maura on the cheek, then gave Rory a kiss.

"Don't do anything I wouldn't do," Zee said, as he walked out the door.

"What the hell is it with morning people?" Maura asked as she laid her head down on the counter. "Conner's always freaking chipper, all smiles and shit. Well, not smiles. Conner hardly ever smiles, except sometimes at me and more when he is around Jillian. He should thank me for that, dammit."

She looked so...cute. Grumpy as Zee had pointed out but cute. Her hair was a mess, her face was still flush from sleep and she had her hand on her coffee cup as if she were afraid someone would steal it. This was a side of her he had never seen. She had always been so put together at the office and she was there early every day. He would have never thought he would see her like this and it made her even more tempting. Seeing the soft side of such a buttoned down perfectionist turned him to goo.

"So what should we do?" he asked.

She yawned, took a sip, and put her head down again, closing her eyes. "Pretend we are sleeping."

"No really. There's gotta be something to do."

"With Mr. Sunshine out of the picture, I think we should go back to bed," she said. It wasn't said coyly, as if she were trying to entice him, and that made it all the more arousing. She still didn't understand her appeal to him or even probably to Zee.

"Yeah?" he asked. She opened one eye and looked at him. He didn't blame her. His voice had already deepened at the idea of a little play with her. She was one of the most amazing subs and they had just started.

"I thought..."

Her voice trailed off and she frowned. Now he knew what Zee meant about her brain. It got her into trouble.

"You thought?" he asked as he reached out to toy with her hair.

"Well, I just thought it was the threesome. I mean, I know you and Zeke do things together, but I thought for the week, it was going to be the three of us."

He smiled. "There are no rules here on how we do things. And, I will point out that you and Zee had sex without me yesterday."

She didn't return his smile and he started to worry. Did she mean she didn't want to be with him without Zee?

"Maura, is there some reason you wouldn't want to play a bit this morning, just tell me."

"No, there isn't. I just didn't know if you would want me without Zee around. I understand that a lot of the excitement is having him watch you."

"That is part of it. The other part of it is you."

She studied him for a few seconds, the serious expression in her eyes made his stomach clench. He knew he could order her to the room and she would do it. But in this, he wanted her to decide on her own, their D/s relationship out of the equation.

A shy smile curved her lips and his heart did that little tap dance he was getting used to when he was around her.

"Yeah?" she asked. He was amazed she didn't understand just how much a man could want her. She might be a genius, but apparently she didn't understand her appeal.

"Yeah. So, love, what do you say? Wanna play?"

Her smile turned into a grin. "Yes."

He took her hand and pulled it up to kiss her fingers. Without a word, he led her into the bedroom they had all been using. He couldn't believe the way his body was already begging to take her. When it came to sex, Rory had complete control, but with Maura, he seemed to lose part of it. He needed to remember what she needed from him.

Rory dropped her hand.

"Take off your clothes, lay down on your back, and spread your legs so I can see my pussy."

She hesitated for a second and he swatted her behind.

"Get a move on."

She did as ordered and he drew in a deep breath. How could he resist a woman who was so damned submissive, and one that Zee loved? *Impossible.*

He went to the drawer where he had stashed the toys and pulled out a pair of nipple clamps. She wasn't large on top, but that was fine by him. Her breasts were sensitive, that much he had figured out last night.

He walked over to the bed, sat down beside her, and clamped them on her nipples. She drew in a breath.

"Hurt?"

"A little."

"Remember your safe word."

She nodded. He knew she did but it never hurt to remind a sub about her options. Maura had been trained but he was pretty sure he was the first Dom she had taken on outside of that training. He would be lying if he didn't say that part of their relationship didn't give him a little thrill. He had never really taken on such a novice, although he wouldn't have been able to tell from the way she behaved.

"You know, when I first met you, I was surprised that Zee had a thing for you. Not because of your looks because you are beautiful." Her face flushed and he found it slightly endearing. "But, well, Zee has never liked prudes and I pegged you as one. After yesterday, you proved me wrong."

He gave the chain connecting the nipple clamps a little tug. She shuddered.

"Like that, huh?"

"Yes."

He tugged on the chain again.

"Yes, Sir."

"I think we need to see just what some of your boundaries are so we know where to push you."

Rory grabbed the egg he had picked up and stood. He said nothing as he walked around the bed. He was still fully clothed and he liked the idea of her naked on the bed. He knew the psychological aspect of it and he thought that maybe Maura liked it. Many subs did.

He slid a finger down her slit. She was already getting wet. He could smell the pungent aroma of her arousal. There was no way he could resist just a taste. He bent his head and licked her pussy. Damn, she was decadent, like the most delicious dessert. Before he got carried away, he pulled back and inserted the egg.

Then, he stood. "It has a remote control."

He turned it on and a low humming noise sounded. She moaned and closed her eyes.

"Stand up."

It took her a second respond so he stopped the egg.

"I told you to stand up, Maura."

She did as ordered and he hit the pulse to give her a reward. She sighed.

"Yeah, you like that, don't you?"

"Yes, Sir."

He slipped his arm around her waist and kissed her. When he pulled back, he smiled at her.

"Did you taste yourself, love? You are like a piece of pie." He had to force himself to step back. "Come."

He slipped his finger behind the chain and tugged gently. Her step faltered but she followed. He knew she could feel it all the way to her pussy. There was a chair and he was ready to play some more.

He stopped by the chair. "Take my pants off. And no touching the cock. You get to touch that only when I think you've earned it."

She frowned up at him, and he had to fight to keep his expression stern. Adhering to his rules, she pulled his pants down, waiting as he stepped out of them.

"Fold them and put them on the bed."

She did only faltering in her steps when he buzzed the vibrator to reward her. She returned. He sat down in the chair then took hold of the chain again and tugged until she was standing in front of him again.

"I don't want to get carried away. I have some ideas for later, but I want to save them so we can share them with Zeke."

He knew she wanted to ask what they were, but when she didn't, he hit the button on the remote again, leaving it pulsing longer. Her knees almost buckled but he righted her. His cock twitched. The scent of her arousal was almost overwhelming him.

"Get on your knees."

She did, but she had to use his knee to balance herself.

He cupped her face and tilted her face so he could see her. Right there, he could have died and been happy. There had been one other person who could undo him with a look, and that was Zee.

"As I was saying earlier, I would have thought you a prude, but you proved me wrong last night, didn't you, love."

She nodded and licked her lips. He knew how much she

enjoyed sucking cock, and he had her level with his. Rory had done it on purpose.

"You liked doing just about anything I suggested. Hell, I bet your cunt is fucking wet right now. I liked watching Zee fucking that tight little ass of yours last night. Just know, I am going to get my time with it again. And you're going to fucking love it."

She said nothing just kept waiting and dammit, that turned him on more than anything. The woman definitely understood the Dom and sub relationship. She might have not tested it that much, but she was perfect for him at least. He took his cock in his hand and her gaze dropped to watch. He stroked himself and watched as her tongue darted out over her full lips again. Oh, she wanted it. In fact, he had never seen a woman who liked having a cock in her mouth as much as Maura. He pulled his cock up, giving her access to his sac.

"Lick my balls."

She set her hands on her knees.

"No. Put your hands behind your back. I don't want you to be tempted to touch."

She did and in the process, her breasts were thrust forward. She leaned down and placed the flat of her tongue on his balls and gave them a long, loving lick. God, she was wonderful. As she licked, nipped, and sucked his balls, she locked her gaze with his.

"You want some cock?"

She pulled back and nodded. He released his cock.

"Suck."

She did it happily. Keeping her hands behind her back, she took his dick into her mouth. He groaned the first time she slipped her tongue up over the tip. Then, he leaned back to enjoy the pleasure she was giving him.

Soon, though, it was a little too much. He almost came once or twice.

"Stop."

She didn't obey him right away, so he turned off the egg. She pulled back.

"You like cock so much, doncha, love?"

She licked her lips and nodded. He almost came right there and then. He helped her up, then grabbed the chain again and took her to the dresser. She was going to have to get used to that because he had a collar he'd bought just for her. He couldn't wait to put it on her.

"Hands on the dresser, Maura."

She did it and he turned the egg back on low as a reward. She hummed and shivered.

He stepped closer, his cock against her ass. He nuzzled her neck.

"God, you smell good. Just soap, I like that in a woman. I also like that you are such a fuck toy. You like that don't you, Maura? You liked being fucked so hard you can't walk."

"Yes, Sir."

There was no hesitation when she gave him the name this time. It was an intimacy he enjoyed before with subs, but this was different. He felt like he had been punched in the heart.

"I am getting my cock up that ass of yours and you're going to love it, aren't you?"

She shivered again and sighed. "Yes, Sir."

He forced himself to pull back and arrange her so that her ass was in the perfect position. Her breasts were easy to see in the mirror. He grabbed some lube and coated his finger with it. As he turned the vibrator to a higher level, he slipped his finger into her ass.

"I was so happy to know that you liked to have your ass

fucked. Zee likes it, and well, of course I like it, but it is always nice to have a woman who wants to be fucked like that."

She groaned.

"Remember, love, no coming until I tell you. You understand, right?"

She nodded as he added another finger. Oh, she was ready, and thank god she had done this before Zee and him had brought her into their bedroom. He didn't have the patience to train her for it.

He pulled his fingers out and then took her by the hips. Then, he positioned his cock.

"Remember, you can show me pleasure. Tell me what you like. I want to hear you scream."

With that, he eased his way into her ass. God, she was tight. She stayed steady and groaned as he slipped past the tight ring of muscles.

"Fuck, yeah," he muttered. He started to move. Over and over he thrust into her ass and he enjoyed every bit of it. Damn, she was the fuck toy he had called her. She was humming and moaning his name over and over. He turned up the vibrator and he felt it.

Soon, he needed to come, needed to see her lose control. He slapped her ass hard then grabbed a fist full of her hair and pulled her back as he leaned forward. He kissed her then, thrusting his tongue into her mouth as he continued to fuck her ass. He pulled back.

"You need to come now. Do it for me, love."

He ratcheted the speed to the highest level and it sent her over the edge.

"Oh, Rory, yes. Oh God."

She screamed his name over and over, her body convulsing with the orgasm. He turned down the egg and just as she was coming down, he turned it on high again.

"Oh, Rory...Fuck."

She came again, and he went with her, thrusting one last time. Moments later, he leaned over her and kissed her neck.

"You are fantastic, love."

"Why thank you, sir," she said with a smile in her voice.

twenty-one

Zeke hung up the phone.

"So, I take it they are just getting out of bed?" Conner asked. Zeke glanced at him and wondered at the question, but Conner was studying his laptop screen.

"Yeah, I guess those two get along in the mornings." He was pretty sure they got along a little more than just not being morning people. But Conner wasn't ready to hear that. "They're going to head down to the swap meet today."

He nodded as he punched a few keys. "She isn't having a problem with you two, is she?"

Jillian choked on her coffee but Conner didn't notice. It took her a few moments to compose herself but she looked everywhere in the room but at him. Zeke had a feeling Maura told Jillian. What was he thinking? Of course she did. They were best friends.

"No. I think you're worrying just a little too much about her. Maura's doing fine."

Conner turned his head and gave him a narrowed look. "Are you telling me the truth, or what she told you to tell me?"

"I hate to tell you this, but we don't sit around the office talking about ways to hide things from you. We're sort of running the Miami office and shit."

Conner's frown turned darker. "I shouldn't have left it up to her. She's taking on too much."

"Hey, whoa, take a step back there, Saint Conner. She's handling everything just fine. And she has me and Jennifer to help her. It's not like she's fifteen. She's an adult who can deal with shit. Let it go."

"You'll call if she starts to drown?"

"No."

"What?"

"I won't because it isn't going to happen. Why do you have such little faith in her?"

Conner's mouth opened then closed. "What the hell do you mean by that?"

"If you had hired a woman with her background, you wouldn't think about leaving her in charge of the office. Hell, you would expect her to contact you. But for some reason, you doubt her at every turn. Why is that?"

"Because she's my sister."

"Which means that you should have more faith in her than you have in strangers, but you don't. Do you know what that does to her?"

Conner said nothing.

"I'll tell you. It makes her second guess everything she does. Ask Jillian. I bet she'd tell you the same thing. Have some faith in the fact that I'm there to catch her if she falls. And have more faith in the fact it would take a lot of shit to make her fall."

He didn't realize he had been yelling until he stopped talking. The room was deathly silent.

"I need a break."

And with that, he strode out of the room, down the steps and out onto the beach. He didn't have shoes on, so he walked across the hot sand. He found an empty spot and plopped down.

Fuck, what was he thinking? Maura didn't want her brother to know what was going on, but there was something in the way Conner had talked about her that pissed him off. Conner had been more father than brother for so long, he couldn't step back and see the amazing woman she had become. And, the way he yelled at his best friend hadn't been smart. He might as well write I love Maura across his forehead.

"So, I take it you didn't plan on yelling at Conner?" Jillian said from behind him. He glanced back her and he could feel his face heat. Dammit, he had acted like a fool in front of Jillian. Great.

"No." He looked back out at the ocean. "I guess I shouldn't have done that in front of you. Hell, I shouldn't have done it at all."

She said nothing as she walked up and sat next to him, crossed legged.

"No, I think it's good that he hears it from someone other than me."

"You said the same thing?"

He sensed her shrug. "He has the problem of still looking at her like she's still that scared teenager trying to deal with the loss of both parents."

"Yeah."

"You know, I said things kind of similar when she was in college with me."

"Yeah?"

"Conner hadn't prepared her for sex. I did."

He glanced at her. "You did?"

"Yeah." She smiled at him. "Conner wasn't happy to find out that I had given her condoms and showed her how to put them on."

He chuckled. "I can imagine."

"It's so easy to see you love her."

He sighed. "It's complicated."

"Naw, it isn't. You love her, she loves you."

"There's Rory."

She snorted. "Please, if he isn't over the moon for her already, he will be soon. I saw the way he looked at her."

"What do you mean?"

"When you all stopped by here the first day. He couldn't take his eyes off her."

"Is that how you figured out we were all involved?"

"No. Maura told me." He glanced at her. "No, I didn't tell the bear in there. He's going to figure it out soon."

"Why is that?"

"Conner can be a curmudgeon but he isn't stupid. The three of you in a room together, anyone can tell you're involved."

"Damn."

"And another thing. Make sure you don't play at Rough 'n Ready."

"Oh, Rory was thinking about..."

He trailed off not wanting to tell her as if he were breaking Maura's trust.

Jillian patted him on the knee. "I know. She's always had a fantasy of two guys who were bisexual and she wants to play in public. But word will get back to Conner. It would be best if it didn't. At least not until you all decide what happens when you get home."

He nodded. Jillian gave him a kiss on the cheek. "Now, you better go make up with that grumpy man because I have a deadline I set for myself."

"Sure thing. You know if Conner hadn't gotten to you first, I would have taken a shot at you."

"And you might have had a shot. Especially with that accent."

He laughed and stood, holding a hand out to her. She waved it away.

"Naw. You go make up with Conner, I'm going to sit here and contemplate my next scene. It isn't really sounding right, so I need a break."

Zeke walked up the hill, which wasn't easy in the sand. He waved at one of the guys who owned the house in front of Jillian's before turning toward the front door.

He opened the screen and found Conner right where he left him.

"Over your temper?"

"Zeke?"

"Yes."

"You want to tell me what that's about?"

He didn't but he probably needed to give some kind of an explanation. "You know we were involved."

"Yes."

"Dammit, Conner, stop working for a second."

He hit a few keys, probably saving what he had been writing and looked up at Zeke. He didn't know what to say now. Zeke had been known as having a cool head. He had to. Growing up in a primarily white area, he had learned to pick his fights. Why he got so hot and bothered over this now was sort of a mystery to him.

"I'm waiting."

"Okay. We were involved but we called it off. You know that. But, it doesn't mean I don't still care for her. I know how she feels when you question every one of her moves."

"I ask her how things go."

How did Jillian put up with such a stubborn mule? Why did he?

He sighed and sat in the chair. "I set up that meeting with Colfax. You asked me how it went."

"Yeah, you said fine. Why, did something go wrong?"

"No, but Maura does something, and you have a list of twenty questions."

"Well I want to make sure--"

"Exactly. Jesus, you don't even see it, do you? Jennifer has been working less time for you and you have more faith in her abilities than you do Maura."

Conner sighed. "I didn't realize she felt that way."

"I'm not sure she does. Not all the time. She is used to it. But some praise from you would be good. And you need to trust her. What's more, she needs you to trust her. She's smarter than both of us put together."

Conner smiled. "That's the truth."

"She's not a little girl anymore."

"No. But it's just second nature to me. I don't even think about it. I didn't realize I was doing it."

"Lay off her and she'll do better."

"You really think that would help?"

"I think it would at least get her back to sleeping at nights. I'm not sure she does much sleeping from the bags under her eyes."

"She never slept much as a kid to begin with." Conner sat back in his chair and studied him for a second. "How did you get so smart about women?"

Zeke shook his head. "I'm not that smart about women. I just know Maura well."

"Because you love her."

He had never really admitted it out loud to Conner. He was never sure exactly how Conner had felt about Zeke and Maura together.

"Yes, and even if I didn't, I care about her and you. It's been a tough few months for you and whether you like it or not, it has an effect on Maura."

"You love her but you can't be with her?"

He wanted to strangle the man. He was Zeke's best friend but there were times he just wanted to slap him silly. He was making this about Zeke and not about Maura. He wasn't even sure if Conner knew he did that.

"I couldn't give her what she wanted." Conner opened his mouth. "And I want you to leave it at that. It's private and it's between us. But that isn't the point I was trying to make."

Irritation was stamped all over Conner's face. "What?"

"Your sister is stressed and you aren't helping. You're making it worse. I want you to back off."

"And just what authority do you have to do that?"

"I'm your business partner and this does have to do with work. You never question anyone like you question her. You need to show some faith in her and her abilities. It's causing problems at the office. And worse, it's hurting her Conner. She doesn't realize it, but it is."

He sighed. "Jillian says I'm obtuse."

"You are. You're also an ass."

Conner chuckled. "I'll take her to lunch tomorrow, show her the offices."

Zeke nodded. "I think that would be a great idea."

"Now, do you have anything else you want to bitch about?"

"I hope not, because I'm ready to get back to work," Jillian said from the doorway. "Did y'all make up?"

"Yeah. I'm going to take Maura to lunch tomorrow. Wanna come?"

She easily plopped down on Conner's lap. It was good to see his friend so happy and relaxed. Well, relaxed for Conner.

"Naw. I think it should be a brother sister day."

Their happiness was something he wanted. At one time, he

had always thought it would be with one person...but now he wanted that fantasy to be real. He wanted Maura and he wanted Rory. Forever.

He pushed that thought aside and gathered up his work and shut down his computer. After slipping it in his briefcase, he looked at Conner. "I think we're done here, then? I thought I would goof off a little bit since I am on Oahu."

"Enjoy it while you can," Jillian said, the double meaning not lost on him.

"I plan on it. Hell, I might find a way to enjoy it for much longer."

She laughed.

"What are you two talking about?"

"Nothing, just joking. See ya' later, Zeke."

He laughed and headed out the door. Jillian was already nuzzling Conner's neck and Zeke didn't have to be told they would rather be left alone.

He was on his way back to the rental house when he made a promise to himself. He would do everything he could to make the relationship he had started here with Maura and Rory last.

If there was one thing the three of them deserved, it was to be happy.

twenty-two

Rory watched Maura walk out of yet another tent. She smiled at him as she walked in his direction. She was so damned cute. There was that word again—but she was. She looked years younger wearing a pair of board shorts and a University of Georgia T-shirt that had seen better days. He didn't like the looks she had been getting since they arrived and that had bothered him even more. He had never been that possessive of a woman, even a sub. But, with those long legs and those tiny shorts, she was getting a lot of looks from men. It had been hard for him to allow her to walk into the tent by herself, but he'd started to avoid them because of the increasing number of shoppers. It had gotten so damned hot he thought he would pass out.

Inwardly he snorted. He hadn't lived in Ireland in over ten years, but he still couldn't stand heat for long. He did it for the job, but he definitely wouldn't do it for shopping.

"So, you brought me here for what reason?" Rory asked amused.

She had another bag full of junk—he was pretty sure it was junk—and normally he would be irritated with doing something that was such a waste of time. But Rory couldn't help but enjoy walking around the tent city that surrounded Aloha Stadium. Maura took such joy in the hunt for a bargain that he couldn't really deny wanting to walk with her.

"To buy something Hawaiian. If you want to buy something to commemorate your trip, you come here. You have a few malassadas—"

"Now, I have to agree that is a good thing to have. Along with that pineapple crack you fed me, that almost makes it worth it.

She snorted. "Yeah, you ate all mine. We need to make another pit stop because I love that pineapple stuff. But, to get back to what I was saying before I was so rudely interrupted, this is the place to come for anything touristy. I always make sure I'm here on the weekend or on a Wednesday. It's too much fun."

He smiled. "And you needed that coconut bra for what reason?"

"It's for Jennifer. She'll love it."

He thought of the former FBI agent. "Uh, do you know another Jennifer? I would never buy something like this for her."

"That's why she'll love to get it. People like stuff like that."

He raised his eyebrows. "They do?"

She stopped and huffed at him. "Of course they do. It isn't the gift, but it's the fact you thought of them while you were gone."

"Is that so?" he asked but she ignored his disbelieving tone. She was already making a beeline to a tent with hats. Normally, he would get irritated with a sub who acted this way. Of course, he didn't spend much time outside of the bedroom

"I need a hat, you should get one too. Not good for people who are fair like us."

"You're not really blonde." He slipped his arms around her waist, pulled her against him and kissed her neck. "I have inside knowledge of that fact."

She laughed and swatted at his hands. "Behave in public. I meant our skin. Turtles!"

She was working her way through the crowded tent by the time he caught up with her. She picked up a ridiculously large straw hat with a turtle pattern on it. She put it on and smiled at him. "What do you think?"

For a second he couldn't actually think. She was smiling at him and his tongue was stuck to the top of his mouth. Her eyes were sparkling with happiness and her grin was bright and wide. He had never seen a human so happy with her lot in life as he did looking at Maura right then. And in that split second, the only thought that came to Rory's mind was he wanted to see that smile every day for the rest of his life.

"Does it look stupid?" she asked apparently not realizing that he had a life altering thought. "I don't care. We are in Hawaii and I can look like an idiot like other tourists." She spied something behind him and grabbed the straw hat off one of the mannequins. She plopped it on his head.

"There, I like that. Now we need to get Zeke a hat. He can't be left out."

He stopped her by grabbing her hand and pulling her back to face him. He still couldn't utter a word.

"Rory?" she asked, her smile dimming just a bit. "Something wrong?"

He shook his head and then brushed his mouth over hers. She sighed. It was noisy in the tent, crowded and hot, but he heard the small sound over everything. It feathered over him as if it had been blasted on a loud speaker.

He pulled back and she was watching him now warily.

"Are you okay?"

"Sure, love. Let's get something for Zee. He really likes red."

She smiled again and he felt like he owned the whole fucking world.

"You're right. That would be fabulous. Let's look."

She grabbed his hand and pulled him through the tent. This time, he went willingly as he tried to figure out just what the fuck he was going to do about her.

twenty-three

"**R**ory and I decided that red is your favorite color," Maura said as he pulled the red straw fedora out of her bag.

Zeke chuckled and took the hat. "It is."

"I thought you would need it to keep you covered while on the island since you decided to go all bald a few months ago."

Zeke nodded.

Maura smiled happy that he liked her gift. Zeke was one of those people who were so hard to buy for. Knowing that he had a rough time after his father had been killed. Money had been tight. So, once Zeke started making money, he never hesitated to buy what he wanted. He had what he wanted mostly.

"Did you and Conner have some good work time?"

He hesitated. "Yeah."

She frowned and stopped going through her bags. She studied him and could tell that something had happened. "What?"

Rory glanced at her then at Zeke. "Yeah, what? I picked up on that too."

"I got irritated with him and yelled at him."

164

Maura didn't say anything for a long time. Her fear was that her brother had found out about them. It wasn't that she was ashamed of what she was doing, but she didn't need a lecture about it. Of course, if Conner knew about it, he would probably be sitting here waiting for her when she got home.

"And, what happened?"

He shrugged. "We worked it out. It wasn't anything important."

"It wasn't that important but it's bothering you?"

He glanced at Rory, then back at her. "Just some issues at the office, stuff we have to work out. You know your brother is a pain in the ass. Once he decides on something, he's tenacious."

That wasn't the whole truth, but she knew better than to push Zeke. He might call Conner hard headed, but Zeke was just as bad. If he decided to hide things from her, there would be no budging him. Maura decided a call to Jillian was in order. She'd know what was going on with the partners.

"Yeah," she said, grabbing up her bags. "I bought some of that pineapple stuff and I am going to put the rest of this away. I want to hit the beach for a little bit. I'm going to change and if anyone wants to come along, come on."

Zeke nodded. "Be up in a minute, love."

She gave them both a quick kiss and hurried up the stairs. Once she was in the room, she started thinking how everything had changed in just one day. One simple day and they were acting like this was normal. Okay, so not really normal, but it was if the three of them had been together for years.

Her phone chimed Jillian's ringer and she picked it up immediately. "Hey, Jillian."

"So, did you have fun this morning?"

She laughed and sat on the bed. "This morning, yesterday afternoon...I'm sure tonight."

"Slut."

Knowing she was joking with her, Maura chuckled. "You would know from experience."

"Really, how is it going?"

"Okay. Rory and I went shopping and I'm going to hit the beach here in a bit. Wanna tell me what went on over there between my brother and Zeke?"

"Nothing much. Zeke was irritated with your brother over stuff."

She sighed. "Just tell me what it was. I know it isn't about what's going on here because Conner would have been here waiting for me."

"Or he would have picked you up at the Swap Meet."

She covered her face with her free hand. "Oh, God, you're right." She dropped her hand. "And quit trying to change the subject."

Jillian sighed. "Apparently Zeke was upset about the way your brother treats you."

"He treats me fine."

"Yeah, well, I wasn't here, but that was what the argument, or I should say disagreement was about."

"Ah."

"And speaking of your brother here he is."

Before she could tell Jillian she didn't want to talk to her brother—mainly because she was afraid that he would figure out what was going on with Zeke and Rory—his voice filtered over the phone.

"Hey, Maura. I was wondering if you had time for lunch tomorrow?"

She frowned. Again, he wasn't acting like himself. Conner didn't plan lunch dates unless it was official work.

"Did we have some work to do? I was planning on goofing off all week."

"No. Is there anything wrong with me wanting to have lunch with my sister?"

She shook her head, and then realized she was on the phone. *Brilliant, Maura.* "Nope. You don't normally do things like this."

There was a pause. "Good lord, all I wanted to do was have lunch and show you the new offices. Why does everyone think I have ulterior motives for everything?"

He sounded so exasperated that she had to bite back the giggle tickling her throat. "I'm sorry. I will be happy to have lunch with you."

"I will pick you up at ten."

Then he was gone. She sighed. Conner was changing but he still needed to learn how not to order her to a social type of thing.

Jillian came back on the phone. "And, now you know sort of what went on. I have a feeling that Zeke told Conner he needed to spend time with you as a brother."

She frowned. "Why would he do that? Does he hate me?"

Jillian chuckled. "Stop. You know both of them love you."

"Please tell me you're coming."

"Nope. It's all Dillon blood tomorrow. I'm going to work in silence for the first time in over a week."

"Okay. We do need to get out together though."

"Will do. We'll hit the town in a day or two. Be nice to your brother tomorrow and don't be too bad."

Maura was smiling when she clicked off the phone. She should go right downstairs, but she needed a second to herself. They guys were so damned overwhelming at times. She watched the people on the beach in the distance as she thought about both of them. Zeke was always going to have a special place in her heart. Maura had realized long ago that Zeke was probably the love of her life. It was a shame that there were so many things in their way.

Now though, Rory was worming his way into her heart. Sadly, he wasn't even trying. Only one day and she was getting tangled up with him. The way he acted sometimes...she had thought he was a prick. Now, though, she had a feeling that he did it as self-preservation. She was sure there was an ooey gooey center to him.

She shook her head and decided to get back to emptying her bags. Wishing for more than this week would be a huge mistake.

twenty-four

Zeke talked about everything but the conversation with Conner. He really didn't want to talk about it, especially with Rory. Zeke knew part of the reason Rory pushed the threesome was because he felt threatened by Maura. It hadn't been hard to figure out. Rory had a "keep your enemies closer" mentality.

"Are you going to tell me what happened or are you going to keep talking about this bullshit?"

"What do you mean?"

"I mean what was going on between you and Conner?"

"Oh."

Rory crossed his arms over his chest and glared at him. *Ballocks.* When Rory got suspicious it usually ended in a fight.

"Yeah, oh. Did he object to us staying here together?"

Zee shook his head. "He hasn't picked up on that. Jillian knows."

"Shit."

"Don't worry about her. She knew the moment we showed up. She did say to put the kibosh on the idea of public submission at Rough 'n Ready."

His frown darkened. "Why?"

"It'll get back to Conner."

"What the fuck does that matter?"

"It would upset Maura."

Zeke expected Rory to say he didn't care about that. Rory had tunnel vision. Once he had his mind set on something he couldn't see anything but reaching that goal. It was one of the reasons he was such a damned good security specialist. It was hell being his lover though. The messes that resulted in that kind of thing were never pleasant.

Now, though, he seemed to be thinking of something other than that one goal...and it was about Maura. Zeke felt his stomach dip just a tad. Not in a bad way, not really. But if Rory was getting feelings about Maura, there was a good chance that he would want more than just a week.

Zeke mentally shook himself. Rory wasn't into long relationships—except for the one they had. Zeke knew he was about the only person Rory kept in contact with outside of Zeke's ma.

But, if he was...

"Okay, so no biggie. We'll do it when we get back to Miami."

Zeke's heart stopped for a second. "What the hell are you thinking? You said one week."

Rory glanced at the stairs and then moved toward Zeke. The crooked smile that always made him hot curved Rory's full, sensuous mouth. His cock twitched.

Fuck.

"Come on, Zee, you know that it's more than that now."

He did, but he was worried there was something else going on. Rory had been rushing toward this threesome. It was as if Rory was trying to burn them out on it and that wasn't going to work for Zeke. He needed Rory to think he was resistant to the idea or Rory would get bored.

"I'm not sure that's a good idea," Zeke said.

It was a delicious idea, but Zeke bit his tongue from adding that. Thinking of having the two people he loved in his life that way...it was more than he could hope for. He wanted it, prayed for it, but if Rory was pushing for it, he saw it as a temporary fix to his problems with Maura. Zeke knew he needed to slow him down or Rory would ruin it.

But as always, Rory saw another way of solving their problems...if only temporary. He stepped behind Zeke and slipped his hands to his waist. He leaned closer, pressing against him. Zeke felt Rory's hardened cock between their clothes.

"You want it as much as I do, don't you? I thought just a week, but the truth is I'm not sure that's going to be enough. Not for me, or you...and I'm pretty sure Maura. I don't think we've ever had a sub like that."

Zeke shuttered and shook his head. Rory kissed his neck as he slid one hand down to Zeke's crotch.

"Ah, that's a nice present you have there for me, Zee," he said, the edges of his voice roughened.

Why did that always get to him?

Rory continued kissing his neck, nipping at the skin. Turning him around, he shoved him against the counter. He took Zeke's mouth in a rough, possessive kiss. Zeke felt the scrape of Rory's teeth against his bottom lip. He shuddered in reaction. He couldn't help it. Rory pressed his groin against Zeke's.

Bloody hell.

Rory paused and looked behind Zeke, who followed his line of vision and saw Maura watching them from the stairs. Damn, she was wearing that tiny yellow string bikini that barely covered all her naughty bits. Whenever she wore it, he wanted to either cover her up so people couldn't see her—or tear the fucking thing off her.

"Don't stop on my account, boys," she said. He would have never known she would be so turned on watching them, but she was.

"Boys?" Rory asked. "I think we've proven more than once that we are a little bit more than boys."

She walked down the stairs, taking her time as she watched them. "No, really, you shouldn't stop."

Zeke knew that most women who came to their bed did it as some kind of challenge and they often became jealous if Rory and he spent too much time together. For Maura it was different. He knew that part of it was her love for him. But, now, there was something else he hadn't expected. She was turned on by his interaction with Rory. Zeke was pretty sure that hadn't happened before now.

"I'm fairly certain you don't call the shots around here," Rory growled.

She stopped a few feet from the two of them and cocked her head to the side. "Yeah?"

He heard the challenge in her voice and he looked at Rory. Their gazes locked.

"I think she's questioning my authority here, Zee."

"I think she is too," Zeke said and they both looked at her.

Her lips curved and his heartbeat kicked up a notch. "So, whatcha going to do about it, guys?"

twenty-five

Z eke almost laughed at Maura's challenge.

"I think girlie here thinks we are supposed to listen to her. Be at her beck and call," Rory said.

Zeke almost wanted to tell him they were already there. One day and he knew that Rory was falling for her, for this thing the three of them shared together. But for some reason, he wanted to hold back. Rory would freak as soon as he told him, or made him face what was happening.

"I think you're right," Zeke said. "She sort of needs to be punished."

She tried to look angry with them. He knew she was having a hard time of it though. Especially since he could see her nipples were already poking against the thin fabric of her bikini.

"I told you I don't like when you talk about me like I'm not here."

Rory growled again, the sexy sound urging on Zeke's arousal. Lord, there wasn't a man who could make him lose it like Rory and now, dammit, he was caught between the two of them.

"I don't think I asked your opinion."

The cocky smile she gave both of them was full of teeth. "Well, I gave it."

Again there was the challenge. The fact that she felt comfortable enough to do this told Zeke that she was already at ease with Rory as her Dom. He just wondered how long it would take her to figure it out.

"Hmm," Rory said, as he turned and opened up the refrigerator and took out the whipped cream he'd bought the day before. He set it on the counter. Zeke knew what he was doing. He was acting casual as if nothing big was going on. But in the next second, he turned with lightening speed and went after Maura. She let out a sound that was half laugh and half scream and ran. Zeke was laughing himself when Rory cornered her in the dining room. They were standing on opposite sides of the table in a standoff.

Zeke had never seen Rory act so free with anyone with well.

"You're cornered, Maura. Come out now."

He knew there were rules to the D/s relationship that he didn't always understand, but this; he would think Rory would be pissed. Instead, there was an unholy gleam in his eyes and Zeke's heart melted just a bit. The man didn't laugh enough and for some reason, Maura had been able to get him to loosen up.

Rory stalked around the table, but Maura took off with another scream. Unfortunately for her, she didn't understand that Zeke was on Rory's side. He grabbed her up.

"I have her, love," Zeke said laughing.

"Zeke, you're supposed to be on my side."

He shook his head and looked down at her. "I'm on the side that gets you naked faster."

Before she could respond, Rory stepped up behind her. "Now, you're going to learn how to behave. No back talking, no running away."

Rory grabbed her up and threw her over his shoulder. He gave her ass a hard smack.

"Some little sub is going to learn not to be such a pain in the ass. Grab a chair will ya', Zee. I think our lover needs a little lesson."

His body already responding, he grabbed a chair and followed Rory into the kitchen. When Rory was in a playful mood like this, there was no telling what would happen.

twenty-six

Maura found herself stripped of her bathing suit and bent over Rory's lap. She was laughing when he smacked her with his hand.

The sting caused her to gasp, but he didn't stop. If there was one thing Rory knew how to do well, it was covering her ass with a lot of smacks. By the time he finished, he'd covered her entire bottom and it felt like it was on fire. He smoothed his hand over her rear end. His palm was cool against her hot skin.

"You do have a pretty ass. It gets so damned pink when I spank you."

She heard Zeke's footsteps and tried to look but Rory pressed his hand against her back.

"You stay there."

"I got everything you asked for," Zeke said, his voice a little breathless. He must have run upstairs to get whatever Rory had asked him to retrieve. They had kept it secret from her. She tried to twist again to see what he had brought, but the smack that landed on her rear this time brought tears to her eyes.

"I told you not to look. I'm not kidding here, Maura."

His voice had lost some of the humor, although she knew

he wasn't truly mad. There was part of her that wanted to give him more trouble, but the bigger part, the one that wanted to submit, had her obeying.

"Hand me that," Rory said. "Put the rest on the counter over there."

Zeke did as instructed then squatted down in front of her. She looked at him and frowned. "You should have helped me."

He smiled and brushed her hair out of her face. "Where's the fun in that?"

She opened her mouth but moaned the moment Rory pressed a vibrator against her pussy and turned it up to a high speed.

"Like that, do ya', love?" Zeke asked. His voice had deepened. She nodded and threaded her lower lip between her teeth.

Fuck, she went from mildly aroused to fucking ready to come in just a matter of seconds. Rory must have sensed it because he turned the vibe down to a low hum.

"Not yet, Maura. You were bad, and while you might have been playing, you need to learn that when I tell you to do something, you do it."

He changed the speeds a few times, going from low to high over and over.

"Hey, Zee, bring me that and the lube."

Zeke gave him what he asked for, then joined her back on the floor. "You know how pretty you look there?"

She shook her head, and groaned when Rory worked his lubed finger up her ass. Damn, that felt good. He worked her a little before adding another finger. She groaned again as he pulled out his fingers and replaced it with an anal plug.

"Now, that will add a little bit of fun to the punishment you're about to get."

Zeke rose and picked her up off Rory's lap. She shivered, her body ready for the fun.

"Well, love, I do like that cock you have there," Zeke said. She looked down and noticed the impressive erection straining against Rory's jeans. "Our lover here likes a good spanking. Gets him really fucking hard."

He smiled. "That it does."

He leaned over her and kissed Zeke. Long, wet and damn it was sexy. While he was kissing Zeke, he slipped his hand up her torso to her breasts, squeezing her nipples. When he pulled back both of them leaned toward her. At the same time, they kissed her. Zeke attacked her mouth while Rory attacked her throat. The dual assault almost overwhelmed her. Soon, though, Rory was apparently ready to get on with it. He stepped back and nodded at Zeke. Apparently, he knew what Rory wanted. He set her on the chair.

"Spread those legs, Maura."

She hesitated mainly because her brain was numb. The guys didn't know what they did to her when she watched them touch each other, then touch her. It was the sexiest thing she had ever experienced.

"Maura, you better spread those legs so I can see how wet our cunt is. Do it."

She ordered her legs to work and spread them.

"Nope." He bent over and spread them so wide, it pushed her up to the edge of the chair. Again, she felt exposed to them in a way she never had been with other men. It was also a huge turn on for her. He hooked a foot behind each one of the front legs of the chair.

"Give me the cuffs, Zee," he said rising from his position. Zeke did then started to disrobe.

"You were naughty, so I am going to make you watch for a bit," Rory said as he secured her hands behind the chair.

She watched Zeke pull his pants down. When he was finally

completely nude, she sighed. His cock was hard, bowed up against his stomach.

Rory leaned forward. "Ah, look at the cock, love. It tastes good doesn't it?"

She nodded her mouth suddenly dry.

"Well, I might let you, but well, that's all mine now."

She shivered as he slid his hands down her stomach and between her legs. A few strokes of his finger had her wiggling on the seat.

"Now, you are going to learn how I punish subs who are naughty."

He walked around the chair and started to undress. Zeke came forward and gave her a quick kiss on the mouth. He said nothing as he turned toward Rory who was now completely nude also. Even this early in the play she was wet, dripping. The plug in her ass added another level of naughtiness to it.

"Make sure to stand sideways, love. She needs to see the whole scene."

Zeke shot her a smile and did as Rory requested. Rory grabbed the can of whipped cream and dropped to his knees. After popping off the lid, he applied it to Zeke's cock. Damn. The white creamy confection was the perfect contrast against his dark skin.

"I've always thought Zee was a treat...the sweetest of sweets." Rory looked over at her with a naughty little smile. "I think you agree."

He set the can down and took Zeke into his mouth. Zeke immediately slipped his hands around Rory's head as he thrust in and out of his mouth. Just watching the act sent another gush of liquid to her pussy. Which of course, they would know if they looked at her. She needed to squeeze her legs together, give herself some relief, but she didn't break Rory's command.

Maura had thought he would only tease Zeke, but apparently, Rory had other plans. He slipped his hands to cup Zeke's ass as he continued to take him in and out of his mouth. Their groans and moans filled the kitchen. Maura thought she might pass out from loss of blood in her brain. She watched as Zeke sped up his thrusts then after two more strokes, he came, moaning Rory's name as he did.

Once he pulled out of Rory's mouth, Zeke leaned back against the counter. Rory rose and leaned forward for a kiss. She watched, again entranced by the way they were with each other. It was easy to see the love, the tenderness hidden in the really hot sex.

Rory looked at her. "Now it's our turn."

Zeke walked over with a key. "I think you can let her go now, right, Rory?"

"No."

Zeke looked back at Rory and she realized this was out of character for Rory.

Rory walked over to the chair. He cupped her face and leaned down until their mouths were only inches apart. "If I wanted to really teach you a lesson, I would leave you here like this while Zee and I went out."

Her eyes widened and his mouth kicked up on one side.

"I won't do that though."

He helped her up then placed her on the counter. Just moving her around had her pussy throbbing. She moaned.

"Aw, darlin'," he said. "You're in a bad way, huh?"

"Yes, Sir."

She saw an emotion in his eyes that she couldn't discern, but it was gone before she could figure out what it was. He leaned forward and gently pressed his mouth against hers—just enough for a taste. Then, he grabbed a condom, tore it open and rolled it on. She thought he might tease her more, but he surprised her again. He pulled her up to the edge of the counter, tilting her just right. Then, he entered her slowly, his gaze on hers. Inch by inch, he entered her and when he was fully seated inside her. He thrust in and out of her, with an unhurried patience that had her ready to scream. With the plug in her anus, it was extra tight. Each stroke inside her pushed her closer. Zeke moved closer, and for the first time in a few minutes, she realized he was still there. He leaned in and kissed her, then reached behind her back to unlock the cuffs. Then, he stepped back to watch.

Rory wrapped his hand around the back of her neck, holding her head steady as he increased his rhythm.

"Yeah, Maura, just like that, love," he muttered. "Touch yourself."

Maura didn't hesitate. Her brain just wouldn't allow her to. She wanted relief, but more than that, she wanted to please Rory. She slipped her hand down between their bodies and pressed her hardened clit. It was all she needed. Rory thrust into her at the same time. Her orgasm slammed into her so hard it scared her.

"Rory," she screamed as tendrils of ecstasy filtered over her.

He followed her after one last thrust. He shouted her name as his release took over. A few moments later, he kissed her as leaned forward, and then set his forehead against hers. They were both breathing heavily.

"That was...wow," Zeke said. She glanced at him wondering if he would be pissed that it had been just she and Rory, but the look on his face told her it hadn't. "We should have taped that."

Rory chuckled. "No way, love. There's just no way I will allow any taping and you know it."

"You're kidding right?" she asked Zeke. She looked at Rory. "He's kidding."

Rory chuckled. "No, sorry to admit it but Zee is a freak. He likes to watch, in person and on video."

Mortified she closed her eyes. "No way. Never."

Rory leaned forward and kissed her again. "There you have it, Zee. Your lovers disagree."

The term lovers had her breath catching in her throat. She covered, or at least she hoped, the fact that he had grouped himself with her...that wasn't something he had done before.

"Well, I'm going to need a shower before I go to the beach," she said.

Rory pulled out of her, and removed the plug. She was going to jump off the counter, but Zeke stopped her. He picked her up and walked toward the stairs.

"I can walk, ya' know," she said amused. Guys didn't treat her like this. Most guys, actually. Zeke had always been kind of romantic with her.

"I know, but I like carrying you. Plus I need a shower too."

She looked over his shoulder and saw Rory following them, a small smile curving his lips.

"I say we all need a little shower before heading to the beach," he said.

And, just like that, everything felt...right. She sighed and set her head on Zeke's shoulder.

"Sounds like a good idea to me."

twenty-seven

Z eke leaned back on his beach seat and watched Rory dive into the surf. He couldn't stop the sigh that escaped in appreciation for the man.

"He is pretty, I will give you that," Maura said.

He glanced at her but she was looking out at the ocean also, probably watching Rory too. She had that ridiculous turtle hat on and her sunglasses so he couldn't discern what she was thinking. She shook her head.

"You don't have to worry about me being jealous. I think I have proven that the way you two feel about each other is a turn on. I don't ever want you to hide your feelings."

He digested that for a moment. "It's hard to do with you around."

She looked at him and he wished he could read her better. He still couldn't read her with that hat and her sunglasses on. Then she looked back out at the water and Rory. He knew she was following him on the boogie board. There weren't that many people out today and there was a bit of surf.

"I often wondered what it would be like to be with two men."

She said it pretty loud. Not shouting, but someone could have heard her. He looked around to see if anyone had. She laughed without looking at him.

"Jeez, Zeke, you're not worried what other people think are you?"

"It's not that." *Not really*.

She settled back on her towel, a small smile on her lips. "Don't worry about it, Zeke. Fuck everyone if they can't accept it."

For a moment he studied her. She was wearing his favorite bathing suit of hers, bright red bikini. She wasn't overly tan because Maura took her skin too seriously, but there was a nice layer of golden Hawaiian on her flesh now. Damn she looked good.

"Maura," he said but could not go on. What exactly was he going to say, he didn't know.

She glanced over at him. "Stop over thinking it."

He chuckled and leaned back on his beach chair. "You think I worry too much."

"You do worry too much. About this, about everything. I'm not a little girl. I can handle it."

"I know. But you're precious to me, love. I don't want you to be hurt."

She didn't say anything for a few minutes, then she said, "That's part of life, Zeke. I know you would never intentionally hurt me. You have one of the gentlest souls I know."

If she knew what he had done when he was younger, she wouldn't say that. He and Rory had done some nasty things in the name of national security. Zeke knew she didn't know much about his work—or at least he thought she didn't know.

"And, while I know you're apprehensive if I can handle it after..." she said nothing for a few seconds then drew in a deep breath. "I'd rather have the memories than always wonder what would have happened if I hadn't the nerve to do this."

Again, she was honest, always. Sometimes painfully so, but he never had to doubt her feelings on a subject. It was one of the many things he loved about her.

"You know I love you, right?"

Her lips curved. "Yeah."

He looked out and watched Rory again as he rode another wave in on his boogie board.

"How did you two meet?" she asked

He glanced down at her. She had set her hat aside and he knew her eyes were closed.

"Actually, Mum found him. He was trying to steal some food from the grocery my Mum and stepda own. We were both about fifteen at the time. Rory was none too happy with the situation, I will tell you that."

"What happened to his family?"

He sighed. "His mother...she had what I think was clinical depression. She had mood swings. Rory doesn't talk about it much, but she took her own life."

"Oh, that's horrible. How old was he?"

"I think he was about eight. After that he was left with an alcoholic father."

She was quiet for a while then she said, "That's why he doesn't drink."

Zeke nodded, although he knew she was looking at him. "That and the control issues he has. I'll let you in on a little secret about our boy. He can't hold his liquor.

She chuckled. "Really? Like in one drink and he's under the table?"

"No, love, he's on the table. Dancing. I hate to admit that I love a stereotypical drunken Irishman on those nights."

"But he doesn't drink anymore."

"Only when he gets mad. And I mean really fucking mad."

"So, you're mother caught him stealing. What happened after that?"

"She dragged him into the house by his ear, sat him in the kitchen and yelled at him. In English and French. Then she fed him. Mum had a soft spot for bad boys."

"It seems that her son has that trait."

He smiled thinking about Rory. "Yeah."

"And I guess I do too."

"Yeah, I guess you do too. So, after she fed him, she told him he would take the guest room and sleep. He was all skin and bones and it was pretty evident he'd been living on the street. Rory tried to leave. He thought Mum was a softie."

When he didn't go on, she groaned. "You Irishmen. Finish the damned story."

He chuckled. "Rory tried to take a few things, including a silver frame of Mum and my Da. He got to the front door and found my mother standing there."

"Where was your stepfather?"

"In the kitchen brewing some tea. Mum ran the house, and he was just standing by if needed."

She sighed. "They sound wonderful."

Zeke didn't miss the wistful tone. Maura had lost both her parents at a crucial time in a person's life. His father died when Zeke was young, but he'd had his mother. He didn't know how he would have turned out without her. At least she'd had Conner.

"I'd like you to meet them. I was just talking to them last week about coming over for a visit."

"I'd like that. I'd like that a lot." It warmed his heart to hear the easy acceptance of his family. He had a feeling his mother was going to love Maura.

"So, he threatened my mother. She boxed his ears and

dragged him back to the kitchen and told him she found him stealing from her store so he was under house arrest. So he stayed."

She laughed. "I think that is probably the best way to handle Rory."

"You're right. So, Rory moved in."

She opened her mouth then shut it. He hated that she didn't feel comfortable enough to ask him questions. He had tried to be open with her from the start.

"No, ask."

"When did you become lovers?"

"We were eighteen. We had gone to London for a week and we got a little drunk. We had both been thinking about it but never acted on it. Then, we did."

"Then you fell in love."

For all her savvy and her protest that she was sophisticated, there were times that Maura was naïve about the ways of the world.

"No, we both freaked a little bit. Being gay or bisexual is not the thing to be doing when you both want to go in the military, not then. But, we didn't do that. We were both in the military, and we both found ourselves in the Special Forces." Conner and he had decided not to tell her of his work for Interpol and MI-6. "And...well over the years we finally got our shit together."

She laughed. "You always sound funny when you use American colloquialisms, but you know more of them than I do now."

He smiled and looked back at the water. Who would have thought two poor Irish boys would be living like this now? He was spending a week in Hawaii, in a million dollar house, and enjoying a sexual relationship that was beyond anything he had ever hoped for.

"So, what does your mother think about the relationship?" she asked, cutting into his thoughts.

"She's okay with it. She does wonder if either of us will give her grandchildren."

"Your mother does understand basic biology, right?"

He looked down at her and wanted to tell her what he really wanted. He wanted them all together, and he wanted to have babies with her. He had never had that feeling about any other woman, but knowing Maura, and knowing Rory, they would both freak if he told them.

"You two should get out on the water. It's fantastic," Rory said as he walked up the beach.

"In a bit. I need some rest because I have these very insatiable lovers and they won't leave me alone," Maura said.

He laughed. He bent down, kissed Maura and leaned over to kiss Zeke. Before Zeke could say anything, Rory was on his way out to the water.

"He doesn't care what other people think and neither should you," Maura said.

He nodded as he watched Rory run back out into the water.

"Zeke?"

"Yeah?" he asked.

"You know I love you, right?"

He smiled. "Yeah, I do."

And for now, that was enough.

twenty-eight

T he next day, Maura walked down the hall to their new offices trying not to be bummed. She had thought the guys would come with her, but apparently they weren't interested in seeing the new offices. Rory she understood, but she thought Zeke would have been interested.

"We're still getting everything settled, but you'll be able to get an idea of the layout," Conner said as he punched in the security code for the door.

Maura stepped in and smiled. The carpets had been laid and she could still smell the paint.

"Wow, this is nice."

It was sleek and elegant, but she didn't expect any less than that from Conner. He'd always had an innate sense of style that sometimes irritated her.

"Yeah, I like it. I wasn't sure if it was going to come through, but we got the bid with the contractors, and the rent isn't that bad—for Honolulu."

She smiled. "Let me guess, Evan Chambers had something to do with it?"

Conner smiled. "Yeah. He said something about a family discount."

She was really happy for Conner. A man who had been a workaholic for years, he was finally starting to take life more slowly thanks to Jillian. Just a few months ago, he had ended up in the hospital and had been ordered to rest. She sent him to Hawaii and to Jillian.

"So, you still like living here?"

He nodded. "I would have never thought I would."

"Why would you say that?" she asked walking toward the ceiling to floor windows. She could see the Honolulu Harbor from where she was standing. The sunlight sparkled on the water below. Traffic buzzed by.

"It's hot here all the time."

She laughed. "Conner, you used to live in Miami."

"That's different. Here nothing ever really changes. Okay on our side of the island we get a bit more of the winter storm season, but that's it."

"But, you love it."

He said nothing and she looked over her shoulder at him. He was studying her as he often did when she was a teenager. Their difference in age had never been a problem. He had treated her with kindness most teenage brothers wouldn't have for their egghead little sister. But, when he got that look on his face, he was trying to figure something out. Usually what she was up to—and that would not be a good thing right now. She was still trying to sort her feelings out for the guys. She didn't need Conner sticking his big nose in and mucking things up.

"What?"

He cocked his head to the side. "There's something different about you."

Maura had to resist the urge to fidget. "What do you mean?"

He shrugged but didn't say anything. God, she hated him when he was like this. He was trying to figure her out like she was some kind of a puzzle.

"Spit it out, Conner."

"It's like you're another person."

That wasn't what she expected to hear. She digested that for a second or two. "Than I normally am? I think not."

"No, just the last few months."

"I've been a bit stressed," she said, hating that she was lying to him but knew it was best. She wouldn't keep Rory and Zeke a secret from her brother if she knew where they were headed. They didn't need the added pressure of her brother judging them before they decided what to do.

He mulled that comment. "Jillian's been worried."

"Yeah, she's mentioned that to me."

"I..."

He trailed off as if unsure what to say next. This was definitely not like him. Conner was always sure of his actions. He never started anything he wouldn't finish, including a simple conversation.

"I've been a little worried."

She settled on the large windowsill and leaned against the window. "You've been worried? Conner, don't lie to me."

He sighed. "We're not good with picking up on feelings, you know that. Both of us are...kind of lost when it comes to all these feelings but Zeke gave me hell yesterday."

"So, you're doing this because Zeke told you to?"

Another sigh. "No. Not really. Both of us are kind of bad about picking up on things like that.

That much was true. She was always too focused on whatever project she was working on. Conner, well, he was just focused on the company. The idea that Zeke had yelled at him about it made her feel better.

"So, Jillian said something to you?"

He shrugged. "Not until Zeke said something. She...well Jillian claims there are times you don't try to tell me anything because I will just ignore it."

She gasped theatrically and put her hand on her chest. "Never say you are...stubborn. It can't be."

He chuckled. "Well, she claims we both are."

"Yeah. She's said that to me more than once. Although, I have to say she's turning into something of an old mother hen. And while we're on the subject, when am I getting a little niece or nephew?"

"Jesus, kid, we just got married."

"You two have so much sex, I'm amazed she isn't pregnant already."

He rolled his eyes. "Probably sooner than later."

"You are getting kind of old."

"Gee, thanks." He studied her. "What about you. Are you seeing anyone?"

Damn, he thwarted her again. Best way to answer was a non-answer. Conner himself taught her that. "No, not really."

"What does not really mean?"

"It means if you aren't careful, I will go into detail about something that will totally embarrass and disgust you."

He sighed. "Are you going to settle down any time soon?"

"Why should I? You didn't do it for a very, very, very—"

"Watch it." He slanted her a look.

"Well, you are a bit older than I am right now. Besides, you know my view about marriage."

"I think you should reconsider that."

She would have argued with him before. She had never thought to marry. Her years in the dating scene had convinced her that she wasn't the type of person to settle down with one guy.

Now, if she could get Rory and Zeke into a happily ever after, that would work.

"Tell you what. I'll reconsider it. But, work on giving me that nephew or niece, okay? I would love to go crazy shopping for little outfits."

He nodded. "Okay. Although, you know Jillian, she'll want to work her release schedule around it."

Maura laughed. "Yeah, but then you can't complain too much, buddy. You will probably come up with a chart."

He chuckled. "Yeah, you're probably right."

God, it was good to hear that again. Conner had been on the edge of something horrible before she'd convinced him to go to Hawaii for a visit. She had almost lost him and while he was thousands of miles away most of the time, she knew he was there all the time for her. She stood and gave him a hug. He wrapped his arms around her and tears burned her eyes. The warmth of the embrace made her feel as if nothing in the world could hurt her—just like it had all those years ago. He had been the hero, the one who had strode through the ER that horrible night their parents died and picked up the pieces of their life. He kissed her head.

"How about you buy me a pork football for lunch?" she asked.

He leaned back and looked down at her. "I'll do you one better. How about Bubba Gumps?"

"Sounds fantastic."

She pulled back and he put his arm around her like he had a hundred times before. Probably a thousand.

"You know I love you, kid, right?"

She swallowed the lump in her throat. "Yeah. And I kind of like you."

Rough 'n Ready was busy, even for a Monday evening. Being the only official BDSM club on the island, it made sense to Rory.

It was a nice club. Huge even. The red and black was to be expected, but not every club could make you feel welcomed the moment you walked through the door. Micah Ross had the ability to do that. He'd never really been one for clubs, except to play out some of the scenarios with a sub. Sometimes a sub needed certain things that only a club would allow for in a safe way. Public submission was one of them. Rory had a feeling that this club had some great playrooms. He was still irritated they weren't going to get to use one of them

"I'm going to say hi to Dee," Maura said. Then, she looked at him. "If that's alright with you."

Rory fought to keep a smile hidden. Maura might say she wasn't that experienced, but she understood that she was his to order around in Rough 'n Ready.

"Yes, love, go ahead."

She smiled, gave both of them a quick kiss, then ran off in the direction of the bar. They both watched her and he would have been amused if it weren't so damned pathetic. Maura had dressed in the tiny little dress he'd picked out. He thought it would be great to see those long legs all night long. Now that he noticed all the other men watching her, he realized he'd made a mistake. It took all his control not to beat the shit out of the men looking at her.

There it was again, that possessiveness he couldn't seem to fight. It had only been three days and he wanted everyone to know that she belonged to Zee and him.

"I don't think that dress was a good idea," Zee said.

Rory sighed. "Not much we can do about it now."

"I want it noted I told you the dress wasn't a good idea."

"Hey, don't tell me that you don't enjoy seeing her dressed like that. A woman with a set of legs like that should always wear short dresses. And you have to admit she looks fantastic." They walked through the club and stopped when they came to a demonstration floor. "They must make a fortune here."

"As a matter of fact, we do," Micah said from behind them. Damn, he was losing it if a six-foot plus man could sneak up behind him.

When he turned Micah smiled. "Welcome to Rough 'n Ready. And don't feel too badly, McAllister, I used to be a bounty hunter. I know how to sneak up on people. Want me to show you around?"

"Maura will be right back."

He glanced past them. "Lord, give that idea up for right now. May's here and they are all over there gossiping."

Rory followed his line of vision and saw Maura talking to Dee and another woman. Even through the darkened club he could see she was stunning. Hawaiian from what he could discern, and with hair as long as Micah's. She said something that had Maura throwing her head back and laughing. Something tickled the back of his throat and his chest suddenly felt tight. Damn, what the hell was happening to him?

Another man joined the group, almost as tall as Micah, dressed in a pair of jeans that looked like they had seen better days.

"Evan, this is Rory McAllister and you know Zeke."

He shook both their hands, and said. "I think we met at the wedding. Does that mean Maura is here?"

Rory had to bite back a growl—although Ross gave him an amused glance. Rory realized he hadn't kept the sound as quiet as he thought. Bloody hell, this was getting embarrassing.

"Don't worry about it, McAllister. May is Evan's wife."

It still didn't make him feel any better. The jealousy he kept feeling in regards to Maura was troubling. He had never dealt with it before when it came to a woman.

"Want to take a look at our store?" Chambers asked interrupting his thoughts.

He had been so focused on watching Maura—and watching the assholes who were watching her—he hadn't realized they had a store. He nodded and followed the owners and Zee into it. He had to fight the urge to look back and check on Maura. It was getting pathetic that he would feel that need. As a Dom, he'd never had a problem with it before. Not just the possessive feelings, but also the worry that she wouldn't obey him. He didn't like the fact he wasn't sure he had complete control over her.

"We have everything you would need here," Ross said.

"Or we can special order anything you want," Chambers added.

"And you take in a hefty profit?" Rory asked.

Ross shook his head. "A bit, but we use a lot of locals for our leather work. In fact, we're working on a deal with Maui Kink about having a few special pieces made up just for Rough 'n Ready. They do some wonderful work. We believe in supporting the Hawaiian economy and what better way to do that than use folks here?"

"Because of that, we lose the hefty profit we would get with a mainland outlet, but for Micah and myself, it's more important to support our adopted home," Chambers said.

Rory walked around the small area. It was well lit but not overly bright. The design was deceptive because you thought you were heading into something dark and dim, but when you approached the shelves, you could see everything easily. The small lights behind every shelf gave them enough illumination to shop.

"It's my design."

He looked over at Evan. "Yeah?"

"I'm a contractor. I wanted to make sure it was easy to shop but people aren't going to walk into a store for sexual toys if it's lit up like a freaking Walmart."

He chuckled. "I have to agree with that."

"We do have an outside entrance for shopping during the day. We just started that. There weren't a lot of places to shop here on the islands, so we decided to test it out."

"And?" Rory asked.

Chambers shrugged. "Business has been steady. We only do a few days a week."

Rory headed over and picked up a nice black leather crop. He had a feeling that Maura would like to play a little like this. Her reaction to the nipple clamps had been a little more than he had expected. He wanted to push it up a notch. He held onto it, turned and then he saw the collars. There was a wall of them, from floor to ceiling. They had everything from the heavy duty to the pink fuzz. In the center there was a bright red collar, smooth leather, with some rhinestones on either side. There was a spot for a name.

Without thinking, he headed over to it. He picked it up off the shelf and realized he'd been wrong. There was a name on it.

Ours.

He smoothed his fingers over the fine leather. It was supple, well made and it wouldn't damage her skin. The letters were stamped into the leather. He could imagine the way it would look around her throat.

"Nice," Ross said. "I remember when that came in a couple days ago. Everyone was in a tither over it."

Rory fought the urge to immediately put it back like he'd been caught doing something wrong. He forced a smile and glanced at Ross. "I've never bought a collar before."

Ross crossed his arms over his chest. "I've never been into it, and I have feeling that Dee would scalp me if I tried. She likes play, but collars...no. I'm pretty sure that's not her thing. But, the right woman...she would like it."

Was he hinting Maura would like it? Zee had told him that Ross hadn't trained Maura, but what did Ross know about Maura's desires? He didn't like that the man apparently speculated on the subject enough to think she would want a collar. And just what the hell did Maura think she was doing telling people about her likes and dislikes?

Apparently the club owner read his thoughts. "Whoa, son. I didn't train her, but she did have a lot of questions. I'm off the market in the training department as is Evan. We're old married men now."

Bloody hell. He drew in a deep breath and pulled his temper back. He was losing it and not in a good way. A woman's past had never really been all that important to him. All of his lovers had a past, just as he had. He always found it hypocritical of men he knew who judged their lovers' past behavior. But, with Maura he was dealing with feelings he had for no one other than Zee.

"Old my ass," Evan said as he walked up. He looked at the collar in Rory's hands. "Nice."

Zee frowned down at it. "Not sure if she would go for that."

He nodded knowing Zee was probably right. He didn't even know if she wanted to be with them past this week and it had only been three days. People didn't get serious that quickly...and he really didn't know if he wanted to.

"Probably not. But the workmanship is first class." He set it back on the shelf. "Let me check out."

He sensed Ross watching him as he walked away. He heard him say, "Let me show you the new security system we want to do."

That was all Zee had to hear. "I'll be up in the office."

Rory nodded as they walked away.

"The stairs are on the left side of the club. Just come on up when you're done." Ross glanced at the collar then at Rory. His lips twitched and he followed his friend and Zee out of the shop.

Rory looked at the collar from the corner of his eye as he moved up in line. He set the crop, along with a box of condoms on the counter. At the last minute he said, "Wait."

Before he could change his mind, he rushed over and grabbed the collar. He gave it to the female clerk who smiled at him.

He didn't have to give it to Maura, but just in case... he could keep it around. None of them knew what would happen after this week. He knew Zee loved her and Rory was man enough that he could admit he was starting to have more than just sexual feelings for her.

Shit. He walked out of the store and decided to take the bag out to the jeep and lock it up. He would decide what to do with the collar later. Hell, he probably wouldn't give it to her but he could always sell it. The workmanship would bring in a pretty penny.

After locking it up, he headed back into the club. He couldn't think about that, about next week, about anything beyond tonight. He was already being seduced by the idea of keeping her with them. Always.

He learned a long time ago, wishing for things like that would lead to heartache.

thirty

Maura took a sip of water and smiled as she watched the best friends banter back and forth. It wasn't enough of a distraction from the feeling someone was watching them. Or her. She hadn't felt it since that night out with the guys, but now, she felt it. As before, it was going to be hard to pinpoint because there was such a huge crowd.

"So, Maura, tell us about living with two men," May said. It wasn't a question. May just said it as if she were asking how she liked her blonde hair.

Dee choked on her drink. "God, May, will you ever learn how to have normal conversations?"

"No. Normal conversations are boring. I'm not boring. I never understood the reason for small talk. People I don't know, sure I'll talk boring shit with them all day long. Friends, I don't see the reason to do it." She smiled at Maura. "So, spill."

She returned her smile. The two friends were so different, but they complimented each other much as their husbands did. Both were striking, but where Dee was a stunning Italian with those quintessential Mediterranean features, May was pure Hawaiian. Long dark hair reached her mid back and her eyes, the blue of them kept catching the attention of just about anyone in their vicinity, man or woman.

In a way, they reminded her of the relationship she had with Jillian.

"I'm not living with them, really. Just while we're here on vacation."

May opened her mouth but Dee stepped in. "I'm going to warn you about May. She wants to know what it's like to be with two guys all the time...and by *be with* I mean in the bedroom. Not like she doesn't know what it's like—ask me about that sometime. But that's what she wants to know. Her brain is always in the bedroom."

"Well, I'm sure those two aren't boring. More than likely, they've used other rooms in the house."

It was Maura's turn to choke on her water.

May scooted forward in her seat and smacked Maura on her back a few times to help her.

"No, I'm fine. Stop, May you're going to leave bruises on my back."

"I'm sorry. I just...we don't have much time before the men will descend on us. They don't seem like they want you away from them for long."

She frowned. "Is it that obvious?"

She wasn't ashamed of being with the men but she wasn't sure she wanted Conner to know what was going on. Not if the relationship didn't make it past this week. His relationship with Zeke would be at stake and that was something she couldn't accept. Conner had few friends in his life—mainly because of his control freak ways.

May's voice broke into Maura's thoughts. "Yeah. Lord, they watch you constantly. So, tell me, do you like it?"

She rolled her eyes and hummed. "You've seen them."

"Yeah. I didn't get the Dom vibe off Zeke when I met him before."

"He's not really into BDSM, at least participating."

"Oh, well I don't like to invade people's privacy—"

"That's a lie."

May gave Dee a dismissive glance. "But what do you mean, not into participating?"

She shifted on her seat. She told Jillian but she wasn't sure if she wanted others to know. May must have picked up on her reluctance.

"Never mind. I won't pry."

"For once," Dee muttered.

"But, good for you. I always thought you and Zeke should be together."

For a second, she didn't know what to say. The idea was too delicious to ignore. It was something she wanted for a long time and never thought to have. But when Rory had moved to Miami, she had thought that it was for the best. It was worse after the last few days. Now, dammit, she wanted both of them.

Before she knew it, she was blinking back tears.

"Oh, honey," May said as she patted her hand. "I'm sorry. What's wrong?"

Maybe it was because it was just the three of them, or maybe because she hadn't really talked to anyone about it since she'd talked to Jillian, but she said, "I'm not sure I'll be with them when the week is over."

"Oh. Oh! They're together. You were invited." May looked at Dee then back at her. "Hmm."

She said nothing else and Maura felt her patience slipping. "What?"

May said nothing as she looked around. It was as if she was searching for something or someone. "I have a feeling that those two do not want a week. They will want more."

"Really? Because you haven't talked to either of them since Jillian and Conner got married," Dee said. She looked at Maura. "Ignore her. She thinks she's some kind of relationship guru."

"You just have to let things happen and let Auntie May help."

Dee's eyes widened with what looked like alarm. "Maylea Aiona Chambers, what are you up to?"

May shook her head as a slow smile curved her lips and she waved at someone in the crowd. Maura turned to follow her line of vision and saw the man she was waving over. He strode through the club with a lazy, laid back walk that was definitely deceptive. If you looked at him closely, you could see the way he scanned the area for threats. He was tall, taller than most, built like a bit of a boxer. His blond hair was cut short, and the kind of tan he had told her he worked outside. And...there was something vaguely familiar about him. That put her on alert. She had a very good memory and sometimes the pictures of men on the wanted posters stuck with her.

"May, that is a really bad idea."

"Naw, Eli likes being used. It's part of his charm."

"Well, hello, ladies," he said. Oh, damn he was Australian. He scanned their faces then stopped when he saw Maura. His lips curved. "And hello to you, darlin'."

"I didn't know you were back on Oahu," May said.

He broke his attention from her to look at May. His smile dimmed. "Bossman is here for a procedure. He's been kind of sickly and I wanted to hop over for a couple days to check him out."

"Aww, is he at Queens'?"

Eli nodded.

"I'll get Cynthia to make some of that monkey bread he loves so much and go see him."

"He'd like that. Now, why don't you introduce me to your friend."

"Elias St. John, this is Maura Dillon. Maura, this is Eli. He runs a ranch on the Big Island. Maura's here visiting her brother."

"It's nice to meet you." Then, she remembered him from her trip over before. "I think we've met before."

He cocked his head to one side and studied her. "I think I would remember a stunner like you, love."

"It was about two years ago." She sensed Dee's glance but ignored it. "I had longer hair, and it was dark."

She knew the moment he remembered. "Yes. And you were with an Irishman."

Maura smiled and nodded and he stilled his movements. He kept staring at her, then his mouth curved slowly. The silence among the four of them stretched out. She glanced at May and Dee. Dee shrugged but May smiled.

"Why don't you have a seat and tell us what's going on over there," May said.

Dee shot her a look but she smiled at Eli. "Yeah, why not?"

"I don't mind if I do," he said, taking the open seat and smiling at her. For a second, she felt all her brain cells freeze. She was accustomed to gorgeous men. Hell, she was having a wild affair with two, but there was something about Eli that stunned her. Women who walked by the table slowed down.

"So, Maura, have you ever been to the Big Island?"

thirty-one

"This is going to kick some ass," Zeke said as he looked at the new set up in Rough 'n Ready. "I knew some of the preliminaries, but Conner didn't tell me you had it installed."

Micah nodded. "He did an excellent job with it. We needed something to keep up with the demand of a growing business. And, well, it sure is pretty."

Zeke didn't take his attention from the multitude of screens in front of him. "We really appreciate you moving your business to us."

"We like to keep it in the family so to speak. At the time, McMasters was the best we could afford. Now that we've grown and we sort of count y'all as family, we wanted a change. With Conner trying to gain some business in this part of the world, we figured it would help. We get a lot of businessmen who buy daily or weekly passes."

"I think that is bloody brilliant, if you ask me," Rory said. "Especially in a locale like this. People constantly coming in for a small amount of time."

"It's been a virtual cash cow for us," Evan said.

Zeke nodded and started playing with some of the cameras. "I can imagine."

"What is that asshole doing here tonight?" Evan asked, stepping up behind him.

At first, Zeke wasn't sure just who he was talking about until he looked at the screen that had caught his attention. He watched as some fucker leaned closer to Maura, smiled as he said something. Maura threw her head back and laughed. Zeke couldn't hear her, but it didn't matter. What the bloody hell did that bastard think he was doing?

"Who the fuck is that?" Zeke asked.

Rory came up from behind him and looked over his shoulder. "I think if he touches her, I might have to break his hand."

"That's one of our members, Eli St. John. I didn't know he was back on the island."

"Well, he can just get the bloody hell off the island," Zeke said as he strode to the door. He knew they were following him but he paid no heed. Didn't Maura understand that she wasn't supposed to be flirting with another Dom? He wasn't even in the fucking life and he understood it.

He ignored the strange looks as he pushed through the crowd to where the women were sitting. Maura looked at him and grinned, but it soon dimmed when she saw his expression. The jackass who had been flirting with her looked over his shoulder and the fucker was stupid enough to smile.

"Ah, just as I expected. Gentlemen," he said, standing. He heard the slight Aussie accent, and he saw the warning in his gaze. This was not just some normal client. This was a guy who had seen some action. He looked past Zeke. "Chambers. Ross. I was just talking to the ladies here."

"When are you not," Dee said struggling to stand up. He moved to help her, but Micah stepped in.

"I allow for a lot, but touching my woman is not one of them."

St. John held up his hands. "No problem, just wanted to help her. Promise."

"Eli, this is O'Brian and McAllister. Guys, this is Eli St. John. He runs the Kaheaku Ranch on the Big Island," Evan said. "Sort of surprised to see you here. Aren't you usually busy this time of year? I thought you had your annual pageant for the guests."

The man's smile dimmed a bit. "Big Joe is here at Queen's. I hopped over to see him. And now that I've done my duty, I think I'm off to hunt for another fair submissive. Good night, ladies. It was a pleasure to see you again, Ms. Dillon."

With that he walked away. Zeke and Rory never had a chance to say a damned thing to him.

"He's so sad," May said, as she stood.

"Sad?" Zeke asked.

"Yes. I have a feeling Joe Kaheaku is dying. They go a long way back."

"And before you think about following him or giving him any problems, O'Brian just know that he's ex SASR," Ross said.

Maura gave them a heated look. "You will not give him any problems."

Rory snorted, his gaze still on the cowboy. "I think I do what I want."

"I think you'll be sleeping alone if you do."

He turned and looked at her. "Is that so?"

She ignored him and looked at Chambers and Ross. "SASR. So, Australian Special Forces. And I am assuming he was probably one of the most lethal of them all."

Evan shrugged. "Not sure. I do know that Joe was a Seal, so that's probably how they met and they run a tight ship over there at the ranch."

She looked at both of them. "Do not cause a scene. He was telling me about things at the ranch and even invited all three of us to visit."

Zeke watch the bastard walk through the crowd to find himself another sub for the evening. It took all of his control not to follow after the bastard.

"I think May and Dee owe you two men an apology," Ross said.

Both Zeke and Rory turned around and stared at the two women.

"Hey, I had nothing to do with it. You know how May can get."

Evan slipped his arm around May's waist and leaned down and said something to her that none of them could hear. Her entire face flushed in embarrassment.

"I apologize."

"I really don't know what everyone is upset over," Maura said as she slipped out of the booth. She stepped in front of them and leaned in closer. "Unless you want some kind of incident to happen."

"Yeah, like I kick him so hard in the ballocks that he has a permanent change to his voice," Zeke said.

Rory glanced at him. "Actually, I have to say that kind of makes me hot, Zee."

She rolled her eyes. "Go ahead. Then you can deal with Conner and explain to him why you want to beat the hell out of a man for no good reason. Or are you ready to tell him what's going on?"

The challenge she gave them was enough to make him cool down.

"And you, Zeke, you got pissed at him two years ago for hitting on me. Get over it."

She turned and Rory grabbed her arm. "Where are you going?"

She shook her hair back. "If you must know. I drank a lot of water." When Rory held onto her arm she rolled her eyes. "I have to pee."

She untangled herself from his grasp and walked off. Zeke knew that it was almost too much for Rory to take. It was a bit of a challenge in front of people at the club, but most of them weren't paying attention.

Dee slipped around them. "Being pregnant, I can understand her predicament."

She hurried after Maura and May started to, but turned to face both men. She settled her hands on her hips. "Now, gentlemen, I see the way you look at her. Don't blame her. I set it up and Eli is always willing to help me. Just remember how it felt to watch her with another man other than you two when the week is up."

With that she followed after the other two women. Chambers clapped him on the shoulder. "Sorry, there, O'Brian. Our women do like to meddle. Just make sure that you don't blame Maura too much."

"Yeah, and knowing Evan, May won't be trying that particular line of matchmaking after tonight,"

Chambers chuckled as he crossed his arms over his chest and watched his wife disappear into the bathroom. "And I am going to enjoy that little lesson in particular."

Maura was still irritated and embarrassed by the guy's behavior at the club. She knew part of it was her fault, but she truly didn't think they would react the way they did. They didn't say much as they left the club and walked to the Jeep. When they were on the road again, the only noise was the wind whipping through her hair. She had never seen Zeke so angry before. Sure he was a little possessive when they had first started dating, but that had been more about protecting her while they were on the island and on a mission than anything else. Or had it?

She had never had a man get jealous like that before. She knew that May had been trying to help so she couldn't truly fault her, but Maura didn't like it.

She watched as Rory downshifted and came to a halt at a light on Ala Moana.

"I don't play games like that." She looked over her shoulder at Zeke. "You should know better. I don't think it's fun to have guys who are jealous over me."

"I didn't say I was jealous," Zeke said, still not looking at her.

"Really? I am kind of confused then why you rushed up to the table then. Were you just hot to have a conversation."

She turned around and crossed her arms over her chest. Men. Seriously, he couldn't admit he was jealous?

"You didn't look like you were pushing him away," Zeke said.

She gasped and turned around. "What was I supposed to do? Am I not supposed to talk to other men at all? Rory is the Dom here, so I'm not understanding why you're going all possessive on me."

"Well, I would have paddled your ass red in public if I had thought you were flirting with him," Rory said.

She opened her mouth to yell at him but the image he created was too delicious. She shivered. He hadn't been looking at her, but he laughed. Damn, he already knew her too well.

"Oh, no. We're going to have to do something in public with you."

"Out of the question here because of Conner," Zeke said. He didn't say anymore and just kept looking at the scenery as it passed by. She had a feeling he wasn't really seeing any of it.

"Give it up, boy-o. You were ready to pounce on that cowboy faster than a tic on a dog."

She looked at Rory and laughed. The southern kind of saying sounded odd given in his Irish accent. His lips twitched. Maura looked at Zeke who said nothing and showed no reaction.

"Zeke, I didn't do anything wrong."

"I didn't say you did, even though you were a little too open to being flirted with. And I am emphatically denying that I was jealous," Zeke muttered.

"Well, I was, and I am going to show you just how jealous when we get home," Rory said. "It might not be in public, but I think you need to learn a little discipline and we haven't spent that much time with the paddle."

She opened her mouth but no sound came out. Her body was already reacting to the threat. No, not a threat, a promise. She squeezed her legs together to reduce the pressure but he tsked.

"Nope, spread those legs, precious. You apparently need to learn a little discipline and I aim to teach it to you."

And just like that her body was humming with need. Maura turned and faced forward. They were driving along H1 and he took the exit for Likelike Highway. He came to a stop at the light and looked over.

"That's not wide enough. Spread them wider."

She knew if she did, her skirt would ride up and she would be exposed. There wasn't anyone around them, but that didn't mean there wouldn't be. Rory apparently didn't like her hesitation.

"Do it now."

She immediately did as he ordered, exposing her pussy.

"Wider."

She complied. The rush of the naughty behavior and the fear of getting caught had her blood heating. They couldn't play in public and this was the next best thing.

"Hands on your thighs and no touching our pussy."

She did as he ordered. They were still alone at the light. He reached over and smacked her pussy. The quick slap sent tendrils of pleasure and frustration rolling through her.

"Now, you sit like that until we get back to the house." He glanced in the back seat at Zeke. "We should have put her in the back with you. You need to see how pretty she's sitting here."

He took off when the light turned green and drove down Likelike. She didn't turn around but she heard Zeke move forward.

"See anything you like, Zee?" Rory asked, his voice dancing over the words.

"Yeah," he said. "Yeah I do."

Just hearing the arousal in their voices had her arousal spiking. God, she wanted to touch herself, give herself a little relief, but she knew the rules. As it was, the cool Hawaiian air was whipping through the Jeep, it kept brushing over her bare labia. Rory had ordered her to spread her legs so wide, she was ready to die. She knew she was already wet, dripping in fact.

Fuck.

"Ah, I think our lover here is frustrated, Zee."

Zeke chuckled. "Yeah, I can imagine."

"Push your ass up a little more in the seat, Maura."

She did as ordered, her legs spreading further apart.

"Yeah, like that. Now, arch your back a little more. I want to see your breasts against that shirt."

He hummed when she did as he ordered.

"I would love to pull over, bend you over the hood and fuck you. God, that would be fantastic."

Again, the image he was creating had her moaning.

"But, we can't. I bought an extra special toy tonight, and I want to use it on you."

Zeke slipped his hands around her seat and covered her breasts. "Shit, her nipples are so fucking hard."

"They hurt, love?" Rory asked.

"Y-yes."

Zeke pinched them. The mixture of a pleasure and pain shot through her and she jolted in the seat. Unfortunately, it didn't give her any relief.

"Do it again, Zee."

He did and she reacted the same way. She couldn't help it.

"Damn, we should have brought the clamps," Rory muttered.

"Don't worry. We're almost back to the house," Zeke said. "And then, you can teach Maura a lesson."

thirty-three

I t only took them less than five minutes to get to the house but Maura was no less affected. In fact, it had felt like hours to get there.

Rory put the car in park and looked over at her and Zeke who was still caressing and pinching her nipples. They had not done anything else really and she was ready to come right there.

"Stay here."

She did as he and Zeke got out of the car. Zeke went to open the door and Rory came around to her side. He opened the passenger door. "Out of the car, hands behind your back and do not adjust your skirt."

The house was gated, but they were still outside and she wondered if anyone could see them. He held out his hand. "Do it now, Maura."

She took his hand, stepped out of the Jeep, and put her hands behind her back. Walking to the house was hard, not because she was virtually naked from the waist down, but the fact that her sex was practically pulsing with need. He helped her along to the door and to Zeke who was standing just in the doorway. Once they were in, Zeke shut the door and then keyed in the security code.

"Down here, Zee. I like the idea of fucking her on the big couch."

Zee walked up beside him. He skimmed his hand down Rory's abs to the obvious bulge in his pants. She watched as he caressed him. Rory leaned his head back, closed his eyes and groaned. Then, he leaned over and kissed Zeke's neck.

"Thanks, needed a little touch. Seeing her sit like that in the car was amazing. But now, we have to get down to the games."

He leaned closer and spoke in Zeke's ear. Zeke was watching her, his gaze moving up her body and his lips curved. "Oh, that sounds fantastic. I'll go get the toys."

Rory gave him a long, wet kiss that had all three of them moaning. Rory smiled at her.

"I think our girlie likes to watch almost as much as you do, Zee."

Zeke walked up to her and kissed her, long and wet. When he pulled back he was smiling again. "I think you do too."

Then, he left them, practically running up the stairs to get whatever these two planned on.

"Now, I need to get you ready."

He walked around her in a circle. He smacked her ass, hard. It stung but it also filtered over her flesh. Her already out of control libido was pushed even higher.

"We have not done enough spanking I think."

She shivered.

Zeke bounded down the stairs toward them. He set the toys on the table but they were in a bag as was the new toy from Rough 'n Ready.

They both sat on the couch.

"Turn around, love," Rory said. She did.

"Take your clothes off for us."

She didn't respond fast enough for Rory. He rose from the couch to reach around and spank her.

"Clothes, now, love, or I'll spank that ass red."

She shivered trying to figure out which she wanted. Sebastian had told her that the discipline wasn't always about what she had done wrong, and most of the time it wasn't. It was about pleasure for the sub. Still, there was something about Rory that made her want to misbehave.

He sighed. "Strip down, Maura."

Without waiting to see if she would comply, he sat back down on the couch. "Oh, and Maura, if you don't hurry, I'll make you wait longer for your relief tonight. You really don't want to challenge me on this, love."

She didn't know what he expected her to do. All she was wearing was the dress and she had lost the heels she'd been wearing. But, slowly, she slipped her hands beneath the bottom of her dress and pulled it up and over her head.

Rory stood and walked over to her again. She heard Zeke's clothes rustling but she fought the urge to look. Instead, she kept Rory's gaze.

"Good girl," Rory said, his voice rumbling over the words. He grabbed the nipple clamps off the coffee table, then continued on. He stopped in front of her and kissed her. She shivered as she let her eyes close and accepted his tongue in her mouth. He cupped her face, the metal of the nipple clamps cold against her skin.

He pulled back, gave her a small smile, and without saying anything, fastened the clamps on her nipples.

"Our girl likes to have a little pain, Zee."

"Yeah, I see that," Zeke said. Rory stepped aside and revealed Zeke. He was naked his cock hard and long and she licked her lips.

"In a second, love. First, though, I need to catch up to speed. Zee...wanna little taste of our pussy?"

He smiled. "You know I do."

Now he walked the same path as Rory. He didn't kiss her though. He slipped a finger on the chain and tugged. The pain shot straight to her cunt. Fuck. She was already dripping wet.

"Never would have thought you would like that, love." He pulled again, then released it. He went down on his knees.

"Spread those legs, Maura," Rory said from behind her.

She complied.

"No coming. You're going to wait for us tonight. We go first since you decided to be so damned naughty."

Zeke set his mouth against her pussy. It was almost casual the way his tongue slipped in and out of her. The brush of his goatee against her overly sensitive flesh ratcheted up the tension inside her. It was teasing, almost enough to make her come but not enough.

"That's enough," Rory said.

Zeke gave her one last long lick, and rose. He kissed her, lightly, leisurely, then he pulled back. The heat she saw in his eyes told her he was beyond aroused. Hell, she didn't need to look down to see that he was ready, she thought with an inward laugh.

Zeke turned and sat back on the couch. Rory walked in front of her.

"Time for a spanking, dear," he said, slapping a crop against his hand. This was the new toy. Excitement lit through her. She'd been paddled, but she loved the crop the best.

"Ah, I see you are happy. Well, why don't you see if you can make our love happy. He's got a nice big cock there and I'm sure he'd like to feel those lips wrapped around it."

She followed him. She had no choice really as he pulled on the chain to lead her over. The little bites of pain from the clamps were almost too much to bear, but she tried. With each tug, a shaft of pain and pleasure moved through her.

Zeke was sitting on one end and she walked to go between his legs, but Rory had different ideas. He tugged her over to the side of the couch.

"Now, bend," he ordered, letting go of the chain. She did, her ass up in the air. "Now, you suck him good, and you don't stop until I tell you."

She wrapped her hand around Zeke's cock as she steadied herself with her other hand and took him into his mouth. There was a small pearl of precum that danced over her taste buds. She began to move, taking him in and out of her mouth. She was just getting into giving him head when Rory smacked her the first time with the crop. The sting of the hit caused her to moan.

"Remember, love, you keep that naughty mouth on him until I say so."

She did as Zeke threaded his fingers through her hair and started to thrust up into her mouth. Rory gave her a series of smacks that lit her ass on fire. Damn, her skin burned her body completely in tune with what the men were doing to her. Her pussy was soaked, her body shaking with need, but she did what Rory ordered her to do.

"Oh, yeah, fuck. That's good, love," Zeke muttered as he continued to thrust into her mouth. "Damn, hit her again, Rory. She moans on my cock when you do."

Rory complied and she did. Not on purpose but she couldn't help it. She wanted to come so badly and every time he smacked her ass she hurt. A good kind of hurt, but she hurt nonetheless.

Then, the smacks stopped and Rory was moving. Zeke thrust up one more time, then stopped. Rory helped her up.

. . .

He twisted the nipple clamps slightly. "That was very good, Maura. Now, we're taking you. Zeke wants his cock up that tight little pussy and I want to fuck your ass, at the same time. You game?"

She shivered at the picture he'd painted. She nodded.

Zeke was already lying back on the couch and he was rolling on a condom.

"God, he's so fuckable, isn't he, Maura?"

She licked her lips and nodded. Rory led her over to the couch and helped her straddle Zeke. The moment he entered her, her pussy clamped down tight on him. Damn, she needed this, needed to feel them inside her. She slid down until he was fully seated in her, then, she started to ride him. Zeke tugged on the clamps, the pain and pleasure even more heightened. She rode him, her moans growing, her orgasm approaching. Then, he stopped.

She felt a smack on her ass.

"Not yet, Maura," Rory said as he joined them on the couch. "I want to be up your pretty little ass when you come."

Zeke slid his hands up to her shoulders and eased her down. "Tell us if it hurts too much."

She nodded just as she felt Rory's lubed finger ease into her anus. She shuddered. He didn't give her much time to prepare. She sensed an urgency about him, one that she had never felt from him before. Zeke spread her cheeks apart as Rory eased his way into her ass.

When he was fully inside her, Zeke looked up at Rory then back at her. They started to move. At first, it hurt, but was a good kind of pain just like before. Soon, though, she didn't care. The men increased their rhythm. She felt her orgasm coming, her body shivering with the need to let it go. She bit her lip trying to keep herself from succumbing. Rory said something, but she didn't hear it. Maura was so lost in the pleasure of having both men in her at the same time, feeling this connection, that she blocked it out.

Zeke cupped her face. "Maura, look at me."

She forced herself to open her eyes.

"Rory said to come, babe. Do it."

For a second, she panicked. She couldn't seem to get herself to come then. All this time she had been yearning for it, and now...nothing. Both men were still working in tandem. Rory thrust into her ass then groaned her name. Zeke kissed her as he thrust up into her one last time. He groaned as he came, and opened his eyes. He was still shaking.

"Come for us, love." He whispered the words against her mouth.

At that moment, her orgasm crashed through her. Over and over she said their names as she allowed pleasure to take over her.

ABOUT AN HOUR LATER, RORY WALKED OUT OF THE bathroom and looked at Zee and Maura. He'd never thought to find a permanent third for their relationship, but Maura was definitely making him think twice about that. Zee had his arms wrapped around her, and she had snuggled against him, her head just under Zee's chin.

Something shifted inside him. Something he had been trying to avoid the whole time he had been in Hawaii. Hell, he'd been trying to avoid it in Miami. He had known about Zee's attraction and he had resisted getting to know her. Because if Zee loved her, there was a good chance he would fall for her himself.

Damn.

"Are you going to keep standing there or join us, love?" Zee asked.

Rory's lips twitched. Zee hadn't opened his eyes. He didn't answer. Instead, he padded across the floor and slipped into bed behind Maura. He wrapped his arm around both of them as he spooned Maura.

Maura had different plans. She shifted then turned around to face him. She trailed her fingers down his face. "Thank you for tonight, Rory."

He kissed her forehead. "Anytime, love."

She smiled and snuggled against his chest like she had done to Zee.

"I love you, Zeke," she said.

Zeke kissed her neck. Just before she drifted off, she said, "I love you, Rory."

She let out a slight snore then. Rory's chest felt tight.

"I love you too, Rory," Zee said, giving him a kiss and settling down to sleep.

Rory lay there trying his best to dismiss the warmth spreading through his body, but it was of no use.

He looked down at Maura.

Just what the hell was he going to do about her? She had wormed her way into his heart and now she claimed to love him.

He sighed and tried his best to brush his worries aside. It was probably just said to make him feel better. Or she had been too sleepy to know what she was saying. No use worrying about it now.

Rory knew he would have plenty of time to worry about it when he returned to Miami.

With that last thought, he closed his eyes and followed his lovers into sleep.

R ory cracked the last egg in the bowl and tossed the shell in the trash. It was already past nine in the morning and Zee was still in bed.

"I can't believe he's still sleeping," Maura said.

"We had a long night, love," he said, giving her a kiss on the cheek. She was sitting on the counter next to the stove watching him make French toast. When she had said it was her favorite thing to eat for breakfast, he couldn't resist making his for her.

"Not that long. There is something very wrong with him being in bed and us being up."

He chuckled as he poured in a little cream in with the eggs. "Nothing wrong with a little private time just the two of us."

She said nothing for a while and he looked up. The look on her face didn't tell him anything. If anything she showed no expression.

"What?"

She shrugged. "You promise not to take this the wrong way?"

Now, he started to worry. "I'll try."

She sighed. "I just didn't think I would like you very much.

Truthfully, I didn't think you would like me very much. I have been told more than once I'm an acquired taste. And, since you admitted to being a little jealous last night, I guess I have to say that it killed me when you showed up in Florida. You know how special Zeke is, don't you?"

Her heartfelt expression and solemn tone told him she was serious. He swallowed. "Yeah. It took me a long time to figure it out but I did."

"Good. I'm glad you do. He deserves someone who loves him. Someone who will give him the world."

And we could, love. His brain stopped functioning for a second as he let the thought seep into his consciousness. He waited for the panic to come but it didn't. Instead, the incredible rightness of the statement settled in his gut. The three of them. Together.

"Are you okay?" she asked.

He looked at her and swallowed the lump in his throat. Zee had been right. There was so much more to Maura than she showed the world. And there was something about her that completed both Zee and him. They belonged together.

"Yeah, yeah. I'm fine."

"Okay." Apparently not wanting to push it any further she looked down at the batter. "I love French toast."

"Any special reason?" he asked as he retrieved the loaf of bread.

She nodded. "My mom made the best French toast. It was just amazing."

"Ah."

She took the bread from him and pulled out the slices. "It was the last thing she made for me before the accident."

He felt the stab to the heart right there and then. Seeing her position the bread on the counter carefully, he could easily see the teenaged Maura suffering through losing her parents, watching them die. She showed so little of that part of her that he held it close to his chest. He blinked.

"Oh?"

"Yeah. We had done brinner that night and had gone to see a movie."

"Brinner?"

She grinned at him. "Yeah, that's what we called it when Mom made it, then on the way back..." she shrugged.

He set his hand on top of hers and she looked up at him, surprise lighting her features. Her eyes widened behind her lenses. He couldn't tell her he knew the feelings, or even express how it made him feel that she had shared it with him. Instead, he leaned in and brushed his mouth over hers. She closed her eyes and leaned into the kiss. It wasn't carnal but it affected him just the same. No, this was more intense. It hit him on so many levels, but the worst part of it was what it did to his heart. It turned over as she pulled away and then trailed her fingers down his cheek.

He'd been fighting it for days now, but he had to admit he was ass deep in love with a woman for the first time in his life.

"Hey, do I smell French toast?" Zee said.

Rory couldn't speak, not yet. He was pretty sure his voice would crack.

Maura grinned at him. If he hadn't known before that, he would definitely know now that he was in love with her.

She turned around. "Yep. He claims it is fantastic."

Rory tried to get his head in order as he went back to preparing the toast. Zee stopped in front of Maura and gave her a kiss, then leaned over to kiss his cheek. "Smells good."

The Georgia fight song went off on Maura's phone. "Hey, Jillian. Having some French toast. No, Rory cooks." She laughed and his heart danced a little.

Damn.

"No, I don't think Conner would let him live with you just for cooking. Sure." She jumped off the counter. "I'm going to check something out on the computer, be right back."

She started up the steps and he couldn't help but watch her as she went. He didn't pay attention to her words, but the tone of her voice, the way she laughed entranced him. The swing of her hips didn't hurt either.

"Earth to Rory."

He shook his head and looked at Zee who was smiling at him.

"What?" he asked. His head was still spinning and his body was still humming.

"Nothing. You just seemed to be lost there."

He shrugged with one shoulder. "We were talking about her family."

"Conner?" Zee asked as he poured himself some coffee.

"No, her folks."

He sensed Zee's stillness. He looked back over his shoulder.

"She did."

"What?"

"She rarely talks about them. I don't know much about them."

He sensed a thread of hurt in Zee's voice. Setting down the whisk, he walked over to him and kissed him. "It wasn't that much. She mentioned she liked French toast, that it was her favorite thing to eat for breakfast."

"Yeah, I know that."

"It was the last thing her mom made her before the accident. That's all she said."

Zee sighed and put his head on Rory's shoulder and for the second time that day he felt that slow roll through his heart, through his soul.

"I didn't mean to act like an ass."

He chuckled. "Really, Zee your definition of acting like an ass is weird."

He pulled back and looked at him. "It's hard at times, this relationship. Most of the time I am okay with it, all the time really. Just hearing she had talked to you about her folks, that's...well, she avoids it."

"And you've known her longer and you love her."

"Just me?" Rory made a face. "Okay, I won't push you but at some point you're going to have to deal with it. Both of you." He gave him a kiss.

"Now, get some breakfast for me, or I might just kick you to the curb."

"I'd like to see you try."

When Rory turned he noticed that Maura was walking down the stairs and she was watching them.

"No, don't stop on my account. I find it very sexy," she said, her voice happy—truly happy. He realized that for all the months he had known her, he had never seen her this happy.

"What did Jillian want?" Zee asked and pulled her into his arms as Rory went back to work on breakfast.

"She's stuck and needs to get out of the house for a bit. She wanted to know if I could run into Kailua Old Town and do some shopping this afternoon. I hope that's okay."

No, it wasn't bleeding okay. He wanted her to stay there with them, not out traipsing around. But he didn't say anything.

"Yes, we need to talk to Conner about a couple things. Did you want to go out tonight?" Zee asked.

She scrunched up her nose and shook her head. "Can we stay in tonight? I can pick up whatever Rory wants to make us for dinner. We have a great place to dine on the lanai and I would rather enjoy the sunset from there and just relax with you two."

He shared a glance with Zee. "Sure. That sounds like a great plan."

She looked at the bread he had in the pan. "That breakfast isn't going to cook itself."

She gave him a kiss and wandered over to get more coffee. He forced himself to focus on cooking. He would have time enough later to worry about the woman who was worming her way into his heart.

JILLIAN SMILED AT ZEKE WHEN SHE STEPPED IN THE door. She was dressed like she normally did. Do rag on her head, cut off shorts, and an old T-shirt. She gave him a quick kiss on the cheek.

"I promise not to keep her long. We need some girl time."

"No problem, Jillian."

"Yay, girl stuff," Maura said. She gathered up her purse and glasses. Then, she stopped and grabbed her hat. As if it was the most natural thing in the world, she gave Rory a kiss then him. "Should be home soon. Text me what you want me to pick up for dinner."

They watched as the women climbed into the Jeep and then headed off for their day of fun.

"So, what do you want to do?" Zeke asked. He was antsy, ready to do something—anything. He wasn't accustomed to long days of leisure.

Rory frowned. "I'm planning on relaxing out back. I think you have a few dishes to clean up."

He glanced over at the kitchen. "Dammit, she left me with the plates to clean up."

Rory laughed. "Our Maura isn't stupid, that's for sure."

For a second he said nothing as he let the words sink in. He had seen the way Rory had reacted earlier. Rory had never had a real relationship with a woman. One night stands or fuck buddies for vacations, but no real relationship. In truth, Zeke was pretty sure he was the only relationship he had ever had that was, well, a relationship.

"Our?"

Rory looked up at him. "What?"

"You used the word 'our' for Maura."

He frowned. "Well she is."

"Come on, admit it. You want to make this permanent."

He said nothing but turned around to find something on the TV.

"I don't know if I can do that."

His heart sank. The only hope he had at the start of this was that somehow they might all make it through the week and maybe they could keep it going. He thought it was a long shot until he saw the way Rory and Maura had interacted. Every time the three of them made love that connection seemed to grow stronger. He had been hoping against hope that they would end up together in the end. The interaction he'd seen this morning at the breakfast table had reinforced the idea that Rory was falling for her. There was only one thing that could be keeping Rory from committing.

"You're afraid."

"No." He stood up and threw the remote control down on the couch. "That's not it."

Zeke watched the man he'd loved more than ten years struggle. He hurt for him, but Zeke was also glad for it.

"Do you want to elaborate?"

Rory's frown turned darker and the look he shot Zeke told him he was trying to think of ways of killing him. It made Zeke want to dance.

"I don't know how I'm going to give her up," he said, the

words seeming to explode from somewhere deep inside him. Rory was good at hiding his feelings but he held onto them so tightly that there was always an explosion of some sort.

Zeke's heart stood up and cheered.

"This wasn't supposed to happen."

Zeke put the last of the plates into the dishwasher. Then started in on the skillet. "What was supposed to happen? Just a few fucks and then walk away. I told you it wouldn't be easy with her. It never is."

Rory let out a frustrated growl. "I can't deal with this right now."

Zeke said nothing although he wanted to. He wanted to push Rory, make him understand that this was supposed to happen. The three of them were supposed to be together, but he didn't. He knew the worst thing he could do was push Rory. So, instead he nodded. With a curse, Rory turned and headed out to the lanai.

Zeke thought it was another important step. They were slow and he was frustrated but to think there might be a chance that the three of them could come to some kind of agreement...he didn't know if it could happen, but just thinking about it made him happier than anything in his life had before.

thirty-five

"I think I bought too much," Maura said when she walked out the door of Lanakai. It was one of her favorite finds in the Kailua area. The Hawaiian made soaps and lotions were some of her favorite things. "But I really don't care."

"That's the spirit," Jillian said with a laugh. "You worry too much as it is."

She sighed. "I feel a lecture coming on."

"Naw, not from me. In fact, there is no way I am going to say that you haven't learned to stop worrying about things. You're in a hot relationship with two men."

An older woman gave them a look and Maura could feel her face heat up. She wasn't ashamed, but she wasn't going to go shouting it out on the street. "You are so bad."

Jillian looked behind them as the older woman muttered to herself and walked down the street. "Hey, these things go on. She's probably jealous that she hasn't had as much fun as you. If I didn't have your brother cleaning my clock every night, I would be too."

Maura closed her eyes for a second. Jillian had always been

willing to share. It had just taken a weird turn when she became involved with Conner. "Jillian, I told you that while I am beyond happy that the two of you are married, please quit sharing things like that."

"You're like one of my few girlfriends. That's what we're supposed to do, right?" She pointed to a little coffee shop. "Why don't we grab a drink and gossip?"

"Sounds good."

They were served pretty quickly, and soon they found themselves sitting at the table on the street. The trades were soft, with just enough to keep her cool.

"God, I love it here."

Jillian smiled and took a sip of her coffee. "You live in Miami."

"Yes, and you know it's different. There is a vibe...a feeling when I am here. Something that just grabs hold of me. I can't live here, but every time I come, I feel centered."

"And that's why I live here. Plus, an ocean between me and the rest of the crazies in my family is good." She set her coffee down and settled a stern look on Maura. "Okay, so tell me, is everything going okay?"

"Yeah."

"No problems?"

"Lord, no. They...well, lord, it's hard to explain but there is something about the two of them that is so sweet."

"Sweet?"

"Yeah. They are sort of yin and yang."

Jillian chuckled. "Sweet. Special Forces dudes are sweet."

"Well, not entirely sweet or they would be boring. Rory is an amazing Dom. Some of the stuff..." She stopped and cleared her throat. "Let's just say that the man is close to being a god."

"Have y'all talked about what will happen when you get home?"

She shook her head. "No, not sure exactly what is going to happen. And for once I am going to ignore my inner voice. I am going to live in the moment. I would like it to go on, but...for right now this is what I am going to do." She took a sip of her raspberry tea and knew the best way to divert Jillian's attention. "So, how's the book going?"

Jillian huffed. "Okay, I guess. I wish this one was as easy as the last one, but, well, every book is different."

As Jillian went into depth about her problems with the book, Maura felt something stir on the back of her neck. The fine hairs sizzled and she got the feeling someone was watching her again. It wasn't odd being with Jillian and being seen. She was a striking woman and with her tattoos she did gain a lot of attention. But for some reason...this felt different. It was wrong.

She casually looked around to see if someone was watching them. She saw no one.

"Then, your brother was being a butthead and said that he didn't want me going to the Big Island."

"Wait, what are you talking about?"

"I want to go learn how to ride a horse on the Big Island."

"Let me guess. Eli St. John has something to do with this."

"He invited us over for a visit and Conner went all stupid Dom on me and said no. Wait, you know him?"

"I met him last night. I met him when I came over here before, but I didn't remember. Anyway, he talked to me, the guys freaked and Zeke—of all people- came over and acted like an ass. Then, well, Rory...well, let's not go into that."

Jillian studied her for a second. When she said nothing, Maura asked, "What?"

Then, slowly, her lips curved and that one hundred watt smile brightened her face. "Nothing. Just...well, I think there may be more to this trio than you think."

Maura shrugged. "I don't want to think about it."

Because when she did it made her so sad to think that she only had a few days left with the guys. Things had been so wonderful that morning, having breakfast. It had been as if they had been doing it for years.

"Maura," Jillian said. She looked at her oldest friend and had to blink rapidly against the tears. "Do they know?"

"Zeke knows I love him. I've never hidden it."

"What about Rory?"

This time when she blinked, the tears fell. "I'm not sure."

"Oh, honey, don't cry. Being in love should make you happy."

"It does, when I'm with them." She pulled in a breath and closed her eyes. She could not be seen on the street in Kailua Town crying like some fifteen-year-old. When she opened her eyes, she had her emotions somewhat under control. "When we're together it's great, but then I don't think about what will happen when we return to Miami."

"Does Zeke know about your feelings?"

"Which ones?"

The gentle smile she gave her took her back to her first horrible week of college, being the underaged geek and tormented more than she had been in high school. Jillian had been the calm in the storm of pain.

"Well, first, does Zeke know you love Rory?"

She shrugged. "I haven't even decided for sure if I love him."

Jillian chuckled. "Oh, honey you do. I just never thought you would because he seems kind of abrasive."

"He is, but there are a lot of things in his past, and, well... he's a sweetheart."

"Rory McAllister? The man you just left. The one who knows how to kill people with his bare hands? Hell, both of them do, but Zeke hides it better."

"I know," she sighed and smiled. "Rory made me French toast."

Jillian studied her for a moment before saying, "I want you to think about saying what you want from them."

"I don't want to cause problems here and seriously, I'm not sure I could do this long term. There is so much emotion there...I'm overwhelmed."

Jillian reached across the table and gripped Maura's hands in hers. "You deserve whatever it is you want. Don't ever settle for less because you think you haven't earned it."

"What do you mean?"

"You don't think I know just how exhausted you were when you got here? You've been trying to keep everything going and it isn't for you. You have to tell Conner no every now and then, and you need to tell the guys what you want."

"I don't know what I want," she said.

"When you figure out what you want you demand it from them. If they aren't men enough to give it to you, tell them to fuck each other and you go find someone who is. Because honey, you deserve to be happy."

She opened her mouth, but Jillian stopped her. "No, don't tell me you're happy. I know you are. Hell, I don't think I have ever seen you laugh as much as you have in the small amount of time I've seen you while you've been here."

"So, why can't you just let it be?"

"I will. I just want you to remember that if this doesn't continue when you return to the mainland, then the problem isn't you, it's them. Remember that."

"Okay."

"Now, I need chocolate because this book has been a pain in the ass."

"That's sounds fabulous."

But as she followed Jillian to the store, Maura wondered if

she would ever have the nerve to ask the guys for what she wanted, or if she would be left alone again?

She shoved those thoughts aside and concentrated on buying some chocolate because if there was one thing she knew, it was that chocolate would make her feel a little better...even if it was only for a little while.

thirty-six

"How do you like your steak cooked?" Rory asked Maura.

She said nothing, just kept looking out over the water from their lanai. He shared a look with Zee. She'd been quiet since she returned from her trip with Jillian. It wasn't that it was alarming but she seemed a little more subdued.

"Maura?" he asked again.

She shook herself and looked over at him. It took a second for her eyes to focus on him. "I'm sorry, what?"

"How do you like your steak?"

"Oh," she said then smiled. "Medium rare. I like a little blood."

He threw the steaks on the grill trying very hard not to freak out. The openness he had grown accustomed to over the last week was no longer there.

"Did you have a good time with Jillian?" Zee asked.

"Yeah, we did a little shopping, had a snack."

She said it absent-mindedly as if she were thinking about

something else. She had been of course. Something had been bothering her since she got back to the house.

"Maura, are you going to tell us what's bothering you?"

She looked at him. "Nothing's really bothering me."

"You've been quiet since you got back from shopping."

She shrugged. "Okay. Something was bothering me a little but I mostly dismissed it. Doesn't seem that important."

"You can tell us," Zee said, his voice as worried as Rory felt.

Sighing, she said, "Well, it felt like someone was watching me again. It was really odd but then, that happens sometimes with Jillian. She gets a few people who recognize her. She's also a striking woman. She stands out so she does draw a lot of attention."

"That's all that was bothering you?" Zee asked, but Rory could tell that even he was suspicious.

"Yeah." She smiled. "I had to work it out in my brain."

Zee took her hand and brought it to his lips.

"Oh, are you romantic," she said.

Zee laughed with her. "You're rarely quiet with us."

She shrugged. "You know sometimes I have to work things out in my head. Once I do, everything is okay. I'm going to wash up and fix a few lazy man's lava flows. Anyone else?"

"Naw, I have a beer," Zee said. She gave him a kiss then touched Rory's back as she walked by.

It was something he had grown accustomed to the last few days. For someone who seemed so singular, she seemed to always want to touch them.

"Stop worrying," Zee said.

Rory glanced at him. "I can worry if I want to."

Zee smiled and leaned closer for a kiss. After brushing his mouth over Rory's, he said, "I thought I would never hear the day that Rory McAllister would worry about a woman."

He shrugged. "I'm used to seeing her be open with us, especially you."

"Don't worry, love. You'll see after dinner, she'll be fine."

But, as he watched her through the meal, he knew there was something else going on. She was a woman with a healthy appetite who never tried to pretend she wasn't hungry.

"You only ate half of your steak," Rory commented.

She laughed and it relaxed him a bit. "It was a sixteen ounce, Rory. You might have a man-sized appetite but there is only so much I can eat. Plus, this way, there is some left for tomorrow morning for breakfast. I'm going to go wrap this up because I do like steak and eggs. And just for reference, I like my eggs over medium."

She picked up her plate and went inside the house.

"I'm not buying it," Rory said.

Zee shook his head. "You need to let it go. Sometimes Maura gets like that. If you push, she'll just close down. I've seen her do it."

He sighed trying to gain control of the emotions raging inside of him. He hadn't been able to come to terms with his own revelations earlier that day. He had never been so tangled up about a woman, but Maura had him tangled up good.

"Hey, do y'all mind if I take a bath. I bought some great bath stuff I want to try out."

"No, go ahead, love," Zee said.

She gave them each a kiss and then headed back into the house.

"Rory?"

"I think she's having second thoughts."

He was proud of the fact that he kept the panic out of his voice. It was crawling down his spine.

"She's not having second thoughts."

He didn't say anything trying to keep his worries to himself. He had already said too much. Of course, Zee didn't let it go.

"Rory."

He sighed. "How do you know she isn't having second thoughts?"

"Because, with Maura, if she truly was thinking about us she would say that when asked. You keep looking for some kind of hidden agenda from her, but there isn't." He stood. "Now, I think we clean up—because if you notice, she left us with the dishes again—and join her up in the tub. Of course, if you want to sit out here and brood, go right ahead. I'll take advantage of having Maura to myself."

Rory sat there for just a few seconds because he pushed his worries aside. There was one thing that would make him feel better for a little while and that was being in bed with Zee and Maura.

thirty-seven

"How did I end up at a bleeding mall?" Rory asked

Zeke gave him a smile and glanced at Maura who was getting a pretzel. "Not much you won't do for her, huh?"

His smug tone irritated Rory. There were several things about Zee that drove Rory crazy—and not in a good way. Zee had never seemed to question his own feelings for Rory or for Maura. He also had one of those work ethics that had him up at six in the morning while he was on vacation. And, worst of them all was that Zee liked being right. He always made sure to remind Rory of the times he was right.

Sure, Rory practically wearing his heart on his sleeve with the woman. Last night had been overwhelming, even for a degenerate for him. It had been the first time in days there had been no real play in the bedroom. He didn't realize it until that morning, and it scared the fucking hell out of him.

"Oh, now I know she has you by the short hairs because you won't even say anything about it."

Rory gave him a mean look but Zee shook his head. "Not scaring me, boy-o. I know what last night meant."

"Yeah, why don't you enlighten me, Einstein?"

Zee wasn't deterred a bit by his nasty tone. "There was no play, none. You don't do that with women."

"Apparently I do because I did last night," he said trying to quell the unease in his stomach.

"Exactly. Face it, Rory, you're falling for her."

He said nothing as he watched as Maura charmed the little Hawaiian woman behind the counter. This wasn't just worry about last night. There was plenty there to keep him on edge, but this was something that had his other senses on high alert.

"What did she say about feeling like someone was watching her?"

"Don't change the subject."

He glanced at Zee, then back at Maura. "I'm not changing the subject. And it doesn't matter. Here she comes."

He still couldn't shake the weird feeling. He'd been off since last night, but it had only gotten worse as they approached Kahala Mall.

"Face it, love. You're in deep. That's all that's bothering you."

He shrugged as he looked around the area trying to detect if there was someone watching them. It was afternoon on a weekday but that didn't mean anything there. Tourists flocked to areas like this in the heat of the day. Kids screamed and ran through the area and there was always a motley crew of teenagers around.

"Rory?"

He shook himself out of his funk and realized Maura was standing in front of him holding a piece of pretzel out to him.

He forced himself to smile. "Thanks, love."

She smiled as she sat down. "I got cheese," she said as she sat down.

"Woman, please, cheese on a pretzel? Did you get mustard?" Zee said.

She tossed a packet his way along with the pretzel she bought for him. "I have no idea what you have against cheese."

"That's not cheese, love. That's processed crap."

"And it tastes delicious."

She dipped a piece of pretzel into the cheese and offered it to him. Rory took it without thinking.

"I told you I didn't need anything, love."

She grinned. "I don't mind sharing, but then you know that."

For a second he couldn't believe she said that out loud. Then, slowly the humor of the situation hit him and he smiled, and then chuckled. All the worries he had dissolved and he leaned forward and gave her a kiss.

"That you do, love. That you do."

thirty-eight

Maura walked down the long hall to the bathroom. She hated mall bathrooms. It always felt as if she were walking to the end of the earth just to pee. The mall had been insane, but the hallway was deserted. Then, she heard a scrape of a shoe against the floor. Alarm bells immediately went off in her head. Before she could turn, someone hit her hard against her back, shoving her into the wall. A large male body smashed her against the wall as a large, sweaty hand covered her mouth.

She was trapped.

"Your boyfriends let you walk down the hall by yourself," he said, the sneer in his voice easy to hear. There was a slight accent, one that sounded almost Irish, but not quite. It sounded as if he were trying to disguise it. Her heart was beating so hard against her ribs. She drew in as much air as she could and then let it out. The stench of his breath, along with cologne and a healthy dose of sweat filled her senses. She felt bile rise in her throat.

He pulled her arm up wrenching it behind her back. It hurt so much tears burned the back of her eyes.

"I think I might like to have a piece of McAllister and O'Brian's woman before I kill her. An eye for an eye."

Fear doubled as he pulled her away from the wall. They were near the back exit, the kind that led to the alley behind the mall. IF he had a car out there, he would get her out of there without anyone knowing. She struggled knowing that if he took her anywhere, it could be deadly. He slammed her head against the cement wall. Stars formed in front of her eyes. Warm blood trickled down from her forehead. He pulled her arm tighter behind her. Maura was surprised he didn't break it. She sucked in a deep breath as pain radiated down from her shoulder. Her fingers were tingling.

"Bitch, you want to live, you might want to start cooperating."

He was dragging her down the hall and she refused this. She would not let this bastard take her out of there without a fight. She kicked back with her legs, connecting with his shin the third time.

"Bloody bitch," he said, his accent coming through more. Voices sounded down the hallway and she knew this might be her only chance for escape. She threw her head back smacking it against his forehead.

"Fucking hell."

He loosened his hold on her as a gaggle of teens came down the hall. Their chatter echoed. She stumbled forward, losing her balance and landing on her knees and hand. She didn't give the bastard another chance. Ignoring the way her stomach roiled and the blurred vision, she rushed headlong into the group of kids. She didn't look behind her and ran to the food court.

Maura ignored the strange looks. She knew she must have looked a mess. The moment Rory and Zeke saw her, they were out of their chairs and running through the milling crowd to reach her. She fell into Zeke's arms.

"What the fuck happened?" Rory yelled.

"Some guy attacked me when I came out of the bathroom."

Zeke led her to a chair and gently helped her sit. She raised her hand to push her hair out of her face and realized it was shaking. Her stomach quivered.

"Hey, hey," Zeke said. She looked up at him and realized her vision was still blurred. Shit, she was crying. In public. She drew in a deep breath trying to control the tears, but that seemed to make her cry harder.

He pulled her up out of the seat and into his arms. As his warmth surrounded her, she was comforted by the familiar scent of his cologne.

She realized then that the mall cops had appeared and Rory was talking to them and leading them down the hall.

"Did you recognize him?" Zeke asked.

She shook her head. "No. He was disguising his voice too."

"Disguising it?"

"He had an accent, like yours and Rory's. I'm sure of it. But he was trying to make it American."

He pulled back from her and stared down at her. "Are you sure?"

She nodded again her stomach turning over as her head started to pound. "And if he was trying to do that it means only one thing."

"He knows you," Zeke said.

She swallowed, still fighting the bile that almost overtook again. "And you and Rory. He mentioned you. It means the bastard knows us all."

thirty-nine

Zeke tied the back of Maura's hospital gown for her then helped her sit on the bed. His fingers were shaking from the anger he was trying to suppress.

"I told you I didn't need to see a doctor," Maura said for the fifth time in as many minutes.

"And apparently, I'm ignoring you."

She gave him an irritated look and he realized he had snapped at her. It was the best he could do. He glanced at their lover and as he had been since they talked to the mall cops, Rory said nothing. He stood as a guard by the door, stoic as he had been since they got to Queen's Medical Center. Zeke knew that he was blaming himself for what happened. It wasn't their fault, but he did understand why Rory felt that way. Maura was a tough woman, but the thought that someone had attacked her so brazenly in the middle of the day in a crowded mall was alarming.

The door opened and Rome Carino walked in. Rory went on alert. It was easy to see why he would be. Rome Carino reeked of deadly force. Even when he wasn't on the job as an HPD homicide detective he looked ready to kill.

"Settle down, Rory. Carino's the guy I called."

Rory nodded and stepped back. Carino's lips twitched. "I take it you don't need protection for Maura."

"Maura can speak for herself, thank you very much," Maura said from behind him. He glanced over his shoulder to find her glaring at all of them. She probably would have crossed her arms but the doctor put her right arm in a sling.

"Of course," Carino murmured as he stepped forward. "You want to tell me what happened?"

She gave the detective a narrowed look. Zeke could almost hear her mind working.

"The HPD sent a highly decorated detective to investigate a simple assault?"

"I recognized the name." There was a beat of silence. "So, tell me what happened."

Maura told her story again, her voice no longer wavering when she went over the details. As long as he lived, Zeke knew he wouldn't forget the sight of her rushing towards them, her glasses askew and terror in her eyes. He had never felt so hopeless before in his life.

She told the story in the same calm tone she had been using since she'd seen the doctor.

When she was finished, Carino studied her. "It seems quite brutal for someone you don't know."

His accusatory tone ruffled Zeke's feathers and he knew for sure Carino was pissing Maura off. Of course, she didn't rise to the bait.

"I don't know what to tell you, Rome. The truth is I don't know the man. He wasn't even familiar to me by scent."

That brought Carino up short. "Explain."

Rory shifted his feet and Zeke gave him a warning glance. A Dom like Rory wasn't going to take a man questioning Maura that way.

"I have a very good sense of smell. I can sometimes tell who a person is if I know what cologne he or she wears, and a basic human scent. It's freaky, but I have always been that way. This guy, I did not know, at least not well. He smelled off, like he had been living on the streets. His breath, well I don't even want to go there, if you get my drift."

"How tall was he?" She opened her mouth but Carino stopped her. "Think back to when he was behind you. Did he seem shorter than you as he stood behind you? Taller?"

She nodded, sighed and closed her eyes. "I was wearing flip-flops so I was practically barefoot. I think he was probably close to my height, maybe a half an inch taller. So, five ten possibly. No taller." She opened her eyes.

"Bastard broke my glasses. It's a good thing I have another pair with me."

"And he said nothing else?"

"No. But his accent was Irish, I am pretty sure of it. More like Rory's, who is from Belfast, so it was definitely from Northern Ireland."

"You said you didn't hear it at first."

She had already been arguing with both Rory and Zeke about it since they had pulled her out of the mall. Zeke thought maybe she had confused the accent because she had been traumatized. She was hiding it, keeping herself together, but he knew it had sent her over the edge.

"Okay."

"Any luck on the security cameras at the mall?" Rory asked. It was the first words he had spoken in more than half an hour.

Carino turned back to both of them. "The security cameras were tampered with. Nothing."

"Fuck," Rory said.

"Exactly," Carino said. "It can only mean that he had been stalking her."

"Excuse me. 'Her' would like to speak right now."

Carino's lips twitched again and he turned to face Maura. "What does that mean?"

"It means there is a good chance he was stalking you."

"Me?" she shook her head. "I don't think so. He mentioned both of you."

"Is there anyone who would like to cause you harm?"

"No. Other than Susan Vincent from college."

"What?"

"Susan Vincent from college. She was mean to me so I replaced her shampoo with Nair."

For a second there was stunned silence in the hospital room.

"Jesus, Joseph and Mary, I don't think Susan Vincent is after you in a mall in Hawaii."

She shrugged. "She was one mean bitch. She was Miss Georgia and you know how those types are."

"This has to do with the Peterson case. Damn, I hate to admit Conner might be right," Zeke said.

Rory nodded and Carino asked, "Peterson case?"

"We helped nab someone who was in tight with the Mexican Mafia and my brother and these two goofballs actually think we are a mark for them. First, it doesn't make sense because my name isn't in any of the information. And, if so, it would be the company and Conner or Zeke at risk."

Carino looked at first Rory then Zeke. He read the answer in his eyes.

"What?"

The detective sighed. "The truth is you might be collateral damage right now. They might use you to get to them."

"I think you are blowing this out of proportion."

"For fuck's sake you were attacked. You need to take it seriously."

The words burst out of Rory. Zeke knew he had been

barely keeping it together since they had left the mall. His anger wasn't truly for Maura. Just like Zeke, Rory felt helpless, and for both of them, it was beyond what they wanted to handle.

She frowned. "I know the attack is serious. And I might be collateral damage, but not for that. He specifically mentioned you two. Not Conner, who I would think he would mention first before Zeke because he's my brother."

"That makes sense. I take it the relationship you are in hasn't been a long standing one?" Carino asked.

"What?" Maura asked apparently stunned by Carino's blunt question.

"The three of you. You haven't been together long have you?"

She shook her head. "Rory and Zeke have been though. They've known each other for years."

Before Carino could say anything else, the door swung open, hitting Rory in the back. He turned, ready to pounce on the intruder, but since it was Conner, he backed down.

Conner rushed to her side. "What the hell happened?"

"Way to show the great bedside manner, Con," Jillian said. She wasn't smiling though. Her face was unusually serious. "How you doing, kid?"

She sat on the bed next to Maura.

"I would be fine if everyone would listen to me."

"I knew something with the Peterson case would come back to bite us in the ass," Conner said.

"I don't think it was a good idea to come here. We should have stayed in Miami," Zeke said.

Conner shook his head. "I'm not sure it would matter."

"Will you idiots listen to me? This was not anyone related to a Mexican drug lord. This was plain and simple an Irishman."

Conner looked at the two of them. Zeke shrugged and Rory did nothing. "Explain."

Even though it was the same word and attitude from earlier from Carino, Rory didn't rise to the bait, thank god. They didn't need to deal with this and Conner finding out what was going on with the three of them.

"He had an Irish accent."

"You said at first it wasn't. It was American," Zeke said.

"Then later it was Irish. After he got hurt."

"How did that happen?" Conner asked.

"I kicked him in the shins then head butted him."

"Good girl," he said and kissed her bandaged forehead.

"Maura, can you be sure? You have a slight concussion according to the doctor. You might have thought you heard it because you've been spending so much time with us."

"I know what I heard. He was Irish." She stuck her lip out, but it wasn't a pout. This was stubborn Maura.

"Where are your glasses?"

She blew out an irritated breath. "They were broken in the attack."

"Well, Zeke can bring them by the house. You're staying with us for the rest of your time here."

"The hell she is," Rory said. Zeke rolled his eyes and knew now there would be no way of avoiding Conner finding out. It didn't really matter. They were going to have to face it at some point.

"What?"

"I said she's staying with us," Rory said, his voice turning dangerously soft.

"You didn't do a great job watching her before. I think I would do a better job."

"Quit talking about me as if I'm an idiot. I can take care of myself."

"The hell you can," both Rory and Conner said at the same time.

"I might want to remind you that the man was dragging me out of the mall and I got away. I didn't need any help."

"You were attacked. You should have been more aware of the situation."

She opened her mouth but Carino stepped in. "Looking at the scene through pictures, I would say that Maura did everything she should have done. I doubt any of us would have been aware of what the guy was up to. He turned off the lights."

"Yes, it was much darker when I stepped out of the bathroom." Maura's voice turned smug.

"That doesn't mean that you should not be particularly careful. If this trial has something to do with it, you need more protection."

Conner glanced at Zeke. "I think she should come home with us."

"No bloody way," Rory said, grounding out every word.

Conner looked from Rory to Zeke then back to Rory. Zeke knew the moment Conner realized what was going on. His eyes turned cold, colder than he had ever seen his friend turn.

"We will talk about this."

Zeke nodded.

"I need to call a few friends of mine and my wife's to see if she knows what's going on with this Peterson thing," the detective said.

Conner turned his attention away from Zeke to focus on Carino. "I'll help. I have a few connections still and I'll have Jennifer call around too. She just left and she had ties to the Secret Service through a family member. She might be able to find out just where they are in the negotiations. I know they were trying their best to get him to turn state's evidence."

Before anyone could say anything else, the doctor stepped in. "Well, this room is just a little too crowded. Everyone out."

Conner opened his mouth at the same time that Rory and Zeke did, but Maura stopped them. "Do you mind if my friend Jillian stays here?"

The doctor smiled. "Of course not. That means all the men need to hit the road."

Zeke wanted to kiss her but from the look on Conner's face he thought it would be best that he didn't. They filed out into the hall.

"As I said, we'll talk about it," Conner said.

Rory stepped in. "Not that it is any your blood fucking business, but if you discuss this, I want to be there when it happens."

Conner's phone rang. "Jennifer calling me back."

Zeke watched him walk down the hall to speak.

"Do you think he's going to cause us problems?" Rory asked.

"He'll try. He's always been too protective when it comes to Maura."

"No more dizziness?" Doctor Akako asked.

"Nope, just tired. I know that's from some of the pain meds."

She nodded. "You won't be alone tonight?"

Jillian snorted but said nothing thankfully.

"No."

"I figured those two Alphas who shot me threatening looks every time you drew in a breath would be hanging around for awhile."

"When can I travel?" Maura asked. She wanted to leave, to get away from there.

She ignored Jillian's stare. Maura had decided during all of the mess that she wanted to go back to Miami as soon as possible.

"I would say at least a few days. You should spend most of your time resting. Traveling would not be good."

"We have a company jet with a bed. I can sleep my way back to Miami."

The doctor sighed. "Okay, but maybe wait a day."

She nodded.

"I'm going to get the nurse to get the paperwork ready for you."

When they were left alone, Maura said, "Stop staring at me and being quiet. You're freaking me out."

"You sure you're okay?"

"Yeah. It hurts, but I think I gave him a few nice bruises too."

"The guys were a mess when they called. I'm surprised it took Conner this long to figure it out, but then he was holding out hope that you were still a virgin."

Maura smiled then winced.

"Oh, sorry," Jillian said.

"How pissed do you think he's going to be?"

Maura didn't have to say who she was talking about.

"It's hard, hun. He sees you like a father would and knowing that you are having some hot freaky sex with two men is going to be hard for him to take. He still sees you as the teenager he raised."

She nodded.

"You're not having any issues here?"

Maura looked up and around the room. Jillian was the only person who really understood the way she felt about hospitals. She hadn't had a true panic attack for years. "I'm doing okay. I think because I was out of it when I came in I didn't freak out. Plus, I've been concentrating on getting those two Neanderthals to listen to me. Why does everyone think this is Peterson? They don't know where we are. We aren't even mentioned in anything in the case, mainly because the FBI didn't want to drag us into it."

Jillian laughed. "Oh, honey, they did. Your brother threatened a few people to make sure that none of you were. I have a feeling he has some dirt on some people at Quantico and he made sure they knew it would come to light if they ever pulled you into the case."

She sighed. "I have to admit, when he does stuff like that, I love him. Now my personal life, I have a feeling this is not going to go over well."

"He'll live with it. He doesn't want to see you get hurt. I don't want to see you get hurt."

"I'm not sure that's possible."

"Maura, have you talked about what's going to happen when you get back?"

She shook her head. "I think we're all afraid to talk about it. We need to and I was going to push for a discussion but now...I just want to go home."

"Conner's going to want to keep you here."

"Well, fat lot of good that did me."

Jillian smiled. "You will call me. Don't hide in the house and pretend nothing is wrong."

One of the best and worst things about having your best friend as your sister-in-law is that she knew Maura too well.

"No. I promise. I don't think this is Peterson. Even if it were, coming here apparently did not help one bit. They found me—whoever it is. I want to go back to familiar surroundings."

The door opened and Conner stepped inside. His face was pale, his eyes cold. Zeke and Rory followed. They didn't look much better.

"We have a problem," Conner said.

At first, she thought it was her relationship with the guys but apparently not. "What?"

"Peterson has disappeared and the FBI doesn't know where he is."

"Didn't they have protection on him?" Jillian asked as she stood up.

"They were trying to back him into a corner and since he would not turn on his former bosses, they left him out to dry. They had a car on his house, but sometime during the night, he disappeared."

"You mean they think the Mafia got a hold of him?"

"That's not the really bad news."

"Dammit, Conner just tell me."

"The name of the company, your name in particular, came up in some documents."

She frowned. "Documents?"

"Bloody hell, this is painful," Rory said as he stepped forward. His expression softened as he took her hand. "Love, there were some transcripts of bugged phone conversations. Peterson mentioned you to his lawyer more than once."

"Yes. He told his lawyer it was you that brought the FBI in," Zeke said.

"What? How did they find that out? There's the confidentiality thing with the lawyer. That's against the law."

"Not when the lawyer is on the take," her brother said, his expression turning even darker. "They arrested him a day ago."

"What are you saying?" Jillian asked.

"Maura might have a hit out against her because the FBI is planning on bringing her in to testify."

"I want to go home."

"We'll get you out of here as soon as we can, love," Zeke said as he sat on the bed next to her hip.

"No. I want to go back to Miami."

He shared a look with Conner. "It might be better to stay here."

"Fat lot of good that did me. No. I want to be home."

She needed her house, the one she felt secure within. Conner opened his mouth to argue but Jillian shook her head. Thank God her best friend at least understood.

"We can wait until tomorrow, but I want to go home, be in my house. The doctor said since I had a private jet where I could recline she was okay with it." She looked at Rory and Zeke. "You can stay if you want, but I'm going home."

forty

By the time they got Maura settled in her bedroom, Rory was sure Conner was ready to kill them all. There was no doubt her brother had picked up on the relationship they all shared. He had never thought to keep it private. He had only done that because Maura had wanted him to.

Jillian had stayed by Maura's bedside probably because she didn't want to see the argument.

He walked into the home office of the house and settled on the seat behind the desk.

"So you want to tell me what was going on?" Conner asked.

"What do you mean?" Zeke asked.

"Oh, for fuck's sake, Zee, he wants to know about the three of us."

Conner glanced at him then back at Zee. "You're my best friend, Zeke. I wasn't really happy when you were together, but this crosses the line."

"I don't think you have a say in the matter," Rory said. His temper was starting to boil, but he didn't want to come to blows with Conner. It would make him feel a hell of a lot

260

better, but he didn't want a disturbance in the house. Maura needed rest.

"I think I do. I'm her brother."

"And we're her lovers," Zee said quietly. He was angry. Rory knew his lover well enough to see the anger in his eyes. And the hurt. Rory knew that Zee thought Conner thought he wasn't good enough for Maura. It had nothing to do with Zee or even Rory. Conner would never think a man was good enough for his baby sister.

"She's not equipped to handle a relationship like this."

"What the fuck does that mean?" Rory asked.

"She's too naive. She doesn't understand what all this means."

He looked at Zee who rolled his eyes.

"I think you still see her as a fifteen-year-old. She's not. She's a grown woman and we left the decision up to her," Rory said. "What you don't like is your sister likes the arrangement."

Conner made a face and Rory felt a little sorry for him. He didn't have any sisters, but he was pretty sure he would beat the living crap out of a man saying that about his sister. Conner had more restraint than Rory would have. Of course, he wasn't going to test it, because there was a good chance Conner was ready to lose it.

"That doesn't matter. She is not sophisticated enough--"

"Stop right there," Zee warned. "She is an adult, one who was given the choice. We didn't pressure her. Your sister might not have had a lot of relationships when she was younger, but she is hardly some wide-eyed virgin. We suggested it and we gave her the choice."

"And if I say I want to buy you out and send you on your way?"

"Then I guess that's the end of the business relationship."

A beat of silence filled the room. Conner looked stunned

but he recovered fast enough. "Shit. You're going to make me accept his, aren't you?"

"Gentleman," Jillian said. They all looked toward the doorway where Jillian stood. Rory wondered how long she had been standing there.

"I think you might want another opinion on the situation."

"How is my sister?"

Her expression softened a bit. "She's fine. She's sleeping right now. And thankfully she missed all this crap."

"Crap?" Conner asked.

"Yes, crap. Lord, you're having a discussion about her as if you have something to say about it."

"I'm looking out for her interests here."

"By dissolving a partnership with your best friend because he loves her."

Zee looked surprised which in turn surprised Rory. Did Zee realize the way he looked at the woman?

"Yes, I've known since the first time I talked to you that first time you were in love with her. It probably makes it easier that Rory is too."

All their gazes swung his way and Rory felt his throat tighten. He had never said he loved the woman, and he wasn't in love with her. Not really. Okay, maybe a little, but he would be damned if he talked about it in front of her brother and his wife. Or anyone for that matter.

"What does that have to do with anything?" he asked. The knowing look Jillian sent him made him want to growl, but he couldn't blame her. Even he heard his defensive tone.

"None of this matters." Conner crossed his arms over his chest and stared both Zee and Rory down. It didn't scare him much, even at all. In a fight, they were about even, but he had Zee on his side.

"Love doesn't matter. Conner Dillon, you want to sleep outside tonight?"

He glanced at her and saw what few probably would ever see. A Dom going soft. Of course, he understood. When a Dom was in love, he would do anything to please his partner. And that is exactly how he felt about Maura.

He waited for panic. Rory had always tried his best to side step love, but Zee had made him think that maybe he was actually capable of love. Adding Maura to the mix had been a way of controlling the situation. But in the process, he had fallen in love. Shit. This was not supposed to happen. He should have seen it coming. He had been attracted to her since they met but there was something else. Something that tugged at his heart just as much as it tugged at his—

"Wake up, Rory," Jillian said. He pulled himself out of his haze to focus on her. Her lips curved in smug smile. "Off in dreamland?"

"This is all well and good, but I think that you need to decide if you want me as your partner still," Zee said.

Rory looked at the man he had loved most of his life. Sure, Zee sounded pissed, but he knew he was hurting. He and Conner went back a long way. Not a lot of people in their business would accept him for who he was. Conner always had.

Jillian threw her hands up. "Lord, grant me patience. Y'all are acting worse than my family. Listen, you're pissed right now Conner—for no good reason. Did you tell your sister all the things you did? Or we do? I mean, that whole honeymoon surprise was probably not something you would personally want her to know about."

"Now, Jillian—"

She ignored him and turned her attention to both he and Zee. "I'm not sure y'all know where this is headed. But, you need to establish something soon because you're going back to

Miami, and I have a feeling Maura found a lot of things she now likes."

Rory couldn't help but smile. Jillian shook her head.

"Don't be going all Alpha on me. Unless you want her joining a club back there and exploring it more with someone else, I would suggest you start figuring it out. She might wait around for you to pull your heads out of your asses but she won't wait long."

That had his smile dissolving. "Point taken."

She nodded. "I brought my laptop and we have a change of clothes so we can stay the night."

"We do?" Conner asked.

"Yes. The only way I will let you stay is if you promise not to give either men, or your sister, crap tonight. And if they all want to go up in that bedroom to be near her, you will allow it."

For a second, Rory was sure Conner would refute her. There was no doubt the former FBI agent was a Dom. The fact that he allowed her to order him around was something Rory didn't think he would see.

Conner nodded. "If that's what she wants."

She snorted. "Oh, I'm pretty sure she does. The stuff is in the car. You can get it now."

Conner hesitated then stepped forward. He kissed her then whispered something in her ear that had Jillian smiling.

"You go ahead and try that, big boy."

"You can bet on it."

When they were finally alone, Jillian's smile dimmed and she crossed her arms over her breasts. Now she didn't look like the loving wife of a Dom who knew how to keep her in line—at least in the bedroom. This woman was ready to kick some ass. Mainly theirs.

"Now, you guys need to take care of her. Conner will try and drag me back to Miami if he thinks you aren't up to the task, or she isn't comfortable with y'all. I hate the mainland. Mainly because my family lives on the mainland, but also because it involves disrupting my work schedule. I am an author and the world revolves around me and my work, so I will become your worst nightmare if I end up back there dealing with that crap. Understood?"

They both nodded. "Good. Now I am going to go find one of the guest rooms and get ready to write. I have a scene I need to get done and I don't have any more patience to calm male egos."

With that, she turned and left them alone.

"She's kind of scary," Zee said.

Rory laughed. "Yeah she is, but now I know how she can put up with Conner."

Zee sighed. "I guess we should go check on her. You don't think we're wrong on this do you?"

"On our relationship?"

Zee rolled his eyes. "No, on the attack. Maura seems very adamant that it was someone else outside of the Petersen case."

"You know when you're scared the adrenaline is pumping through you that you can mistake things. The voice could have been anything and she could have heard Irish."

"We'll need to make some calls, check out things in our past just in case," Zee said.

"Okay. And we agree. We don't let her out of our sight."

Even if she doesn't like it.

forty-one

In the ten days since they returned from Hawaii, Maura had yet to talk about the attack. It worried Zeke on so many different levels. Worse, she was barely talking to anyone. She was talking at them, but not to them. And she had cut off Rory and him. Rory was off licking his wounds being an ass and Zeke was left to try and piece it all together.

His phone buzzed and he rolled his eyes when he saw the 808 area code.

"Yes, Conner?"

"Wrong, this is Jillian."

"Oh, sorry, Jillian. How are things going there?"

"Well, living with a grizzly has been so much fun the last few days. How's our girl?"

"Our?"

"I guess I should say your, but she never mentions you when I call. In fact, she never talks at all."

"That's the problem. She's not talking to anyone."

There was a pause. "That's not good with most people but it is a disaster with Maura." She sighed. "Maybe we should make a trip."

That bothered him. Conner was barely talking to him except about business and to check up on Maura. Other than that, they weren't talking at all.

"I don't know if that would help or shut her down more."

"Hmm, that's true. Have you talked to her about the attack?"

"Yes. Well, I tried. She refuses to accept that this might have anything to do with the Columbians and the Petersen trial."

"And Conner said they can't find anything on that. Even Jennifer can't get an answer from anyone. It's odd how that has all shut down."

"So, the last time we talked about it was two days ago and now she refuses to discuss it."

That was the nicest way of saying it. She had screamed at them. He didn't know how to deal with that. She didn't do things like that, and she didn't just walk away and ignore people she cared about.

"Have you and Rory looked into anything else. I know the mule I live with isn't ready to do that, but have you guys found anything?"

"No, because nothing else makes sense. Rory and I have a past, but our past transgressions are mostly dead and the rest are in prison."

"Are you sure?"

"Yes. The guys we put away got life sentences."

She waited a beat. "So, how are you doing?"

The concern in her voice touched him. He didn't know her that well, but what little contact he'd had with her had told Zeke that she was a caring woman. She let everyone think that she was a ball breaker but when she cared about someone, she was very giving.

"I'm doing okay."

"Oh, it doesn't sound like it. I take it that Rory and Maura have stuck you in the middle."

He chuckled. "That's not hard to figure out with those two. They have a do or die kind of attitude."

"So, tell Auntie Jillian all about it."

"Nothing much to tell. We got back to Miami, Maura shut us off, and Rory shut down. That's where I am right now. I think she might need some counseling."

"I have to agree with you there. And she has a therapist she can call."

"Maura has a therapist?" He was stunned. She had never mentioned it to him. He had been pretty damned close to her the last few years and she never mentioned it.

"Oh, I thought you know. She keeps up with the therapist she had after the accident."

"Since I didn't know about the therapist to begin with, I guess I would have no idea if she was talking to him."

"Her. And don't get your feelings hurt, Zeke. She doesn't tell a lot of people."

"Including those she's apparently just fucking for fun."

The silence on the other side of the phone had him closing his eyes. Dammit, he didn't mean to yell at her. Jillian wasn't the person he was mad at. Hell, he didn't know who he was mad at.

"Oh, sweetie, don't be so hurt by it. She's so private and it has more to do with impressing you than keeping you out."

He opened his eyes and looked out of the apartment window. Usually the view of the Atlantic would calm him, soothe him. But, today, there was nothing. The two people he loved in the world were starting to come apart.

"What do you mean?"

"Maura has always tried to pretend that nothing is ever wrong. I have no idea why. Conner said one time that it wasn't this bad until his folks died. Then, she became overly worried about perception."

"She spent a week with…"

Jillian laughed. "Yeah, but that's different. Sex is healthy and she understands that. If she admits she has a therapist though, she thinks it shows her weakness."

"For being human?"

"Yeah. I don't know what their parents were like, but you've worked with Conner. Is there anyone with a more disgusting work ethic?"

"You?"

"Pfft. Not me. He had strep a few weeks back and was trying to go into work. That's just insane. Me, I know when to take a break. The Dillon's…they don't. They're kind of freaks about it. And one of the things is that they can never admit they are weak. Talking to someone about nightmares or the fact you think someone is following you--"

"What do you mean?"

"Maura said she felt as if someone was following her. She's had that feeling the last few days."

"She said the same thing in Hawaii."

"You all are following her, right?"

"We've been taking her to and from work."

"That's good."

"So, I shouldn't worry?"

"No, you should. You love her and she is shutting down. But it might be that she needs a few more days to deal with it. The most important thing you can do is be there when she falls."

He heard the door crash open and closed his eyes. Rory was home and Zeke wasn't in the mood for him.

"I've got to go."

"Remember, Zeke, take care of yourself. Those two are a lot of work."

"Thanks, Jillian."

He turned his phone off just as Rory sauntered into the bedroom.

He was a fucking mess. He had been out riding on the bike. He hadn't shaved today, but for Zeke that made him even sexier. Being so fucking drunk he could barely stand up sort of took the sexiness out of it though.

"Hey, lover," he slurred.

"So, you've decided to drink again."

"I can do what I want."

He looked at him and his heart wept. Rory avoided alcohol and drugs. He hated it for the most part. Except when things went bad. He was hurting, thinking he'd been rejected by Maura. For a man whose mother committed suicide leaving him with his bastard father, rejection and abandonment issues were always there ready to fuck things up.

Rory pulled his shirt off and threw it on the floor behind him.

"And apparently, that means being disgusting."

"It's just a shirt on the floor." Then he burped. Zeke would have laughed if he didn't know just how much Rory hated this. He wasn't someone who willingly would get drunk.

"So, you've decided to become an alcoholic?"

Zeke said, crossing his arms over his chest. He was trying his best not to reach out for him. Zeke knew that he would just reject him, and that would hurt too much.

"I'm not an alcoholic."

"You're on your way. Three nights, three drunken nights, Rory. That's an alcoholic."

"I am not an alcoholic. I'm just blowing off some steam."

Hearing those words tore away any patience Zeke had.

"Isn't that the phrase your father used all the time?"

"Watch it, Zeke."

He ignored the warning.

"Tell me, did he say that before or after he beat you?"

"I said to fucking watch your fucking mouth."

But he didn't care. He couldn't see Rory do this to him. He had a lot of other issues but drinking had been one thing he had never engaged in. He hated the loss of control, and he didn't trust himself.

"So, you've just decided to drink yourself to death like your father."

He jumped up from the bed and grabbed his shirt. "I don't have to stay here for this."

He pulled the shirt on.

"No, run just like your father. A coward unable to accept the fact that he was a bastard. Jesus, I can understand why your mother did it."

Rory turned and faced him, anger lighting his face but Zeke was past being nice.

"What the fucking hell do you mean by that?"

"Your father was a drunkard coward, petty criminal who couldn't keep it in his pants. Not unlike you, but at least he married your mother so apparently he had some decency in him. Can you imagine the embarrassment she felt being married to him? A drunk. A man who couldn't keep a job. Then, raising a son in his spitting image, some fucker who couldn't even make it through school. Jesus, no wonder she committed suicide."

He was so gone in his diatribe he didn't see the punch coming in time to avoid it. He had enough time to move a bit and Rory's first connected to his jaw.

They tumbled down onto the ground, cursing and screaming at each other. He got a good hit into Rory's nose, but he felt a few jabs to his ribs. Rory was drunk and not able to fight that well. It only took him a few moments to pin his hands down and dominate him.

They were both breathing heavily. On any other day, this would be sexy. Now, he wanted to throw up.

"Get a hold of yourself."

The dangerous look he was leveling at Zeke didn't deter him. He straddled him then took him by the shoulders and shook him.

"You can't do this. I can't watch you do it."

Something he said must have hit Rory. The anger on his face slowly dissolved.

"Oh, babe, I'm sorry."

He blinked. "What?"

"I'm sorry."

"You're sorry?"

"Yes." He studied him. "What?"

"I mean this is momentous. Rory McAllister just said he was sorry. This is close to admitting you were wrong."

Rory toppled Zeke over and switched positions, clasping his hands above his head.

"You're such a bleeding smart ass."

He chuckled then sighed as Rory kissed him. It was the first real physical contact he'd had since they'd returned. They had slept in the same bed every night, but not once had they reached out for each other. He reveled in the kiss.

Rory kissed his way down Zeke's body, grasping his shirt and tearing it open. Buttons flew everywhere, but Zeke ignored it. All that mattered was Rory's mouth on his skin and the way his tongue slid against him as he moved down his body. He pulled Zeke's pants off and took his cock in his hand and then into his mouth. Zeke spread his hands into his hair. He knew this wasn't the answer, but right now, he needed the connection, the primal instinct of connecting with one of his mates.

He thrust up into Rory's mouth, over and over again. Finally, Rory pulled back and tore at his own jeans. Zeke sat up and grabbed the waistband and yanked the buttons lose. Rory's cock thrust out into Zeke's greedy hands. He pumped him, fast and furious. The edge he'd been feeling, the need to connect drove him. It was frantic and overwhelming.

Rory groaned and pulled back, turning around, he straddled Zeke's head upside down. Zeke took Rory's cock into his mouth willingly. Rory groaned and did the same to Zeke. Both of them were so close it didn't take but a few strokes and they were both coming, their ecstasy overtaking both of them as they gave themselves over to the joy of their primal connection.

LATER, THEY LAY IN BED AND RORY SIGHED. HE HURT Zeke in so many ways over the years, he couldn't really fault his lover for what he said.

"Love, it's okay. I...deserve it."

Zee shook his head. "No, no one deserves that."

"I do a little. I just...I hate seeing her that way."

Zee studied him for a second, then said, "Love sometimes hurts."

"I didn't say I loved her."

"Jesus, there is no one here but us. Admit it."

"I...okay, I sort of love her."

Zee chuckled. "I guess we can take that for now."

He settled his head on Rory's chest and snuggled closer. "So what do we do?"

"We can't do anything right now. She's in pain and she's hurt. Yelling at Maura will not work."

"You yelled at me and it worked."

"You're an asshole, she's not."

Rory couldn't argue with that. "So we just wait?"

"She needs some time."

"How much?"

Zee looked up at him a small smile playing over his lips. "Not sure, but we have to be there when she figures it out."

"What if she doesn't figure it out?"

"Then we yell at her."

Rory smiled. "That, I can do."

"You have to understand that Maura was not raised to confront and that is part of her personality. Well, she does confront, but not in the way other people do. She thinks things through, then goes for what she wants. She doesn't do much without thinking it through."

"And so we wait."

"For a little while."

The phone rang and Rory saw the number. "Shit, probably Conner."

Zee picked it up. "Hey, Conner. Yeah. I was busy, that's why I didn't answer my phone. What? Oh, so...the threat is over?"

"Okay."

He hung up.

"Well that was short and I am assuming not so sweet."

Zee clicked the phone off. "Yeah. Well, apparently Conner found out that Petersen's been taken into witness protection."

"He found that out?"

"Officially, he seems to have been killed in an accident, but Conner still has a few connections. He's turned state's evidence. They got some little nobody to turn on the big guy. We're no longer in danger. So, that's that."

"You think he called Maura?"

"Yeah. Probably before us."

"You should call her still."

He glanced at Rory. "Why don't you?"

"She needs you more."

He frowned. "That's an asinine thing to say. She needs both of us. She's being stubborn, which is nothing new. As Jillian pointed out, she hates anyone to know that she is weak."

Rory said nothing to that, just stared up at the ceiling.

"I talked to her before you got home."

"Maura?"

"No, Jillian. Apparently, Maura's been seeing a shrink."

Rory glanced at him, then back up at the ceiling. "She is?"

"Yeah, I didn't know. She talks to her all the time, apparently."

Another beat of silence.

"She hides things from a lot of people, Rory, not just you."

"She's not hiding. She's just not there, Zee. I don't know how to deal with that."

It hurt to say the words—worse than the gunshot wound he took in the chest a few years earlier.

"You have to give her space, but I guess we should call her."

Neither of them moved.

"You do it, Rory."

He glanced at Zee. "Why me?"

"Because, she will expect me to. If you call, it might surprise her a little."

He got up out of bed and searched for his jeans. He hit the contact icon for Maura and waited for her to answer.

"Hey, Rory."

"I guess you talked to your brother."

She sighed. "Yes, but then I never thought it was all that important. Petersen wasn't involved."

He wanted to argue but he didn't. She retreated completely when he confronted her.

"So, I guess we don't need the detail anymore," she said.

Something told him he should just do it, to ease her mind, but with Maura, Zee had told him being up front and truthful went a longer way than any pretty words.

"Yeah, I guess not. You still have that kick ass security system."

She said nothing.

"Maura--"

"Look, I have some work here to do."

"Okay. I'll talk to you tomorrow."

"Sure," she said and hung up. He turned off his phone and looked at Zee. "She's not happy."

"You got to see Maura at her best, but I've told you, love, life isn't about just being happy. You have to make it through those tough times to appreciate the good times."

"And when do the good times come back?" Rory asked. The moment he said the words, he wanted to call them back. Even with Zee he hated showing his vulnerability—especially when it came to Maura.

Zee held out his hand and waited for Rory to take it and join him back in bed. He pulled him close and Rory settled his head against Zee's shoulder.

"I'm not sure, love, but I hope not long," Zee said.

Rory just prayed Zee's wishes became reality. He wasn't sure just how much he take.

"I love you, Zee."

"I love you too."

But now the love seemed incomplete...as if something was missing. Something was—or he should say someone. They needed Maura, because Rory wasn't sure how long Zee and he would last without her.

forty-two

Maura gripped the wheel tighter as she drove home. Maybe the guys were right. Maybe she was imagining things. But something was wrong. *Really wrong*. Could be that she hadn't had a good night's sleep since the attack. The only time she had slept had been the few nights Rory and Zeke had stayed over.

She was not about to admit that though. She thought they might be one step away from calling her brother to commit her.

She pulled off the highway and rolled to a stop at the light.

Why did men always think women were hysterical? They all seemed to have thought she lost her mind in some way. She hadn't, she knew that without a doubt. But, they all seemed to think she did. She rubbed her temples trying to will away the perpetual headache that seemed to follow her everywhere these days.

Someone honked behind her and she took off. Damn, she was tired. She needed a long night's sleep, and maybe tonight she would just take some of the meds they gave her. She had abstained from the heavier pain relievers because she was afraid to sleep too deeply.

277

Maura took a right turn and for once, noticed the car behind her followed her. She blew out a breath and ordered herself to calm down. So, the person behind her took the same turn. That happened every day all the time. It wasn't something new.

Did the bastard need to get so close to her? She slowed down a bit, hoping the guy would pass her. The road was dark and deserted. Why had she waited until late to go home. Instead of passing her though, the car slowed down so much he was almost a spec in the distance.

She was going crazy. Her brother and the guys were right. But before she could follow that line of thinking, brights flashed in her rearview mirror. She looked up and the car was coming so fast behind Maura was sure it would hit her. She couldn't get out of the way fast enough. She jolted from the hit, and worked the wheel like her brother told her, turning into the way the car was spinning to even it out. He was coming at her again, when she saw another car coming in the opposite direction. She turned down the street she knew would lead her to the local police precinct. Her bother had always told her if she were being followed to go to the closet police station or military base. She floored it, breaking the speed limit and getting as much space between the bastard and her as she could. She turned down the next street and sighed when she saw the police building. She sped into the parking lot, paying no attention if the car followed her or not.

forty-three

Zeke slammed the door of his truck and stalked to the front door of the police station. Rory wasn't far behind him.

"You go in there looking like that and she's going to be pissed," Rory said.

"She's already going to be pissed. If Frank hadn't rung me up, then I would have never known."

And damn her for not calling them...him. He had been her friend all these years and now she acted like she didn't want to have anything to do with either one of them. She was in danger and she went to the police. She didn't call them. He knew that she was trying to keep her distance now that they returned, but Zeke was sure she was trying to hurt him by not calling him.

He continued stalking. He couldn't help it. He was fucking pissed...and hurt, but he would deal with that later.

He saw her in the conference room and headed in that direction. Before he could make it there though, Frank stepped in front of him.

"Hey, man, calm down. She's fine."

He looked at him. "What kind of damage was done to the car?"

He sighed. "Not much and seriously, I hate to say this about your woman, man, but I think she might be delusional. She thinks there's someone after her."

"There is."

His eyebrows shot up. "Oh, well..."

"We broke the Petersen case."

"Oh, she mentioned that, but she thinks it is someone else. Someone who is after her personally. She said she was attacked in Hawaii."

"She was. But, we're convinced it had something to do with the government's case."

"Ah. And she had a concussion?"

"Yeah."

"She's not mental if that's what you're thinking," Rory said.

"Hey, buddy, I was only saying that sometimes an injury like that takes some time to recover. Her fender is dented though."

"Can we see her?"

"Sure, she's not in trouble. She was really shaken up though and I didn't want her going home alone. Dillon would never forgive me and believe me, that is one guy I don't want on my bad side."

Zeke said nothing as he turned and walked to the door. Rory followed after thanking Frank. Before he could open the door, Rory caught up with him.

"Now, babe, keep your voice calm. Maura reacts to your anger in a totally different way."

He glanced at Rory. "Yeah, what way is that?"

"She sees it as a challenge. Or something like that."

"Okay, I will remain calm."

He opened the door and his heart melted. She'd laid her

head down on the table and she had her eyes closed. She was so damned tired. It was easy to see from the dark smudges under her eyes. She was pale too. In less than a week, she had seemed to lose the tan she had gained from her beach time in Hawaii. And that pissed him off.

"What the bloody hell, Maura? You didn't call us?"

She jolted awake. She blinked a couple of times, her gaze focused on the two of them.

"What are you doing here?"

"Frank called us," Zeke said, his voice vibrating with anger. He couldn't seem to keep it completely beneath the surface.

She looked past them with a glare.

"Office Duggan, I expected better."

The fifteen-year veteran flushed. Maura could make most men feel like naughty boys when she was disappointed in them. "Ms. Dillon, I couldn't release you after you said you had a concussion less than two weeks ago. Especially since you refused to go to the hospital."

"I can fix that," Zeke said. He stepped forward to grab her arm but she jerked away from him. It felt like a fucking knife to his heart.

Before he could just haul her over his shoulder, Rory stepped between them.

"Hey, why don't I take Maura home and you follow."

Zeke hesitated. Rory didn't always offer to do things like this. Hysterical women were not his thing; although, looking at the woman who was glaring at him at the moment he probably wouldn't put her in the hysterical category.

"Okay."

She had her arms crossed over her chest and she wasn't budging. He could tell from the stubborn set of her chin and the mutinous look in her eyes.

"I can take myself home."

"You can. And I can call Conner and talk to him about it. He might just pull out of active status and put you on...well, I guess you could call it house arrest."

He knew she was smart enough to know it wasn't a good thing for her to drive right now. Zeke also knew she needed an excuse to follow his orders. Threatening her with Conner was the only way to get her up out of that seat and into the car. Truth was, Zeke would do it in a heartbeat and he wasn't too sure he wouldn't do it now. Conner would be pissed if he found out what happened from someone else, so he would probably call his friend—even if he weren't really talking to him.

"Fine."

She stood up and marched out of the room and through the crowded outer office. Rory gave him a grim smile and followed her.

"I hope Ms. Dillon isn't too mad at me," Duggan said.

He shook his head. "No problem. She'll get over it. She's not been herself since the attack in Hawaii. Once they clear all this Petersen shit up, she'll settle."

forty-four

The car ride back to Maura's house was silent. Not the comfortable silence between two lovers, Rory thought. No, this one was heavy on the tension and it had been that way since they returned from Hawaii.

"I was not imagining it. There is someone stalking me."

"I didn't say there wasn't," he responded calmly.

More silence. He wasn't sure there was someone, but wasn't about to admit that to her. He knew just how badly the mind could play tricks on you after something like what happened in Hawaii.

Rory glanced over at her. She was staring out the window, slumped in the seat. She had dark circles under her eyes.

"We're going to put someone on you. I don't like the idea of you riding around out there if this truly is a stalker."

She said nothing to that and he noticed she had closed her eyes.

"Maura?"

"Please, don't patronize me." She opened her eyes and the back of his throat tickled a bit when he saw they were watery.

283

Damn, he hated when women cried. "I am not an idiot. I know people think I am stupid."

"We don't think you're stupid."

She sniffed at that and looked back out the window. "Sure."

He stopped at a red light. "I'm serious."

"Sure."

"No, I believe you. There is someone messing with you. But, in my mind, I think it is probably someone with Petersen."

"It has nothing to do with that. I told you in Hawaii the guy had an Irish accent."

He pulled up to her driveway and punched in the code. The gate opened. He drove through and parked the car before he spoke.

"Maura, we checked. Anyone who would be after us is either dead or in prison." Most of them were dead but he wasn't going to admit that to her. Zeke and Rory didn't leave behind many people when they were hunting terrorists. It had been one of the reasons they had been paid so well by the British government.

"What?"

"We called around. We talked to everyone. All of our cases are accounted for. No one should be after us. Most of them wouldn't have had the means to do it by the time they got out anyway. And, just so you know, most of those people didn't know our names."

She stared at him for a second, and said, "Are you sure?"

"Yes. We called all our contacts, all the officials. No one with a grudge for one of us is running around out there."

"How can you be so sure?"

He sighed. The strain he heard in her voice was disheartening, and he knew she was near a breaking point. Zeke and he agreed on one thing, they wanted her to get some rest. They knew part of this was the fact she hadn't slept since their return.

"Zee and I didn't leave a lot of witnesses, and most people don't know our names."

She said nothing for a moment as if she was digesting the information. The door opened beside her and Zee was standing there. She gave him a nasty look but took his hand as he walked her to the door.

"We're going to put a car on you."

She said nothing as she pulled the keys out of her purse. They entered the house and Rory followed, knowing that Zee wasn't going to go home tonight. Neither of them would. They were not about to let the woman stay home tonight by herself.

"Why don't you take a bath?" Zee offered as they walked into the kitchen.

"Something to quiet the crazy woman?" Her tone had an edge to it and it was getting sharper by the minute.

Rory glanced at Zee. They were both worried about her. From the time she had been attacked she wouldn't accept their comfort. It twisted something deep in his gut.

"No, but you've had a scare and I think a hot bath might relax you. I can get you a glass of wine."

She looked at them both, then nodded.

"Go on, get the water going and I'll bring you a glass," Zee said.

She left them, not saying a word, not asking for comfort. They'd both offered it up the last few days, but she hadn't taken it.

"She's not taking the news that no one is after us well."

Zeke opened the refrigerator. "She needs to work it out in her head."

"I think you're not taking this seriously enough."

Zee set the wine bottle down and looked at him. "Listen, Rory, I've known her longer than you. She's had her world altered. Maura isn't accustomed with being wrong. She needs time to get herself in order. We just need to be here to support her."

Anger churned in his belly. Zee was being too laid back, too ready to let her handle things on her own. And he was being too fucking calm.

"Whether something happened today or not, she is skating a fine edge. She needs more than just a couple of blokes checking in on her. She needs to be watched."

He had seen it up close and personal. His mother had been the same way before she died...before she took that fucking gun to her head. And he would be damned if he would watch another woman he...cared for do that.

One of the bad things about having a lover as long as he had Zee, he knew all of Rory's secrets.

"She's not your mother. Your mother was—"

"Weak."

Zee sighed. "No. She was sick. She needed help and she didn't know where to go."

He said nothing to that. Rory couldn't. Fear for Maura and the memories of his mother were too overwhelming.

"How did I fall in love with two such stubborn people." When Rory continued to be quiet, Zee threw his hands up again. "I'm not going to rehash this right now. I'm going to get some soup going and then take this wine to her."

"Eating and drinking, that will help."

"Dammit, Rory, she needs someone to take care of her. You said so yourself. So, that's what we need to do."

"I think she needs professional help."

"She doesn't need professional help. You're mental if you think she does. Maura is a focused woman. She's been thrown off balance."

He wanted to argue, but who was he to say. The truth of the matter was that Zeke was the longest relationship he had ever had. Everyone else had been short term. He would take a step back like Zee suggested but he would definitely keep an eye on her.

Rory wasn't losing another woman in his life that way. He would do everything in his power to prevent it.

forty-five

Maura looked out over the water and sighed. She was smart enough to understand what she was doing to herself. Dr. Obenhaus had explained it a long time ago. Throwing herself into work avoided the issues and she got sicker by the day. But, thankfully, Dr. Obenhaus also understood that she needed time to get through it.

"Why do you think there is someone watching you, Maura?" Dr. Obenhaus asked, her calm patient voice soothing Maura.

"I don't know. It's a sense I have. I felt it again when I went to work. I thought it was because of the detail that Zeke and Rory put on me."

"So, you knew they were there and dismissed your worries."

Not really, she thought. If only she would have gotten sleep the last few days. As it was, she'd only gotten snatches of sleep since she returned from Hawaii. She avoided the pain pills the doctor there had given her.

"Maura?"

"They didn't know I knew, though."

"So, you kept it from them. Why?"

"I don't know."

"You know."

"Power."

"Yes, I am sure a lot of that has to do with the attack. It's okay as long as at some point you come back out of that shell you always build."

The bad thing about having a therapist who had known her so long was that Dr. Obenhaus knew exactly what she did wrong. But, then, it was one of the reasons she went to her.

"Are we going to talk about the men?"

"Men?"

"Tsk, tsk, tsk. You think I don't know you are involved with these men?" she asked, her voice a little lighter.

"Did Conner talk to you?"

"No, but then I would never discuss you with him. Once you turned eighteen I told you that I wouldn't tell him things. I didn't tell him much when you were younger. So, these men."

"Yeah. Hmm, well, it was just a bit of fun."

"Oh, Maura, don't worry about upsetting me. I know about going against people's wishes."

She accepted that. Dr. Obenhaus was a lesbian who had been living openly for years in Georgia.

"It's just...I can't deal with it right now."

"You love them."

"Yes. But that's not always enough."

"I agree. Just make sure you take the time to figure out if it is enough for you."

"Okay."

"So, are they good looking?"

She laughed. "Yeah, and Irish and bisexual."

"Good for you. Now, make sure to check in with me, but don't use me as a crutch. You need to talk to the people in your life, Maura."

"I will."

They hung up and she stared out over the traffic again. She didn't hear the knock at the door until the door squeaked open.

She turned and saw Zeke and Rory standing just inside the door.

"Did you need something?"

"We just wanted to check on you," Rory said surprising her.

Damn, they looked good. She wanted nothing more than to crawl into their arms and seek some kind of acceptance and love, but she couldn't. They thought she was crazy. They hadn't said it out loud but they got the same tone in their voices that Conner did. They thought she had lost her mind about the attacker.

"I'm fine."

They said nothing.

"Is that all?"

Zeke walked closer. "Maybe you should go home and get some sleep this afternoon."

She looked up from her computer screen. "What?"

"Love, you look worn out."

She frowned. "Way to make me feel good, Zeke."

"No, seriously, how much sleep have you gotten?"

She glanced at Rory who was watching her closely as if worried she would break down in tears.

"Not much. I have insomnia most of the time when I return from Hawaii."

Which was kind of true. Okay, not really, but she figured she wouldn't go to hell for a lie. Considering the things she'd done in Hawaii with these two, God would probably be more upset with that than her little white lie.

"Still, you look really tired. Why not at least work from home? It might do a little good to get out of the office."

She looked from one to the other and hurt. The pain in her

chest was worse than when she'd been attacked. Going home wasn't what she thought she would do today, but maybe a break from seeing the two men she loved but who apparently didn't love her, might be a good thing.

"Okay."

She started shutting down things.

"Maura," Rory said, his voice annoyed.

She didn't look up from her work. "What?"

"Look at me. At us."

She forced herself to do it. "What?"

"You can talk to us."

She didn't know what was behind that comment, but she couldn't deal with them. Not now. She was raw. She knew what she had agreed to when they had been on vacation, but she had fooled herself while they had been there.

"What do you want me to talk to you about?" she asked wondering if they really knew just how much this was hurting her. They had each other. She had no one.

She had walked around the desk but Rory stepped in front of her.

"Don't make me order you to answer questions."

She gave him what she hoped was a condescending look. "Don't try that with me, Rory. I don't play games out of the bedroom and you know that."

"I seemed to remember a little incident in the kitchen...and one that started in the car."

The memory of that was like a jab to the heart. She had thought they were moving on to something more than just a fling. But the guys had proven her wrong. Trust in your partners was needed for a real relationship and they and proven that they didn't believe in her.

"I'm not in the mood for this."

He opened his mouth but Zeke interrupted them.

"I think you need to get some rest, love."

She tore her attention away from Rory to look at Zeke. The pity she saw there hurt more than losing them both. Of course she had never really had them, had she?

"Yes, I do." She picked up her brief case. "I'll have my cell, but I might just take a nap first."

She hurried out of the room.

———

Zeke let the door shut with a silent snick and said nothing. He was still pissed. He was also worried. The fact that Maura had left without argument wasn't like her at all.

"What's up?" Rory asked.

"She's not acting right."

"She's tired. And I think she's still embarrassed about yesterday."

"No, you know her, she wouldn't go home without a fight before."

"Those two are crazy buggers."

"Those two?"

"Her brother and her. It makes you wonder what their Da was like."

He brushed that thought away. "Anyway, it's odd. Really odd."

"Do you think we should set another trail on her again?"

Zeke shook his head as his personal assistant beeped in.

"Sorry to bother you, Zeke, but there's an Inspector Forrest on the phone. He says he needs to talk to you ASAP."

He picked up the phone. "Jerry, I haven't heard from you in months."

"And I wish it was under better circumstances. I just found out myself or I would have called you earlier."

"What's up?" he asked dread inching down his spine.

"O'Connell escaped from Germany a month ago."

"What?"

Rory was looking at him now. Worry etched his features.

"I didn't find out about it until twenty minutes ago, but apparently, he paid off a few guards, who ended up dead in the end. The bastard was always cold. He escaped but we weren't told here at Scotland Yard. Hell, I'm not sure I'm supposed to call you, but the truth of the matter is MI-6 always fucks these things up. I know that bastard was hot to kill you and McAllister. By the by, have you talked to him?"

"He's here now."

"Good. If I were you, I would make sure that you take extra precautions."

"Sure, sure. Thanks for the call."

"No problem, you know I owe you."

He hung up and tried to get his brain wrapped around the news. O'Connell had been an IRA bomb specialist, one who went mercenary several years ago and had worked with anyone with the cash. He and his brother had been good, until Rory and Zeke had found them, killed his brother and caught up with O'Connell to arrest him. Germany had called dibs on him though for a bombing in Munich that killed twenty people. Still, he blamed Rory and him for his brother's death and for being in prison.

He had vowed to kill them both.

"Zee, what the fuck is going on?"

"O'Connell, he escaped."

"Just now?"

"No. A month ago."

He saw the recognition on Rory's face. It was O'Connell all along.

"Maura," Rory said and turned and ran out of the room. Zeke followed.

"Call her. I need to call my mother and stepda."

Jennifer stepped out of her office. "Call Conner, tell him "O'Connell". Then you lock this place the fuck down."

He got a hold of his mother and was assured everything was fine by the time they were heading toward his car.

"Okay, ma. I've got some other calls to make."

Rory started up the car with a grim expression. "Maura's not answering her phone."

"Dammit, you drive, I'll call."

Her phone rang and rang. No answer.

"She's ignoring us. Hopefully."

"Hopefully?"

"Yes. The alternative is she is separated from her phone. That never happens."

If it did, they both knew it meant trouble.

Rory sped through a red light. There were a lot of honking horns but both of them ignored that. All that mattered was getting to Maura and making sure she was okay.

MAURA'S HEAD WAS POUNDING BY THE TIME SHE GOT home. She was so damned tired she might force herself to take the stupid pills the doctor gave her for pain. But that seemed so weak.

She didn't seem to give a damn.

The men in her life were treating her as if she were going insane.

It was too bad she couldn't just curl up in a ball and sleep for three weeks. She knew the signs of depression. Dr. Obenhaus had helped her through all of that before, but one thing the doctor had taught her was sometimes...just sometimes...you needed to escape from the world you were in.

Life wasn't supposed to hurt this much, was it?

She sighed. Sitting in her hot car feeling sorry for herself wasn't going to make anything better. After grabbing her briefcase, she slipped out of her car and shut the door. After reaching the front door, she punched in her security code, but when she stepped into the foyer, she knew something was wrong immediately. She stepped back, but stopped when she saw a man step from around the corner in her house.

It was the bastard who had attacked her in Hawaii.

"So nice to see you again, Ms. Dillon."

Before she could react, he rushed forward. She turned but it was too late. She felt the shock to her left shoulder and it jolted through her body. Then, she fell, hitting her head on the pavement. Pain exploded and then her world went to black.

forty-six

Fear turned into terror when Rory pulled into the driveway and Zeke saw the front door was left open. He was out of the car and running even before Rory put it in park.

"Shit," he said. "Maura! Maura!"

No answer. *Fucking hell.*

"She's not here?" Rory asked.

"Let's search the house and grounds. I'll talk to Conner."

He dialed Conner's number. "I can't find her, Conner. She's missing."

"Fuck. He has her, I know it," Conner said, voicing Zeke's greatest fears.

"This isn't his stomping grounds, so I have no idea where he would have taken her."

Rory ran up, shaking his head. Then, his phone went off. It was Maura's ring.

"Maura, love, where are you?" He frowned. "Maura? She's not saying anything."

"Maybe she can't."

"Can't what?"

"Maura called Rory."

"She might be trying to give you the opportunity to trace her. I'll call it in and then get back with you."

The phone clicked off.

Rory was still trying to talk to Maura. "Maura, love, we know you're there. Just let us know where you are."

Still no answer. They felt helpless as they stood in front of her house and waited for her brother to call back. It didn't take long.

"He's heading to the docks," Conner said.

"We got a location," he said and Rory started up the car.

"We'll get her, Conner, don't worry."

"I'm calling the FBI and I am sure they will call Miami PD. If anything happens to her, I will kill you."

And that was the end of the conversation.

"He's pissed."

"I'm sure he is. Gun in the glove compartment. You have yours?"

"Yes."

"We'll get there, Zee, I promise."

He knew that, he just hoped they got there in time.

forty-seven

Maura sucked in a deep breath and winced from the pain. Fuck, she was pretty sure the bastard cracked a rib or two when he tossed her in the trunk of his car. She slowly opened her eyes. She tried to move her arms but found them tied behind. She was in some sort of storage area or warehouse. She didn't know the area, that was for sure.

"It's about time you woke up, girlie," he said.

She turned in the direction of the voice. A shard of pain radiated from her head through her body. A wave of nausea hit her and she closed her eyes for a second.

When she knew she had it under control, she opened them again and looked at the man who attacked her. It wasn't anyone she had met before. This man was tall, dark, with blue eyes. If he hadn't abducted her she might be attracted to him. Until she studied his eyes. There was something so cold that she shivered.

His accent hit her.

"You have nothing to do with Petersen."

His lips twitched. "No, I don't."

"Then who the fuck are you?"

"Tsk, tsk. American women are so coarse. I have no idea what those two see in you."

She sensed he was from the same part of Ireland that Rory was from, just from the rhythm of his speech.

"So, this has nothing to do with me."

"In a way it does. You are the one thing they want. The one thing they love in this world. I'm going to enjoy taking you from them...watching their pain."

She wanted to argue with him. They didn't love her. When things got tough, they both questioned her intelligence and in a way, abandoned her. But arguing with her abductor would not get her any more info.

"Your plan is to get them to come here?" She shook her head, trying to ignore the way pain sparked through her. "They won't fall for it."

The smile he gave her was so evil she knew she was dealing with a true sociopath. "But they will. Where you are concerned, these two will do anything."

"And you plan on killing them."

He shook his head. "They killed mine...I will kill theirs."

So, he meant to kill her not them. All she had to do was get out of there before they got there. "At least tell me your name."

His smile faded. "You do not need to know."

"Unless you're afraid you will fail and then I will tell them your name. I can understand where a coward like you would fear that."

He said nothing but stepped forward. She didn't expect the slap. The back of his hand came so fast and hard, she didn't have time to brace for it. She could taste the blood in her mouth.

"Again I say American women are so coarse."

His voice never rose. He didn't show a temper at all. *Fucking psycho.*

But, he had a temper and she could use it.

"I don't see what's so coarse about pointing out the obvious. Apparently, you have some kind of agenda against Rory and Zeke, but you can't tell me because of fear."

He smiled. "You want to know? Fine. You will be dead in the next hour, so I don't see that it matters. Does the name Frances O'Connell mean anything to you?"

"No."

"That was my brother's name."

"Good for him?"

"Your two lovers killed him. Cold blood."

"I take it this has to do with their time before they were hired by my brother?"

"See, love, your lovers are killers. They like to pretend they aren't but they are. They killed my baby brother and then laughed over it. They mocked his death, to me, to anyone who would listen."

"And because of that, you terrorized me, abducted me and now are sitting here hoping they will find me and you can kill them, then me?"

"All of it but the last." He held up her cell phone. She could barely read it because she had no idea where her glasses were, but it looked like he had called someone. Probably one of the guys. Hopefully they weren't listening because they would go ballistic. "I want to see their faces when I slit that lovely throat of yours."

She tried her best not to show her reactions. She knew he was serious and planned to do that. While Zeke would think things through, there was a good chance that Rory would not be able to be contained. They would be at risk and put her at more risk if they showed up there, guns blazing. Her training from her brother kicked in.

Maura knew she needed to be free of the chair. Her arms

were tied behind the back of it and she couldn't get up without a struggle. She had to get him to get her out of it so she could surprise him.

"In review, you abducted me in hopes they would come here. I call that a coward. Why not face them right off? You go after a woman. Coward." It took everything she had to let her disgust drip from every word.

"I am not a coward."

"Why was your baby brother killed? Where were you?"

"I was out on a job."

"Sounds like you didn't do a very good job protecting him."

"Shut up," he said, his voice rising just a bit.

"It seems to me you are more at fault for your brother's death than Rory and Ze—"

She broke off when he backhanded her again. This time he did it with such force that the chair tipped over. She landed hard on the cement, her head struck it with such force that she saw stars. But, it had done what she wanted. She was free of the chair.

Maura rolled over onto her back. Her abductor was walking toward her and now she knew she had him. He pulled back his booted foot to kick her, but she swung around out of his way. Then, she kicked him in the back of the knee. He stumbled but did not fall down.

He let loose a roar of rage and turned to face her.

"You fucking bitch."

Now, his temper took hold of his emotions and it was just what she'd hope for. She was ready for him this time. He came at her and she kicked out, connecting first with his thigh. He stumbled again but turned on her easily. He got one swift kick in, then another. Soon, she lay still as she tried to fight the pain radiating through her entire body.

He made a mistake. He crouched down, his face inches

from hers. "Now you are going to make this an enjoyable experience for me. You were just a means to an end but it will be a pleasure to kill you."

She used what little strength she had left and pulled herself up. Then, as he leaned in closer she drew back and smacked her head against his. The pain of it made her dizzy and her vision blurred. She gritted her teeth and kicked the bastard in the knee again. He fell to the ground and now, she knew she could stand up. She swayed and almost fell over once or twice, but she pulled herself up to her feet.

Fear, loathing and rage surged. She pulled her leg back and kicked him right in the groin. After that, she didn't truly remember what happened. She kept kicking him, over and over until she felt someone grab her by the arm. Maura turned ready to hit the bastard who touched her and came face to face with Rory. Zeke was right behind him. Miami police were pouring into every opening.

"Maura," he whispered. Even with all the noise she heard the words and the horror in his voice. The room was spinning around her as Zeke walked up to her. Gently, he took her in his arms.

"It's okay, baby. We're here now."

And for the first time since the ordeal began, she let the tears fall.

Rory walked over to the man and sneered. "O'Connell."

Zeke looked over her shoulder and she could feel him shake. It wasn't fear, it was rage and there was a good chance that one or both of them would have killed the man for what he had done to her—if the police had not been there.

Zeke shifted as if to join Rory, but she stopped him.

"Oh, damn," she said. For the second time that day, her world went completely black.

forty-eight

"You didn't believe me." She tried to sound angry but it came out in a hitching breath. She could tell that both of them knew she was near tears.

"We wanted to, love," Zeke said as he tried to take her hand.

"Wanting to and doing so are two different things. I can't deal with men who can't tell the difference."

The doctor glided into the room. "It looks like you can be released today. After a talk with your brother on the phone and the fact that your trip to Hawaii will be restful since you have your own jet, I'm going to allow it. But, I called a colleague at Queen's Medical. You are to check in with her while you are there."

She nodded.

When the doctor left them alone, Rory stood up. "What's this crap about going to Hawaii?"

"Conner wants me there, and Jillian does too. He wants me to take a rest."

It wasn't what she wanted, not really, but maybe it was what she needed.

"You can't think that you need to be there, away from us," Zeke said. His voice was low, and his accent deepened.

Looking at him hurt. It hurt more than the three cracked ribs that bastard gave her. She wanted to think that they wanted her on some other level, but when push came to shove, they didn't. She couldn't stay with men who couldn't at least believe in her a little.

"I think it would be best for me. For...all of us."

Zeke glanced at Rory and she could feel his need to argue rise. Zeke would argue just because he felt guilty. Thankfully, someone knocked at the door. It swung open and her brother strode in. His face was stern and there were bags under his eyes.

He didn't stop until he was by her side. She could tell he couldn't decide what to do.

"Maura," he whispered. She wasn't sure he even knew he said her name. She took his hand in hers.

"It looks much worse than it is."

He swallowed and she knew that he was barely holding it together. Conner had a world-class temper when he let it loose and she was waiting for him to explode. He had probably been holding onto it the entire ride over. She didn't have a long wait.

He looked at Zeke and Rory. "How the fuck could you let this happen?"

Zeke winced but Rory crossed his arms over his chest.

After a long moment of silence, Zeke answered. "We were looking at the wrong person."

"You two are trained in the field of security and you let this happen? What the hell else can I think but you are incompetent."

She knew her brother was upset, even scared. But she would not lay the blame of the entire episode at their feet. "You are the one who would not listen to me when I said it had nothing to do with Petersen. The cartel wasn't going to care about Petersen and if they were going to go after someone it would be the federal prosecutor."

By the time she stopped talking, she was exhausted. Apparently, once again, the cooler head in the room was Jillian.

"Guys, why don't you take it outside?"

Conner opened his mouth but apparently after seeing Jillian's expression, he thought better.

"Okay. Come on," he ordered without waiting to see if they would follow. Typical Conner. She would have smiled but her split lip was still throbbing.

Rory gave her a glance, and said nothing else before walking out. Zeke hesitated, leaned down and kissed her forehead. "Get some rest, love."

Then he walked out.

Jillian waited until the door shut to approach her bed.

"So, you really know how to throw a party," she said.

Maura laughed then groaned. "Don't make me smile. It hurts."

"Oh, baby." Jillian sat in the chair next to the bed. She slipped her hand into Maura's. "How bad does it hurt?"

Maura squeezed her hand. "Pretty bad. Although, they keep me drugged up."

"Let me guess, you don't want to be drugged so you are making sure you only take in so much. You will take some drugs for the trip back. It will be too hard on you, honey."

She nodded knowing that was true.

"Plus, they didn't want me sleeping last night because of the concussion."

Jillian sighed. "Now, you want to tell me how much the rest of it hurts?"

She glanced at Jillian and wondered not for the first time how strange fate was. The two of them had been thrown together in college. She was pretty sure that no one in their right mind would have paired the two of them up. The tattooed bohemian and the nerd. But, they had become good friends and now they were sisters.

The bad thing about that was that Jillian knew her all too well.

"I don't know what you're talking about."

"Listen, be straight with me. Your brother would get upset if I slapped you around considering the condition you're in."

She smiled, just a little so it didn't hurt.

"They didn't believe me. Even while they were all checking out the Petersen connection, they ignored what I said, and they doubted what I claimed. They didn't really believe someone was stalking me."

Jillian leaned forward and brushed some of Maura's hair from her forehead. "And that hurt more than being dumped."

It was so good to finally have someone understand. Tears filled her eyes and her vision wavered. Jillian said nothing. She picked up a tissue and handed it to Maura.

"To have someone doubt me like that...I am not sure I can deal with that. No one has ever doubted my intelligence."

"They called you stupid?" Jillian asked, outrage sparking through her voice. "Isn't that just like men? If it were someone else, then yes, but you...you never overreact. Zeke knows that."

"So, it has been a rough couple of weeks."

"Yeah, I can tell. Basically because you look like shit." Maura laughed through the tears.

"I've missed you."

"You just saw me ten days ago and if all of this was going on, you should have called."

Maura sighed. "Promise me you won't get mad?" Jillian nodded. "I was afraid you would tell Conner. He wasn't happy with the situation of me being with two guys to begin with. I know he has serious doubts about Rory. This just made it worse."

"Tell you what. As long as I think you are not in imminent danger, I promise not to tell Conner."

"The two women in my life plotting against me?" Conner asked from the doorway. He was alone.

Jillian smiled when she saw him. For once in a really long time, Maura felt the sharp sting of jealousy. She was happy for her brother and her best friend, but their happiness saddened her even more.

"Not plotting, but we have to establish rules for friendship again. Where are the guys?" Jillian asked.

"They had to go talk to the police again. They want all the information they can get on O'Connell. Interpol is very interested in him. He is suspected in doing some very bad things overseas."

"In Ireland?" she asked trying her best not to let anyone see just how much it upset her that they left her. They just left the hospital knowing she was leaving soon. It sealed the end of the relationship she had with the two of them.

"There and then he became a gun for hire. He's suspected of teaching some terrorists in the Middle East, and then some in Somalia. He's a very bad man."

"And Maura beat the shit out of him," Jillian said with more than a little pride in her voice. Maura fought the smile because it would hurt again.

"I did. So, I guess, I am better than the FBI and Interpol. They can suck it."

Conner smiled then it faded. "You're coming with us."

She nodded. "I think it will do me some good to just hang out on the beach, rest."

Conner and Jillian shared a look of worry.

"Don't freak. I'm in a lot of pain and I'm smart enough to know rest is the best medicine."

Conner nodded. "I'm going to call Brett and tell him we are going to be leaving soon."

He left them alone and Jillian sat back down.

"You can do it now."

"What?"

"Cry."

"You think I am going to cry over those jackasses?" The last of it came out on a sob.

"Yes, and then we can plot revenge." She took Maura into her arms. And for the first time in days, Maura broke down and cried.

forty-nine

A day later, Rory was climbing the walls. He just didn't know how hard it would be without having Maura in their lives. And it had been less than twenty-four hours. When they had returned and she'd ignored them, it had been bad. This was impossible.

"Quit pacing, you're making my head hurt."

He snarled at Zeke. The man didn't understand. He was always so fucking calm and cool. Rory used to think that he could read him, but right now, he couldn't. He thought the bastard would be ready to go get Maura, but he wasn't. He was sitting there behind his desk. Damn fool.

Rory stopped in front of the large window and looked down on Miami. He never would have thought a city like this would appeal to him. So many people, hot weather...but he realized for the first time he was home. Or he had been before everything had gone to hell. Without Maura with them, it felt wrong. He needed her as much as he needed Zeke, and that scared the fucking bloody hell out of him.

"You know, if you would work, it would be easier."

He rolled his shoulders. It was the only thing that kept him from hitting Zeke in the back of the head.

"I don't have anything to work on right now."

"Yes, you do. Sanders wants an estimate on the security for that fundraiser. You need to come up with how many men we need for it so I can work it up."

"And just like that, you expect me to go back to work, pretend everything is alright?"

"What else can we do? She chose to leave. We have to let her go. Besides, it wasn't like it was more than an affair."

"What the fuck does that mean?"

Zee sighed. "From the beginning you didn't want anything to happen. But then, all the sudden you were interested. You don't think I know why you did that? Come on, after knowing you most of your life I think I know you well enough to understand your motives."

Rory shook his head. "I did it for you. You were sitting here pining over her."

For a moment a flash of anger slid over Zeke's face. The fact that it made him satisfied, also made him feel small.

"Really? So it has nothing to do with controlling the situation?"

"I was attracted to her."

Zee snorted. "Any man would be, if they were smart. But, that wasn't it, was it? You were worried about my relationship with her. It's the only reason you came here. You knew that there was something there between Maura and me and it was driving you crazy that you couldn't control the situation. So, you come here, hook back up with me, then bring her in."

"I came back because I love you," he said. It was the truth. There was no sense hiding it because he knew that Zeke already understood the depths of his feelings for him.

"Ah, but what of Maura? What do you feel about her?"

"Fuck, I love her too," he shouted. Then, he stopped his pacing. Dammit, he did love her. She was a goof, someone who could always crack a joke. Seeing her pain the last few weeks had been one of the most debilitating things he had confronted. When she hurt, he hurt.

"About bloody time you admitted it," Zeke muttered as he stood. He turned off his computer and started toward the door.

"Where the fuck are you going?"

Zee turned and faced him. "To Maura."

"Wait."

He jogged to catch up with him. "What are you doing? Dammit, Zee, stop."

He stopped in the hall and turned to face him. "What?"

"What the fuck is going on?"

"I've been waiting for you to come to your senses. Can't believe it took so long but I guess I shouldn't be surprised. It took you long enough to admit you loved me."

Rory frowned. "You're not upset I admitted to loving her?"

Zeke shook his head. "No. Why would I when I love both of you?"

He said it as if it was simple and for Zee, it was. He could always look through the shit life handed him and see what was really important. Other people got bogged down in the details, but when something was this important, Zee didn't. He loved both of them and it was all that mattered.

"People will think we're freaks."

Zee shrugged. "They already think that. This way, we have Maura and they think we're freaks. Besides, when did you decide to worry about what other people think? Seriously?"

He sighed. "I thought you would."

Zee smiled and walked forward. Rory felt his heart turn over. The man had him by the ballocks and Zee knew it. Hell they both did. And there was something so bloody sexy about that.

Zee cupped his face in his hands and kissed him. Slow, long, and wet. When he pulled back, he smiled.

"Let's go get our woman."

Warmth spread through Rory. For the first time in days, the feeling of rightness shifted through him. He gave Zeke a quick kiss.

"Let's go."

"She might say no."

"Too bad. I'll drag her back by her hair if I have to," Rory said.

"There's the man I love," Zee said as he pulled out his phone.

"You're calling her?"

"Nope, but we need a flight, love."

"Good. Get the flight, then we get Maura," Rory said.

But he did have something he needed to pick up at home before they left, then off to their future.

He just hoped they hadn't waited too long.

fifty

"Wat are your plans today?" Conner asked at breakfast. Jillian knew that he was trying to engage with Maura but she knew her friend wasn't ready.

Maura shrugged as she played with her cereal. She hadn't been eating enough to keep herself alive, but Jillian knew she needed her space. Unfortunately, her brother didn't understand that. He wanted his baby sister to be better. Now.

The physical bruises were just now starting to fade, but the wounds to Maura's pride were going to take longer. *Much longer.*

"I think I'll go for a walk on the beach," she said.

Conner rose with her and she looked at him. "What are you doing?"

"Going with you."

She glanced at Jillian and she could see Maura wanted to be alone. Conner had been hovering like a mama. Jillian was of the belief that brother and sister needed to set their own boundaries. She was not getting in the middle of that.

"I want to be alone, Conner."

"I think that you might—"

"I didn't ask. I just told you, I want to be alone. Deal with it."

With that she left the kitchen, letting the screen door slam behind her.

There were a few moments of stunned silence. Jillian wasn't stunned. She knew that Conner and Maura had their own issues to deal with and they were starting to come to a head. Trying to sooth either one of them was going to leave Jillian hurt...and Conner and Maura wouldn't heal. Of course, her stubborn husband wanted everything to be all right right now. Like Maura was going to feel better overnight.

"She's starting to get on my nerves," Conner said.

Jillian ignored him. He had been saying the same thing for two days. But for once he didn't go on. She glanced over at him. He was staring at the screen door. She looked down at the Honolulu Advertiser again. When he didn't go on, Jillian figured he would just sit in the house and stew in his irritation. She didn't have time for that.

"She isn't getting on your nerves."

"Yes, she is."

"No, you're angry and you want to hurt someone because she hurts." She took a sip of coffee and looked at him. "You are just going to have to deal with it right now. She needs to be alone."

He frowned and rose from the chair. "I want to hurt someone."

"I know you do, babe. There are just some things you have to let her work out on her own."

He said nothing. She could tell from the way his shoulders were tensed that he was contemplating his next move and it would not be what she suggested. She sighed and walked over to him, setting her coffee cup down on the counter. Jillian slipped her arms around his waist and laid her head on his back.

"You have to let the children grow up some time, Conner."

She felt him relax slightly.

"She's hurting because of them." He spat out the words. Anger dripped from every word and she knew there was a good chance his friendship with Zeke was over...if Maura didn't work it out.

And, Mr. Man needed to learn that Zeke and Rory were not the only ones at fault here.

"Truthfully, she is hurting because of a whole lot of things."

He moved and she released him. He turned to face her. His frown was even darker. "Explain."

"Your sister, the level headed-most of the time-girl you raised came to you and said she was attacked."

He rolled his eyes. "Yeah, I remember. I called Rome, he did the report."

"From the very beginning, she said she knew it wasn't the Petersen case. She was positive. She said she knew the man spoke with an Irish accent. Even after you were told Petersen had nothing to do with it, you questioned her. The reason she didn't really come to you about being stalked was because of you ignoring her. Of course, you weren't the only one. Rory and Zeke didn't do a good job of backing her up. Y'all treated her like she was some bubble headed idiot. She started to question her own intelligence—worse, her own instincts. That is something Maura has never done before. It unraveled her world."

"Well, we all have more experience than—"

"No, it isn't something to brush off. Maura might not have had a lot of dates and being the egghead she is, she didn't really care. But she did believe in herself. When the three most important men in her life questioned her aptitude, it crushed her."

"You make it sound like I'm at fault."

She slipped her arms around his waist again. "You are to a point, babe. But, her big problem is with those two men. Still, you can't really just blame them. You need to start taking her opinion as a valued asset."

"I do."

She shook her head. "To a point, but it's just what Zeke was talking about before. You question her every move. Another person with her intelligence wouldn't have to explain herself to you over and over."

He sighed. "She's my baby sister."

He said it with such love it made her heart skip a beat. One of the best things about her husband was his love for his family. Maura had been the center of his life for so long, but he needed to let go.

"She's not a baby anymore. You need to show her more respect."

He nodded.

"Granted, I expected more from Rory and especially Zeke, but I have a feeling Maura will take care of them."

"I'm seriously thinking about shooting Zeke. He should know better. I'll just kill Rory."

"Shooting your business partner is probably not a good idea." She saw something out the window and was relieved to see a rental car drive up. It parked behind her jeep and both men stepped out of the car. "Besides, she would probably get mad at you."

"Figures. Women." He said it with such disgust she smiled.

She gave him a quick kiss. "And, just like you, they didn't do it on purpose. You were trying to protect her."

He sighed. "Maybe I won't feel like kicking their asses if I don't see them for a month or two. Or a year."

"You're going to have to deal with them sooner than that."

316

His brow furrowed. "What?"

"They're here."

His head whipped around and he growled. She tried to hold onto him, but he escaped her grasp and stalked outside. Jillian hurried behind him and almost got slammed in the face with the screen door.

"You have some real fucking nerve showing up here," he yelled.

Both men readied for a fight. She glanced toward the beach and was thankful that Maura was far enough away so she wouldn't pick up on the fight.

When Jillian turned around, she was alarmed to see Conner grabbing Zeke by the shirt.

"Stop," she yelled running toward the three of them.

Her neighbor Adam was already running down the path to help Conner.

She inserted herself between the two friends.

"Move, Jillian, I can take him," Zeke said.

"No you won't. I'm not going to have you brawl out here like a bunch of seventeen-year-old assholes. Let go of Zeke."

It took Conner a second or two to finally look at her. "They hurt her."

"And how do you think she'll feel when she finds you two up here rolling around on the ground."

"I can take him," Zeke said again, his voice vicious. "He is getting a little old."

She rolled her eyes. "Can it, Zeke."

With a disgusted huff, Conner shoved Zeke away. Rory, who had been quiet up until then, stepped forward.

"Tell you what. Let us talk to her. If she's still pissed at us, you can kick Zee's ass."

"Thanks a lot, you ass," Zeke said.

"Fine," Conner said.

Rory looked at Jillian. "Where is she?"

"On the beach," she said nodding her head in the direction where she had seen Maura.

"Thank you."

"Just one thing, guys." They turned to face her. "If you hurt her again, you won't have to worry about Conner. I'll shoot both of you on the spot. In the groin. And don't think I can't do it. I might look harmless, but I grew up in Georgia. I know how to hunt and I know how to shoot. Just understand I will do both to you if you hurt her again."

They said nothing and headed down to the beach. Conner slipped his arms around her waist and set his chin on her head. "I still want to hurt them."

"Oh, babe, they're already hurting. Hopefully they don't fuck this up or I will shoot them."

He chuckled and kissed her head. "That's my woman."

fifty-one

Maura knew they were coming up behind her before they said anything. They both moved like cats like usually, but she sensed them. And that made her mad. She didn't fucking want to be in tune with them. She wanted to be left alone. Why did no one seem to understand that but Jillian? Probably because she was surrounded by idiot men.

"What are you two doing here?" she asked without turning around. She sensed they paused as if surprised.

The silence lengthened. The only sound she heard was the crashing of the waves and the few people scattered on the beach. She braced herself and turned to face them.

Her heart hitched and tears burned the back of her eyes. Dammit, how did they do this to her? She should be mad, but something in her wanted to comfort both of them. Sure, they looked tired, as if they hadn't slept at all, and lord knew if they were there in the morning, they had a long flight from Miami. Still, she was mad. Or was.

She shook those thoughts away and asked, "Are you going to answer me?"

They looked at each other, then back at her. She rolled her eyes. Without another word, she turned and started walking down the beach. The sun was just getting warm and the trades were pretty strong. She walked into the wind welcoming it. It was still another sign she was alive.

"Maura," Zeke said jogging up to her. She knew without a doubt Rory was with him.

"If you can't say anything then go back to Miami."

"Be reasonable for a second, baby, we need to talk."

"Don't baby me, you idiot. Both of you had a chance to tell me to stay there. You had a chance to tell me you wanted more and you didn't. Go away."

"Maura, you need to stop right where you are," Rory ordered. It was the same voice he used when they were playing and it pissed her off that he used it now. It pissed her off even more that it turned her on.

She did stop, but she did it to turn and face him. "You ass, do not even think that I am going to allow you to order me around outside of the bedroom. I've told you before that I don't go for that."

He was frowning at her, but she couldn't see his eyes, as they were shaded by his mirrored sunglasses. Zeke looked between the two of them.

"Maybe we should take this conversation inside."

She shot him an angry glance. "I don't care who hears. Besides, it doesn't really matter. There aren't that many people out here and I am not taking either of you back. Together or separately. Go away."

"You told us that you loved us. Was that a lie?" Rory asked.

"No, but it doesn't matter. I gave you a chance, you blew it."

She turned and started walking again.

"If you do not stop walking away I will smack that ass until it burns."

"Go suck an egg, Rory. I'm not interested in a Dom who doesn't have the balls to admit when he's in love."

She didn't hear them approaching this time until it was too late. He grabbed her by the arm and turned her around.

"Goddammit, we flew over half a day to be here. You could at least give us some consideration," Rory said.

"Consideration?" Everything she had been feeling for days, for weeks even, welled up. The pain, the loneliness and the fear exploded and she couldn't hold it in. "You have some fucking nerve. Damn you. I don't owe you anything. *Anything*. I gave you both everything you could have ever wanted, but apparently it wasn't enough."

The last was said on a sob. She tried to hold it back, but she couldn't seem to do it. The tears started to fall.

"Oh, baby," Zeke said as he reached for her. She backed up and almost stumbled down.

"No. Don't touch me."

"You will stop that right now," Rory ordered.

She stopped and so did Zeke. "What?"

"Crying. I can't stand a woman who cries."

She was so surprised by the comment she opened her mouth but nothing came out. Zeke was smiling.

"I will cry if I feel like it."

He crossed his arms over his chest. "Well, I don't like it and Zeke doesn't either."

"You're on your own there, Rory."

She shot Zeke a nasty look. "And just what the hell do you mean by that?"

His smile widened further. "I have no problem admitting that I love you. Rory, there, he does. Big bad Dom doesn't like saying the words."

"Shut the fuck up," Rory said.

"See."

Hope sprung but then the last week came back to her. His distance, and the way he pretended that she didn't matter. And tears welled up again.

"Shit, okay. Stop that," Rory ordered, yelling this time. She had never been the kind of girl who cried, but this time, she could not stop herself. They spilled over, streaming over her cheeks.

Rory grabbed her by the arms and opened his mouth to yell at her, but in the next instant, he fell onto the sand in front of her. He pulled her against him, laying his head on her stomach. She looked at Zeke who was grinning at her.

"I love you, Maura," Zeke said. "Please, love, I'm so sorry we doubted you."

Her heart melted but she tried to ignore it. They were only doing this to get her back. She didn't want them to say things to get her back. She wanted them to actually believe in her. Words meant nothing if they truly didn't believe in what they were saying.

Zeke shook his head. "I can see those wheels turning in your head, love. We made some mistakes but you have to know that we both really love you."

She looked down at Rory who then looked up at her. "I love you. Please, take us back. We aren't anything if you aren't with us, love."

A fresh set of tears welled up.

"Oh, Rory," was all she could say.

"We should have believed you. We should have stood behind you," Zeke said, his smile fading. "We love you and we should have been there for you. We failed."

He grabbed a bag from Zeke and pulled out a leather collar.

"I'm not saying this just to get you back. I bought this when we went to Rough 'n Ready."

She looked at it and at the word. *Ours*. It was before she told Rory she loved him...before everything went bad.

Maura looked at him, then at Zeke.

"We were complete and utter asses," Rory said.

"Speak for yourself," Zeke muttered.

"No, we were. Both of us wanted forever with you but we didn't have the nerve to deal with it. And I know Zeke waited for me to agree, but then he never asked."

"Oh, I see, this is my fault." Rory stood up but he kept his arm around her waist and pulled her against him. "You always blame shit on me. I think maybe you should have said something about all of us moving in together, but you didn't."

Zeke threw his hands up in the air. "You would have freaked."

It was so normal listening to them bicker.

"There you go again making grand plans and expecting us to skip along behind you."

She giggled. They both stopped and looked at her.

"I'm sorry, but I can't believe you flew all this way to convince me to take you back just to stand on the beach and bicker."

Zeke's mouth curved. "Sorry, love, but Rory and I like to bicker."

"Way to sell the whole living together. Are you saying I'll have to play referee?"

They glanced at each other.

"Oh, God, I will." She sighed dramatically.

"Love, if you take us back we will never bicker," Rory said.

She laughed. "Really? Starting off forever with a lie, Rory?"

He stepped back and took her by the shoulders. "Are you saying you're taking us on?"

She nodded. "Yeah, I think you need to be saved from each other. With your knowledge of weapons, one of you will end up dead at some point."

He smiled as he pulled her closer. A soft brush of Rory's mouth had her heart tumbling. She sensed Zeke walking up behind her. She turned and accepted a kiss from him.

"People will think we're freaks," Zeke said.

"I told you before, Zeke, fuck them. All that matters is us."

Zeke looked up at Jillian and Conner's house.

"Don't worry about him. He'll come around. And if he doesn't, don't worry about it.

"He's your brother," Zeke said.

"And you two are the loves of my life. He has to accept it."

Rory kissed her again, pulling her close as Zeke stepped up behind her.

"So," she said with a smile, "tell me you came with a plan of where we're staying, 'cause there's no way I'm going to deal with my brother in that little house."

"Not really, but I'm sure we can find a room for the night, Maura," Rory said.

"All we cared about was getting here and getting you back," Zeke said.

"Well, I suggest you figure it out soon." She slipped out of Rory's arms. "Because one of you is going to have to get me to wear this." She shook the collar at them.

Rory grabbed her and pulled her back into his arms. "So, is that a challenge, Dillon?"

She smiled. "You betcha."

She heard Zeke talking and she realized he was calling one of the hotels to reserve a room.

"I guess we can't complain too much about his planning at this point," Maura said.

"No, love, we'll let him plan all he wants, as long as he let's us sleep in."

Joy filled her heart, her body already warming under the sensual assault of Rory's sweet kisses.

"Sounds like an excellent plan to me," she said deepening the kiss as the warmth of their love filled her.

THANK YOU SO MUCH FOR READING ROUGH FANTASY! Eli St. John is coming next in Rough Ride.

If you loved the book, please think about leaving a review at your favorite online store!

twisted emotions is coming!

The final book of the Task Force Hawaii series is coming May 17, 2024!

BUY THE BOOK

She has always been the woman for him, but he thought he lost her forever until a cold case brings them back together.

Adam Lee is a man at the top of his game. Or he should be. He's ready to take control of TFH Team Alpha, and he should be happy, but he's not. There is something missing–someone in particular.

Jin Phillips made one mistake years ago, and she paid for it. After enduring something that would break most people, she was too broken for a man like Adam. He didn't turn away, but was there as her friend supporting her. But when a cold case she covers on her podcast turns hot, Adam and Jin have to work together to find a killer.

Each minute they are together remind Adam why he fell in love with her all those years before. For Jin, she discovers that she still has it in her heart to find love and take a chance on love. But someone is hunting Jin, and Adam will do anything to protect her—even sacrifice himself.

Come along as the entire gang comes together to solve a cold case murder and help Jin and Adam find their happily ever after!

love free books?

Hey, there. I want to encourage you to sign up for my VIP newsletter. I stuff it with all kinds of fun things, including sneak peeks at upcoming books, insights into what I am working on at the moment, and newsletter only contests!

Best of all, you can get a free book for joining. Check out The Sweet Shoppe Collection today. It's three stories about magical chocolate or you can grab Only For Him!

If you aren't interested in all the goodies I have in my newsletter, you can sign up for my RSS Feed. It is a just the facts kind of email that will tell you about new releases, preorder, and appearances.

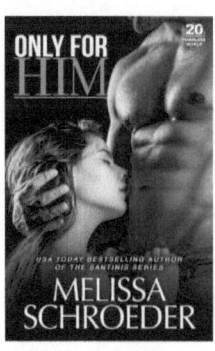

about the author

From an early age, USA Today Best-selling author Melissa loved to read. When she discovered the romance genre, she started to listen to the voices in her head. After years of following her AF Major husband around, she is happy to be settled in Northern Virginia surrounded by horses, wineries, and many, many Wegmans.

Keep up with Mel, her releases, and her appearances by subscribing to her <u>NEWSLETTER</u>. If you want to keep up with cover reveals, new behind the scene info on her writing, and when new excerpts are posted, follow her MelissaSchroeder.net News News. Or you can do both! They are low traffic, so you will not get tons of emails.

Check out all her other books, family trees and other info at <u>her website!</u>

<u>If you would want contact Mel, email her at: melissa@melissaschroeder.net</u>

instagram.com/melschro

amazon.com/author/melissa_schroeder

facebook.com/MelissaSchroederfanpage

bookbub.com/authors/melissa-schroeder

goodreads.com/Melissa_Schroeder

tiktok.com/@melissawritesromance

www.ingramcontent.com/pod-product-compliance
Lightning Source LLC
Chambersburg PA
CBHW051947240626
47153CB00005B/1659